STRANGLE HOLD

Books by Jerome Doolittle

Body Scissors
Strangle Hold

Published by POCKET BOOKS

STRANGLE
HOLD

Jerome
Doolittle

POCKET BOOKS

New York   London   Toronto   Sydney   Tokyo   Singapore

POCKET BOOKS, a division of Simon & Schuster Inc.
1230 Avenue of the Americas, New York, NY 10020

Doolittle, Jerome.
    Strangle hold / Jerome Doolittle.
        p.   cm.
    ISBN 0-671-70754-X : $20.00
    I. Title.
PS3554.0584S77   1991
813'.54—dc20   91-790
                                                                                CIP

First Pocket Books hardcover printing December 1991

10   9   8   7   6   5   4   3   2   1

For Toby

STRANGLE HOLD

— 1 —

I WAS DEHYDRATED FROM TWO HOURS OF WORKING OUT WITH one of Harvard's good new wrestlers and another forty-five minutes in and out of the sauna. I had carried my thirst back home with me untreated, up the stairs, over to the refrigerator for a bottle of India Pale Ale, and then into the La-Z-Boy recliner. Now the bottle of India Pale Ale sat on the table beside the recliner, waiting to be poured into the frosted mug from the freezer. Dusk of another bright October day—football weather with the leaves crackling under your feet.

The phone rang, a friendly sound because only a half-dozen or so good friends knew the number. It's not only unlisted, but it's unlisted under another name than my own, which is Tom Bethany. The phone was sitting on the table alongside the beer, and I picked it up on the first ring.

"Hi," I said.

"Hi," a man said. He wasn't one of the friends. "We're conducting a survey on behalf of a *Fortune* 500 financial services corporation and we'd like your answers to a few questions . . ."

"Sure," I said. "Let me just finish pouring myself a beer, okay?" He had no problem with that, and so I watched the frost melt as the beer level rose in the mug. When all the frost was gone except for the ring around the top where the foam was, my answers were ready for the kind of survey I knew he had in mind. I told him I was in the age range from thirty to forty, owned my own condominium and two cars, earned between $200,000 and $300,000 a year, and was a physician. Physicians have money and tend to think they're a lot smarter than they really are, and so financial services guys tend to like physicians a lot. This particular guy wanted to come by and visit me this very evening, so we could talk over investment opportunities.

"Listen," I said. "Why don't I come by your place instead?"

"Oh, that won't be necessary, Dr. Butcher. I can drop by any time this evening, at your convenience. Let me just jot down your address there at home."

"No, really, Jack . . . It is Jack, right?"

"Bill, actually."

"Bill, right. Look, Bill, I'm inside all day, you know how it is. Nurses and patients, all that shit. Bottom line, I'm always looking for a chance to take the Beemer for a run in the evenings. Where you located, Bill?"

"Way out past Dedham, but—"

"No problem. What did you say your last name was, Bill?"

"Underwood, but—"

"Just give me a minute here so I can get the South Suburban directory, make sure there's a William Underwood out there in Dedham, you know? I mean, this could be a joke, right?"

"Dr. Butcher—"

2

"If it turns out you're in the book though, Bill, I'll call you now and then, odd hours. Maybe I'll get lucky and catch you taking a dump or something. That ever happen to you? You wipe your ass like a goddamn madman, but it's still not fast enough? Time you make it to the phone the son of a bitch hung up already?"

But by then Underwood himself had hung up. I grabbed my beer with one hand and the *Boston Globe* with the other. The phone rang again. I put down the *Globe.*

"Listen, Underwood," I said, "if you *do* turn out to be in the book, you just fucked up big-time."

"Am I interrupting something?" said Hope Edwards.

"Oh, Christ," I said. "I'm sorry, Hope." I would have said darling or sweetheart, but we don't often say those things to each other, however much we mean them.

"Who's Underwood?"

"A guy doing a cold canvass from Merrill Lynch or something. Some bucket shop, anyway."

"You're not in the book, though."

"Probably computer dialing. Don't your fund-raisers use that?"

"Computers? Are you kidding? The ACLU is just phasing in electric typewriters. This office is probably the only one in Washington that still uses carbon paper. Some guy gave us a truckload of the stuff ten years ago."

"What are you doing still at the office? Why aren't you at home, being a good mother to your kids?" She has three of them. They, her job, and her husband are all down in Washington. I am in Cambridge, on the other side of the Charles River from Boston. This means that much too much of the time we are four hundred and some miles apart.

"I'm tying things up. Something came up and I'm flying to Boston tomorrow morning."

"About time, too. What's your flight?"

"No sense meeting it. I'll just take a cab."

"Stop suffering and tell me the flight number."

"USAir seven-five-eight. Gets in at 8:19 A.M. But really, don't come. I'm going straight to Toby Ingersoll's office. Be busy downtown all day." Toby was her local counterpart; he ran the Boston office of the American Civil Liberties Union and she ran the much bigger Washington one.

"What's all day?"

"My last appointment is at four-thirty. I should make it out to Cambridge by six-thirty, at the absolute latest. Meet me then at the Charles?"

"The Charles, huh?"

"I know how you like those little refrigerators in the rooms."

"That and the fruit baskets. What's going on, you're coming to Boston?"

"That Morty Limbach business."

"Is there a civil rights angle to that? The papers said it was autoerotic asphyxia."

"The insurance company is saying it was suicide, and they won't pay off. The ACLU is his beneficiary."

"How much?"

"A quarter of a million."

"Jesus. No wonder they're sending up their heaviest hitter."

"It's not that. What it is, I spent my last law school summer interning for the same insurance company. Fighting off claims, basically. I hated it."

"But you know a little bit about the business? Maybe you even know some of the players at the company?"

"One or two. Can we hire you to look into this for us?"

"No, but I'll look into it. What do you want to know?"

"For the moment, mainly the exact circumstances of death. I thought maybe your friend, the woman in the Cambridge crime lab?"

4

"The one with the nice tits?"

"Stuff it, Bethany. Just stuff it."

"Yeah, right. Okay. Now about this Gladys Williams, the dog that works in the crime lab. Why don't I take her to lunch tomorrow, while you're having fun with the adjusters?"

Tomorrow turned out to be another fine day, when a light sweater was all you wanted. A breeze made the river sparkle. The eights were working up and down the Charles, with the coaches following alongside in their launches and shouting at the crews through bullhorns. The brightly colored blades of the oars lifted and swept and dropped and caught and lifted again. The wakes from the launches sloshed onto the banks.

I had told Gladys to meet me on the little grassy patch sheltered between the Weld boat house dock and the Anderson Bridge. You got a sense of the real speed of the boats there, where they swept under the bridge. They moved faster than most men can sprint, as I knew from my early-morning runs along the river. A crew from Northeastern vanished under the bridge. The vaulted arch amplified the creaking of the rigging and the grunting of the oarsmen as they drove the oars full power. Once at a regatta I saw a rower pass out from the effort just as his boat crossed the finish line. Tough sport. For all I knew, tougher than my own sport. I never saw anyone pass out at the end of a wrestling match.

I spread out a beach towel from my gym bag and weighted it down against the breeze with groceries. I had brought cheese and cold cuts and pâté from Cardullo's on Harvard Square, along with bottles of hot mustard, pickles, sweet peppers, and mushrooms. I had two loaves of French bread from Au Bon Pain, and bottles of sparkling cider and wine that I left in the bag, out of the sun. I was a quarter of an hour early, but I was able to pass the time constructively by watching large young women launching their racing shells from the Weld dock.

"I should do that shit," said Gladys from behind me. "Boat rowing. Maybe it would make me tall and blond and healthy."

"Sure, give it a shot," I said, getting up. "Meanwhile I brought some cholesterol and alcohol and stuff." Neither of us cared—me because I worked the calories off wrestling, and Gladys because she didn't measure her self-image in pounds. And so we got rid of everything except a little bit of the second loaf of bread.

After lunch she got a stack of color photos out of a manila envelope and showed me the crime scene. "Very nice," I said. "Good, sharp focus here, Gladys. You take these?"

"No, a uniformed photographer has to take all the pictures," she said. "Probably union rules or something. What I am is a crime lab technician, different thing entirely. Much more class. Comb pubic hair, collect fluid samples, observe at autopsies, that kind of thing."

"Observe, my ass."

"I'm giving you the job description here, Bethany, not the job. The actual job itself, I do what has to be done."

"And the fact is Dr. Karpegis has got the shakes too bad to do autopsies or even autopsy reports."

"Why, whoever told you a thing like that?"

"Lieutenant Curtin."

"I guess you'd have to go with it, then."

"Is Curtin handling this?"

"No, just a couple of his guys. Nothing to handle, right? An accidental death."

"The insurance investigators say suicide."

"Bullshit. I was there."

"Tell me about it . . ."

6

A lot of it I knew from the papers. The dead man was Morton Limbach III, a rich young guy who owned an old mansion off Mass. Ave. in the direction of Central Square. He used it as the headquarters for an improvisational theater troupe he sponsored, called the Poor Attitudes. Morty had died, according to the police and the medical examiner, while playing weird masturbation games in an unused bedroom on the ground floor of the mansion. Once the bedroom had belonged to Kathy Poindexter, the TV star. In those days she had been with the Poor Attitudes, playing gigs like Central Connecticut State College. Nobody had lived in the room since she went off to New York and got famous.

"Take a look," Gladys said, showing me one of the pictures. "It's almost like the fire alarm went off and whoever lived there ran out without taking anything."

A table held a cheap makeup mirror, with four small light bulbs, two on either side. Around it were pots and jars of cold cream and makeup, bottles of lotions and oils, manicure instruments, combs and brushes and rollers and curlers, perfumes and nail polish.

"It was all stuff from the drugstore or the K Mart," Gladys said. "Not the stuff you get from the department stores with the pretty demonstrators in the doctor coats. Some of the clothes in the closet and in the drawers were good, but it was all old. Most were like the things on the dressing table, cheap. Nothing was outright filthy, but it wasn't all that clean, either."

The decorations I could see in the photos dated back to the late sixties, very early seventies. Psychedelic stuff, Max Ernst posters, a poster that said FUCK COMMUNISM, and another that showed a man puking into a toilet bowl. There was a huge official portrait, a little larger than life, of Lyndon Johnson. He was posed, stern and manly, standing with his hand on the back of a chair. In his lapel was the little red and white device of the Silver Star medal, which he had won for riding along as a passenger on a bombing run in World War II.

Morty Limbach was sitting over by the left-hand wall of the room. He was slumped to one side, saved from falling on the floor by an extension cord looped around his neck. It was strung up to an old-fashioned wooden curtain rod, thick as a broomstick, that ran along the top of a tall window behind him. The socket end of the cord dangled down his shirt front, like a string necktie with a cylinder on the end of it. The extension cord was the heavy-duty orange kind, with sixteen-gauge wires; the cylinder was its socket, which was a little bigger than a regular flashlight battery.

Limbach was wearing a striped rugby shirt that looked to be from L. L. Bean. His only other clothes were dark-colored socks, and a pair of the kind of boxer shorts that fasten at the waist with snaps. They were unfastened and gaping open. His bare legs stuck out straight in front of him, flat on the floor and spread wide. Chino pants and a pair of topsiders, probably also from L. L. Bean, sat in a clump at his feet.

"Can I get copies of the pictures?" I asked Gladys when she had finished telling me about them.

"These are extras. Just don't tell anybody you've got them."

"His face looks pretty normal," I said. "I thought your tongue was supposed to stick out when you're hung."

"Autoerotic asphyxia doesn't really work that way. The point of the ligature is to cut down on the blood flow to the brain. You can still breathe, but the brain isn't getting much oxygen. Supposed to make the orgasm more intense in theory, but hey, what do I know? I'm just an old-fashioned girl."

"Yeah, sure you are." Gladys kept two, sometimes three,

men on her string at all times. Each of them knew about the others, which she figured kept them better motivated.

"Anyway," she went on, "what can happen is the same thing that cops sometimes do to people by accident, with the carotid choke hold. The ligature presses on the carotid artery just enough to cut the supply of blood to the brain. Ten seconds or so, you pass out. You slump forward, the pressure keeps up, the brain dies. Not really strangulation. Probably painless."

"So there wouldn't be any damage to the windpipe, that kind of thing."

"Might be a little, might be practically none. Hard to say."

"Why is it hard to say? Couldn't you tell when you carved him up?"

"We didn't bother with an autopsy. Doc Karpegis was on the scene. He signed off on it as an accidental death, and the hell with it."

"No chance it was suicide?"

"Sure there's a chance. I guess there's a chance Elvis is alive."

"Physically, though, it's possible the guy killed himself?"

"Sure. All of a sudden he's had it with life, okay? He's jerked off one time too many. So the hell with it, he decides to end it right on the spot . . ."

Gladys paused for a second the way Joe Isuzu does. Then in his voice she said, "Yeah, yeah, that's it! He killed himself! *That's* what must have happened!"

In her own voice again, she said, "Yeah, and maybe Elvis lives."

"It's more or less what the insurance company says happened," I said.

"Look, Tom, the jobs I've had you see a lot of weirdness. But nobody gets ready to kill themselves by jacking off."

"Unless he's setting the stage for an insurance scam."

9

"I doubt even the insurance company believes that shit," Gladys said.

Hope showed up in the lobby of the Charles Hotel at just about the time she had said she would. Among other virtues, she was punctual and reliable.

"Hi," she said.

"Hi," I said. She offered her cheek to be kissed, and I kissed it. We hadn't seen each other for three months and six days, but neither of us came from warm, demonstrative Mediterranean cultures. It was enough that we both knew that the other knew it had been three months and six days.

Hope was wearing her hair up in a bun, as she does when she's out facing the world and offering her cheek for fleeting contact. She was not compulsive enough to make a bun that was perfectly wrapped and constructed, though, and she would no more use hair spray than she would use gold nail polish. Or any nail polish at all. Consequently, strands kept coming out of the bun. She kept shoving them back up as she checked in and went through her messages. I watched the unconscious dance of her hands, loving it.

As soon as we got upstairs and the door of her room closed behind us she kissed me properly. And immediately went to work unpacking. While she worked, she talked.

"—the point I'm making," she was saying, "although I might as well be making it to a brick wall, is that it would be completely normal to pay a fee for this investigation, and we'd expect to do it, and the ACLU has the money, and we'd have to pay it to anybody else to do the work, so why not pay it to you?"

"Because it would make me feel funny, that's all."

"What kind of a reason is that?"

"A good kind."

"Well, all right. You want to donate your services. What

10

about expenses, then? At least you shouldn't go in the hole."

"If there are any expenses, the ACLU can pay them."

"Good. At least I'm not coming out of these negotiations empty handed."

"Dinner, too. You can buy me dinner. And give me a place to sleep."

"Is that the kind of girl you think I am?"

We ate an expensive dinner downstairs. It was good, too, or at least it seemed good. Of course, things taste better on an expense account. Working for the nonprofits is generally a nonprofit proposition in itself. But a few of the jobs at the very top pay pretty well in salary and perks, and Hope had the second-best job in the organization.

Over coffee—tea, in my case—we talked about our days. Mine hadn't been very productive. After driving Gladys back to work, I had gone to the reference room in Widener Library and read all the newspaper accounts of Morty Limbach's unappealing death. Then I looked up Limbach, and his rich family, and all I could find about autoerotic asphyxia. It wasn't much. Most of the relevant material turned out to be in the law library, or in the medical school library, across the river in Boston.

Hope's day had been much more active. She had met with her Boston opposite number, Toby Ingersoll, and with a roomful of insurance company executives determined to keep her quarter-of-a-million bucks in their own hands. And she had met with Jerome Rosson, who taught at Harvard Law School.

"Sure, I've heard of him," I said when she asked. "I've got a TV."

Rosson was on the guest list of every assistant producer of every news and talk show in the country, filed under constitutional law. The professor gave great sound bite.

"He was Morty Limbach's attorney," Hope said. "Now he represents the estate."

"Which means he thinks the estate should get the money instead of you?"

"No, he's on our side. Morty asked him for advice when he took out the policy in the first place, so he knows what Morty's intent was."

"What was his intent?"

"Nothing complicated. Just to support the ACLU." Limbach, as I knew from my afternoon at Widener, had been a great backer of liberal causes.

"Sounds pretty complicated to me. Why take out a life insurance policy? Why not just send you a check?"

"It was a scheme our fund-raiser dreamed up a few years back. The idea was that young or relatively young supporters could buy term life very cheaply. So they'd donate the premium money to us and we'd use it to buy policies on their lives. They'd get a charitable deduction for the amount of the premiums and we'd get a big pile of money if a truck hit them."

"Did it work?"

"Not too well. It turned out people didn't like the idea of betting that a truck would hit them. Something about it didn't work, anyway. We've been the beneficiary of a few fairly small policies, but this will be our first really big payday. If we can roll over that bastard Westfall."

"What bastard Westfall?"

"I'm sorry. Warren W. Westfall. He's the president and chief executive officer of Pilgrim Mutual."

"He's slow pay, huh?"

"Maybe no pay. We screwed up royally when we switched carriers last year. These things are group policies, and Pilgrim offered us slightly lower premiums than our old company. The suicide clause didn't seem important at the time."

"The new company doesn't pay off in case of suicide?"

"Everybody pays off in case of suicide nowadays. Suicide exclusions aren't standard anymore, except for the first two years of a policy's life."

"And that's when you bought Limbach's policy?"

"No, it's much older than that. Only with group policies like this, when you switch carriers the new company treats all the old policies as new policies. So the clock on the two years starts running all over again, on every one of the policies. That's what gave Westfall his chance to try to screw us."

"Why would he want to screw you? You're not just some starving widow with orphans, you're a big customer. And the cops say it was accidental death anyway. Why not just pay off?"

"You never ran across Westfall's name?"

I shook my head.

"If Westfall's got any chance at all of keeping that money from a bunch of Commies like us, he'll take it. He's one of the major angels for the far right. Not quite in Scaife's class, but he isn't as rich as Scaife, either." Richard Scaife, I knew, was a fat rich kid from Pittsburgh. Actually I didn't know if he was fat, but same idea.

"Why did you switch to Westfall's company, then?" I asked.

"Nobody on the business side thought to check with us ideological types. And nobody on our side was paying attention. What did we care what the bean counters down in the business office were doing?"

Hope picked up her coffee cup, examined the last little bit of cold coffee in it, and put the cup back down. "Now we care," she said.

"Want another cup?"

"No, let's slip into something comfortable."

And so we took the elevator back upstairs, to Hope's

13

room. " 'I always have to slip around to be alone with you,' " I said on the way. "Know that one?"

"No. What is it?"

"Old country western song."

Hope had stayed at my apartment once, but no more. For one thing, it was awkward to tell lies to her associates about where she was staying. For another, she had been nervous the whole time that something might happen to her children, that her husband might be trying to reach her. Of course, she might have just given him my number, right up front about it, since he almost certainly knew what was going on between us anyway. They had had practically no love life at all since he discovered, after their third child was born, that his real preference was for men.

But I could understand why she didn't want to confront him openly with the truth about our relationship. Once as a kid I was riding a freight train in December, down south but not so far down that it wasn't freezing cold. By three or so in the morning, I was getting close to hypothermia in my empty boxcar. During a stop in a little town, I was dumb enough to go back to the caboose and ask if they would let me in to warm up, since a brakeman had seen me sneak aboard hours before and hadn't shouted at me. But naturally they ordered me off the train instead. It was one thing to pretend you didn't notice when somebody snuck onto your train; it was another for the somebody to shove himself right into the crew's face and force a decision.

And so I always moved into the Charles Hotel when Hope found an excuse to come to Boston. Besides her, there was the attraction of the fruit basket on the night table. There was also the small refrigerator full of over-priced drinks that would appear on the room bill later if we drank them. And the maids turned down the bed, although this one had only done it on one side. And she had left only one chocolate on the pillow.

"Let's be honest here," I said. "We both want that chocolate."

"You take it," Hope said. "You're the guest."

"No, you take it. It's your room."

"Negotiations are deadlocked again," Hope said. "What will we do now?"

"Let's arm wrestle for it."

"No, let's share it."

There you had it, the essential difference between the male and female approaches to conflict resolution. The difference, essentially, between stupid and smart. What the hell, just this once I agreed to sharing.

"What's that I taste?" she asked a few minutes later. "Have you been eating chocolate?"

"Who are you to talk?" I said.

And then neither of us said anything for some little time. Finally, though, we got up to get ready for bed. After that we lay there side by side while we watched something dumb on TV. To improve the show, I turned the sound off. The cars crashed and the guns blasted in silence, as we turned back to each other. We had been apart, once again, too long.

Hope handled the wake-up call next morning, since she was the one who had to join the rush hour to Boston, not me. Besides, it might have been her husband or one of her kids calling. On her way to the shower she turned the television on so that I could power up for the day by watching the idiots chirp and chuckle at one another on "Good Morning, America." I thought about getting up and changing to the "Today" show, but that seemed like a lot of effort just to watch Willard Scott. Mirrors reflecting mirrors. The morning shows all trying to be like the sitcoms that tried to be like morning shows trying to be like sitcoms. Candice Bergen playing Barbara Walters playing Murphy Brown, Deborah Norville playing Jane Pauley playing Mary Tyler Moore playing God knows who. Rosalind Russell, maybe, playing Hildy.

When Hope came out of the shower her hair was up for the day, each hair precisely where it belonged for the moment. The effect was of calm confidence, total control— or no doubt would have been if she hadn't been naked.

"Step over here a minute," I said.

"Can't," Hope said, swaying her hips out of my grasp as she went by. "Got to dress for success." As she was putting on the double-breasted blue, I asked her if she wanted breakfast sent up.

"Sure, but I won't have time," she said. "Why don't you have some? You're not seeing Rosson for a while, are you?"

"Not till his first lecture is over, no. A little after ten." As the dead man's lawyer, Rosson was supposed to give me whatever access he could to documents and records that might bear on the death.

"What would you order for breakfast if you weren't going to be eating a candy bar from the T station instead?" I asked. "Just tell me and I'll eat it for you."

"I don't know," Hope said. "Probably dry toast and a cup of hot water with a slice of lemon. Cottage cheese, maybe."

"You got it," I said. As she listened, I ordered orange juice, two pots of hot chocolate, Cream of Wheat with maple syrup, English muffins, and corned beef hash with four poached eggs.

Hope kissed me good-bye, grabbed her briefcase, and turned back for a moment on her way out the door. "I hope you explode and die," she said. "I just wanted you to know that."

— 2 —

I DID FEEL A LITTLE FULL WHEN I HAD FINISHED OUR BREAK-
fasts, as a matter of fact, but the walk through Harvard
Square and on to the law school settled the load down.
Jerome Rosson's office was in Langdell Hall, which also
housed the law school's library. Once in a while I had
done research there, a privilege that Harvard extends to
most members of the public for twenty dollars a day. Harvard extends it to me for nothing, since I carry a university
ID card. A teaching assistant gives me one each year, once
the university has issued him a duplicate to replace the one
he supposedly lost. In return I work out with him now
and then and give him a few pointers. I can't give him
many, since he used to be a pretty fair wrestler at Lehigh
himself.

Rosson's office was locked, but I saw the professor at the
end of the hall with a couple of students in convoy. As
they came nearer, I could hear that the question before the
court was whether a trespasser could sue the owner of a
dog that bit him. I was on the dog's side. It turned out,

from what the professor was telling his students, that the law was, too.

When the students took off down the hall, he turned to me, stuck out his hand, and said, "Dr. Bethany, I presume. Come on in."

Rosson turned out to have a saloon keeper's passion for celebrity photographs. Wherever there weren't bookcases, photographs covered the walls of the office. Rosson with famous athletes, authors, performers, businessmen, and, mainly, Rosson with politicians. He was shorter than most of them, a much smaller man than he seemed to be on television. A lean little man with a big-nosed, homely face, a Jiminy Cricket. I sat down in the chair he waved me to—a Roche-Bobois production with soft, black leather upholstery. They go for a couple of thousand, and the matching sofa was probably three times that. Law school professors, unlike U.S. senators, can make as much outside income as they want. Rosson's fees from Morty Limbach alone had probably been more than enough, over the years, to furnish a dozen offices with these things that always look to me like oversize dog beds.

Professor Rosson touched down briefly on one of them himself, and then bounded up again. "Terrible stuff," he said. "Absolutely terrible stuff." He moved over to the window. He moved back. He sat on the edge of his desk. He got up again. He lifted a paperweight and put it down. He tested the point of a letter opener. He went to the window again. He touched the sash, then the cord on the blinds. He crossed back behind me, to the door, then back across to the desk, talking nonstop. Energy zinged along all his wires.

As he talked I began to understand that the terrible stuff wasn't the furniture he had been sitting on earlier, but the whole business of Limbach's death. "Young man," he said. "Relatively young. Relative to me, anyway. Baby boomer.

Never got it quite right, poor Morty. Comes into his money in the early seventies, just as our national children's party is ending. Wants to be an angel for the counterculture, and now they're all getting fitted for pinstripes. Borrowing for that first condo. Along comes poor Morty, patron of the arts. What's happened? Too late, Morty. The train just left. All the rebels are on 'Saturday Night Live' now, getting filthy rich. Nothing daunted, not Morty. Turns the old family mansion into the Poor Attitudes House as ancestors revolve in their graves. Stumble, lurch. Year after year. Nothing clicks.

"Finally the real thing comes through the door, great, terrific. Two geniuses. Leo Grasso, Grasso the Great. Kathy Poindexter, loyal sidekick. Troupe finally catches fire, becomes household word. Locally. But not local for long. Grasso takes off to the big time, his own sitcom. Networks. Off to New York, see you around. Along with Kathy and everybody else in the company who's got an ounce of talent. Leaving Morty behind. At last a real party gets going in his house and then everybody splits on him. Poor Morty, nothing to do but take out the empties. Clean up the mess, mop the toilet."

Rosson flopped down heavily on the big black sofa, as if he had just been doing all that mopping himself. "Well, what about it?" he said. "I pay top dollar. Want to go to work for me?"

"Doing what?"

"Prying the ACLU's insurance money out of that fascist son of a bitch, Westfall."

"I already told Hope I'd do that pro bono."

"No reason for that. Look, I've got a fiduciary responsibility to carry out the decedent's wishes, expressed to me both orally and in writing, that his insurance benefits go to the American Civil Liberties Union. Seeing that those wishes are carried out isn't just my personal inclination. If

19

I was Rehnquist, God forbid, I'd have to do the same thing. It's my professional, legal, ethical, and et cetera duty, is what I'm saying here. So how much do you charge?"

"Sixty dollars an hour, for friends. And I work slow."

"That's high."

"I don't know. How much do you charge?"

"More than that. Okay, you're hired."

"Not yet. Let's talk about something. Where does my fee come from?"

"The estate."

"Aren't there other heirs?"

"Other than who?"

"The ACLU."

"Oh, I see what you mean. Yes, there are others who benefit, too."

"And the others wouldn't benefit from the insurance policy?"

"No, just the ACLU."

"So it wouldn't be fair to charge the whole estate for the costs of collecting benefits that would only go to the ACLU?"

"It would be questionable, certainly."

"So my fee would come out of the ACLU's quarter million?"

Rosson smiled. "We were hoping that wouldn't occur to you," he said.

"Who's 'we'?"

"Hope and I."

"Well, it did occur to me."

"Regardless of where your fees ultimately come from, it would be preferable for you to work for me rather than the ACLU. Or, more precisely, through me for the estate. It would give you standing to make inquiries. It would protect whatever you found out, under the attorney-client relationship."

20

"Okay, hire me. I'll charge you a dollar. I work just as hard for a dollar, when I want to. And just as slow." I probably sounded nastier than I meant to.

"You don't like me, do you?" the professor asked.

"It doesn't matter, does it?"

"Not too much, no. Plenty of people don't like me." He didn't sound worried about it.

"Actually, I kind of do like you, so far. I'm pissed off about something else."

"Nothing to do with me?"

"No, not you."

"Good," he said. He took a dollar out of his wallet and gave it to me. "In exchange for a consideration of value," he said, "you are now employed by the estate of the late Morton Limbach the third."

"Fine," I said. "Then you better tell me all about him."

I knew some of what he told me. A lot of it I didn't.

The original Morton Limbach, two generations back, had been a chemist who was smart enough to invent a new type of refractory brick and tough enough to keep control of the patent on it. By the time he died, in 1962, he owned large holdings in the tobacco industry, several distilleries, a pharmaceutical company, a chain of nursing homes, and the country's second-largest manufacturer of caskets. Limbach got you coming and going.

He had had a son, Morton Junior, and two daughters. None of them amounted to much in the old man's view, by which he meant they had no interest in making money. The senior Limbach therefore left the major part of his money to the third generation, on the theory that its worthlessness was at least still in doubt. He left the income from large annuities to his five grandchildren, as each of them turned twenty-one. When they reached the age of thirty-five, which all of them had by now, the grandchildren got equal portions of the whole estate. Even split five ways, the amounts were enormous. Morty's share was in the neighborhood of $30 million. " 'In the neighborhood' is about the best you can do," Rosson explained. "A fortune that big is a moving target, money going in both directions all the time. How I'd explain it to Morty, I'd tell him it was like trying to figure out not just the population of Los Angeles at any given moment, but what its total weight was."

When Grandfather Limbach bet that the third generation would take more of an interest in the business than their parents had, he lost. None of the five cared a bit about where the money came from, although four of them figured it was their due. Like George Bush, they were born on third base but thought they had hit triples. Except for Morty.

In a vague way, uninformed but well-intentioned, Morty had always worried about the folks back on first and second, and even about the ones who never seemed to be able to get on base at all. "Didn't go to St. Paul's like his cousins," Rosson said. "Not St. Paul's material. Putney material."

"What's Putney?"

"Kind of school where they have a farm and the kids play milkmaid. Modern dance. Throwing pots. Prepares you for Bard College."

"That's where Morty went?"

"Yeah. He wanted theater but he didn't have the marks for Yale."

"Not too bright?"

"Compared to the rest of his family, he was a genius. But bright and marks are different things. Morty just wasn't too focused. You don't have to be, when you know your allowance is going to go up to something like five thousand dollars a week during your senior year."

After graduation, Limbach had moved into what the

family called the Old House, in Cambridge. It was a four-story Victorian mansion on Ellery Street that the grandfather had bought when he first hit it big. But when he hit it even bigger he moved out into one of the showpiece Colonials on Brattle Street and chopped the Old House up into apartments. For years the building had been full of graduate students and teaching assistants and other low-rent tenants, living in one or two rooms and sometimes sharing bathrooms down the hall. When Morty took over, he told the rent board he meant to use the whole building as his own residence and eventually got rid of his tenants. He made them as happy as he could by buying up whatever furniture and decorations they wanted to leave behind, which meant that the mansion wound up full of cheap junk from the sixties, which accounted for the period posters in the death scene photos. The place was a time capsule.

The Old House turned into the Poor Attitudes House pretty much the same way a shell develops to match its owner. Limbach's energies at Bard College had gone mostly to a student improvisational troupe. Once out of college and back home in Cambridge, he found his way to another improv company. This one was made up of college dropouts, other recent grads like himself, and graduate students. The company called itself the Poor Attitudes, since most of its members had one, or so they had been told from kindergarten on. And of course most of them were poor—waitresses, busboys, graduate students, and that kind of thing. Morty would let them move into his houseful of spare rooms whenever they needed a place to stay, which usually happened because they had been evicted from someplace else for nonpayment of rent. In theory they were supposed to pay a minimal rent to him, but in practice he didn't need the money and what the hell. Sometimes they paid and sometimes they didn't.

23

Somehow he had become the patron of an unorganized, constantly changing, but nonetheless functional improvisational theater troupe. "Morty became a sort of business manager for them," Rosson said. "You'd have to have known him to realize what an absurd idea that was. Still, though, in that crowd he was probably a fiscal genius. And actually it wasn't too costly. At least he wasn't backing Broadway flops or producing his own movies, which would have run into real dough.

"In fact it worked out reasonably okay. Hell of a tax write-off, as it turned out. I incorporated and loaded everything onto the corporation. Rented the mansion to it. Charged most of Morty's personal expenses to it. I even put the community shrink on the payroll. I wasn't sure the IRS would stand still for that one, but so far they have."

"How do you mean, community shrink?" I asked.

"Dr. Mark Unger. One of the kids that first moved into the mansion was in analysis with him and couldn't continue. Lack of funds. Translation was that her daddy wouldn't keep on paying unless she moved back home. Morty took over the payments himself until she drifted on a few months later. But Unger himself stuck around. Turned out the doctor is kind of a ham himself. Which it seems is pretty common among shrinks. So he attached himself and even moved in. Rents an office for peanuts in the upstairs rear. I think he's pretty good, actually. Helped some of the kids. In addition to his regular practice, he became kind of a resident shrink to Morty and the troupe."

"To Limbach, too?"

"Oh, sure. Morty developed an early dependence on psychiatrists. His parents sent him to one when he voted for George McGovern in '72."

"So Dr. Unger would be the one to talk to about suicidal tendencies. Or would he have some kind of an ethical problem with that?"

24

"Apparently not. At least he didn't have any problem telling the insurance company their suicide theory was full of shit."

"Now that I work for the estate, how about asking him to tell me the same thing?"

Professor Rosson set that up with a phone call, and then made a couple more calls for me. At the end, Dr. Unger and the insurance company's chief investigator were expecting me. So was the maintenance company that employed Maria Soares, the maid who had discovered Limbach's body.

All the while Rosson was on the phone, he held the machine in his hand and quick-stepped back and forth, as far in every direction as the cord would let him. The professor was like a wild animal on a rope, frantic that its energy is confined.

I had found Maria Soares through Sani-Kleen Building Maintenance Services, which had the contract to swamp out the Poor Attitudes House three times a week. She lived in a triple-decker in Somerville. Like a lot of what are called triple-deckers, it actually had four floors. Hers was the top one, but you don't pay extra for the view, not in Somerville. It isn't like Central Park West. There are no views in Somerville, and the higher you live the hotter it gets in summer, and the more climbing you have to do.

The door had been answered by a teen-age kid wearing stone-washed jeans, dirty socks, and a T-shirt advertising an out-there local thrash band called the Pixies. He said his name was Tony Freitas, and that Maria Soares was his aunt. She was in her own room like she always was, playing with her stupid rosary. Already I liked Tony.

He took me down the hall and shouted something in Portuguese through a closed door. Without waiting for an answer he went on in, leaving me to follow behind. Whatever Maria Soares might have been like as a young girl back in the Azores, not much vitality was left in her now. She sat still in her darkened room, her hands quiet in the lap of her black housedress, wasting no motion. Probably years of drudgery and day laboring had geared her down like a tractor, for the long slow haul. On seeing a stranger, Maria Soares got up from her chair. She sat down again only when I had settled into the chair she indicated.

She said something in Portuguese, and Tony answered.

"What did she say?" I asked.

"Nothing," Tony said.

"Sounded like something."

"Nah, nothing. She just said why don't I put some shoes on."

I looked at him just long enough to make him uncomfortable. "Does she pay the rent here?" I asked.

"Some of it. She's a widow woman."

"Widow women get to pay rent, huh? How about you?"

"How about me what?"

"Do you pay rent?"

"Pay rent?" He sounded puzzled. "I live here."

"But you don't pay any of the rent?"

"Of course not."

"And your aunt does?"

Tony nodded. He looked like a dog that can't figure out what he's supposed to have done wrong.

"Then go put your fucking shoes on," I said, hard and sharp.

He stood there, as if nobody had ever given him an order before and he couldn't absorb the whole concept. I wondered if his folks were from the old country, too, like his aunt, maybe speaking broken English so that he could think they were dummies who didn't really signify. I stood up and moved too close to him.

"You want, I can help you," I said into his face.

26

"Hey, I'm going, all right?"

When he had gone I sat back down and watched Maria Soares sitting with her hands quiet in her lap, in the dim light that came through the lowered shade on the window of her small bedroom. There was a rosary on the table beside her, sure enough, and a small statue of Christ Crucified on the wall. It was made of plastic that tried to look like ivory. I asked her how long she had been working at the Poor Attitudes House, but she just gestured toward the door to say that I should wait till her translator got back.

When he did, he had Reeboks on. He had left them unlaced and gaping open, to show that nobody pushed Tony Freitas around.

"Don't fuck with me, Tony," I said. "Tie 'em."

He was the kind of pathetic kid who would probably find a home in the marine corps. All he needed was a drill instructor to be his daddy, and care what he looked like, and what time he went to bed and got up, and what he did every single minute he was awake. While he was tying his laces, I looked at his aunt with a would-you-believe-kids-today expression. Her face stayed impassive, telling me what I should have known: that I wasn't doing her any favors. Tony would still be here after I was gone, no doubt treating his wounded machismo by adding a little extra something to the daily ration of shit he fed her. That's all I had done with my own display of machismo. When will they ever learn?

Once Tony had got himself all laced up and tidy, we started out with the interview. It was a flat conversation, both the part I could understand and the Portuguese part. Tony was trying to sound bored, cool, and uninterested. His aunt sounded like a prisoner, who knew better than not to answer when a guard asked her something.

"She says she been there four years. Sani-Kleen six years but this place, what do you call it? . . . Right, Poor Attitudes House . . . Anyway, only four years there. She goes other places too, only goes this place the guy died three days a week. Monday, Wednesday, Friday . . .

"Okay, she doesn't know nothing about it, the place. She never heard of this group, whatever it is, Attitudes. She figured at first it was, what the word means is whorehouse, only it don't sound so bad, you say it in Portuguese. Then she figured the place was too dirty for a whorehouse. Everybody lived like a pig pen except the doctor. Is there a doctor lives there or something? . . . Okay, that's it, then. The doctor's office. He was normal, this doctor. You know, clean . . .

"Okay, what she figured instead of a whorehouse was maybe students. Or maybe one of them what-do-you-call-its, like the assholes with their heads shaved. The orange guys, what do they call guys like that? . . . Cults, right . . . Maybe it's a cult, she figured . . .

"No, she never asked what the place was. It's a job, you go where they tell you. When she figured it out, it was when she saw Leo Grasso on TV when he first come on and she knew his face and some of the other ones on with him. So she's got a friend, my aunt does, another old woman, only this one talks better English, so anyway she explains it to her, the friend does. How Leo was an actor when he lived where she worked, a comic, whatever you call it. Her friend read it in the newspapers and told her it was a comic house, like . . .

"Well, that day she goes to work at nine like always, it's a Monday, all right? Huh? . . . Okay, she says it was unlocked. A lot of times they don't lock it. Nobody cares, she says, it's like they're living in the street. She starts out downstairs like always. Upstairs where most of them sleep, they don't get up till noon, maybe later. Downstairs they only got one bedroom, only like nobody sleeps there . . .

Yeah, she says locked. It's always locked, that room, only her and the dead guy got keys. The boss, I guess he was.

"So inside, she always starts there because nobody lives in that room and it's clean so it's easy, inside she sees the guy . . ."

I got Tony to go over and over this part with her. To his credit, maybe, he seemed embarrassed at passing on some of my more clinical questions. Probably he couldn't get his mind around the idea that a female relative in her fifties might once have been human, just like him, and might even have had some kind of sex life.

The lock on the bedroom door, Maria Soares said, was the kind that locked automatically when you closed it behind you, unless you pushed in a button below the latch. The front and back doors of the mansion had locks like that, too. So did the office of Dr. Unger, the psychiatrist. All the other locks were the old-fashioned kind, with keyhole-shaped keyholes. Most of the keys were lost, so that anybody who wanted privacy had to go down to the hardware store and buy a bolt.

Maria Soares remembered clearly that the door to the downstairs bedroom was locked that morning. As she pushed the door open, it blocked her view to the left so that she only saw the body when she was fully inside. With the door standing open, she took a step or two toward the body. She bent over and then got down on her knees to look more closely, which sounded pretty unfazed to me. "She says she ain't afraid of bodies," Tony translated. "When she was a girl in the old country she had to help wash and dress the dead people when they died."

What she described was exactly what the police pictures showed: Morty Limbach's body slumped forward and to one side, kept from toppling by the extension cord that ran from the wooden curtain rod to his neck. Pants on the floor at his feet. Underpants open, spotted with dried semen. More semen stains on the rug. The spots hadn't been evident in the police photos, so I had the boy ask Maria Soares how she happened to notice them. Again to his credit, maybe, Tony sounded embarrassed asking. She didn't sound embarrassed answering. "She says she been changing the sheets in that place three years, she seen plenty of it."

"Three years?" I asked. "I thought you said she was there four years."

It turned out that maid service hadn't been provided when she first came to work until she complained to her bosses at Sani-Kleen about the smell in some of the bedrooms. Presumably the bosses passed on the news to Limbach, because her original two days a week became three. The added day was to give her time to launder the sheets and any dirty clothes lying around. A washer and dryer were in the basement, but they hadn't got very heavy use until she took on the chore. Nor had the communal kitchen's big dishwasher, which was always full when she came in.

"Ask her what went on in the room where she found the guy," I said. "How come nobody lived in it?"

Maria Soares didn't know. She called it the museum, because nothing had been moved or even touched in there, as far as she could tell, since Kathy left to go on TV. Before that it wasn't the museum, just the place where Kathy slept. Once after Kathy had been gone for a while, Maria had let herself in the room and found Mr. Limbach there, just sitting on the bed, and another time she had spotted him coming out of the door. But she didn't have any idea what he was doing in the room. He didn't use it as an office, because there was no phone in it and no desk either, unless you counted the dressing table, all covered with bottles and jars. He couldn't have been doing any work on the table, though, because there was no room to. And there was no room because she, Maria, was just supposed to dust the junk on the table and everything else in the place, then put everything back the way she found it. Not to clean up the dressing table, or put away the clothes and other belongings that Kathy had left, or to disturb anything in any way.

Kathy, I knew, was Kathy Poindexter. She had been the long-suffering wife of Leo Grasso on the "Leo Grasso Show," and in real life she had also been his long-suffering wife, if the supermarket tabloids were right. She had been his wife before they both went to New York and got famous, and yet there was no evidence of a male presence in the police pictures.

Tony passed on my question.

"She don't know where any of them slept upstairs," he reported back. "They moved around, like, except for Kathy, who was downstairs. Then she gets married to Leo and sometimes she sleeps in her old bedroom downstairs, sometimes she's upstairs God knows where. Upstairs my aunt don't know. All she knows is when Kathy slept downstairs she was always alone. According to what my aunt could tell, anyway. Back then, there wasn't no baby."

Everybody knew that. The baby was practically born on TV. Kathy Poindexter's pregnancy had been just starting to show when the "Leo Grasso Show" itself started. The whole thing—the situations, the plot line, the jokes—revolved around the pregnancy, the birth, and eventually the baby. Even before his father died, barely off camera, Little Leo had the highest name recognition of any baby in two thousand years, nearly. By now he had probably moved into first place, since Baby Jesus didn't have his own brand-new sitcom. The "Little Leo Show," on the other hand, had been at the top of the Nielsens right from the first episode.

I had watched that first episode myself, one of the mil-

31

lions who did. I'm able to give the Superbowl and the World Series and the Academy Awards and the Miss America contest a pass every year, with no regrets. But no way would I miss the debut of a grieving real-life widow and her orphaned baby starring in their own half-hour comedy. Could our two great native art forms, the sitcom and the soap opera, be successfully married? And not just to each other, but to the docudrama as well? The answer had to be no.

And yet it wasn't.

In that first episode, as in real life, the husband and father had died not long before in a dressing room accident. He had been talking and eating at the same time, when a hunk of meat lodged in his windpipe. When he began to gesture wildly at his throat, then, the man he was talking to figured it was just old Leo again, clowning around. The man was Teddy Elliman, up from Cambridge for a visit. At the time he was the resident director of the Poor Attitudes. Elliman didn't catch on that Leo's performance was for real till the star turned red in the face and crumpled unconscious to the floor. Then Elliman started pounding Grasso on the back, which did no good at all and might even have made things worse. By the time Elliman gave up and ran for help, it was probably already too late. When the emergency personnel got there, Grasso was dead.

Elliman stayed on in New York as the creator and director of what became the "Little Leo Show." Two months later, which was apparently an incredibly brief time, the first episode aired and Elliman became a genius. In his world, anyway. On the "Leo Grasso Show," Kathy Poindexter had played the latest in television's long series of comically abused wives. One of these days, Alice, right in the kisser. Archie Bunker's better half, Eat-it. That kind of thing. Leo's stage job in the old show had been as the tyrannical manager of a fast-food joint, with a constantly changing cast of dippy employees. In the first episode of the new show, Kathy was seen recovering from the blow of his tragic death at the hands of a Hugee with all the trimmings. But Kathy was no longer a foil and a straight woman for her hyperkinetic husband. Her husband's death had set her character free to face the world with tentative, hopeful courage. Her focus and the focus of the new show, as its name indicated, was not on her husband any longer but on her baby.

The baby was too young to talk, but that didn't keep him from stealing scene after scene on both the old and the new shows. He was a cheerful, outgoing, unafraid little kid who had no trouble expressing what was on his mind, words or no words. The impossibility of teaching him lines was the strength of both shows. Little Leo was working from his own unpredictable script, and everybody else had to adapt on the spot. And the shows were shot live, like the old "Sid Caesar Show," which made them even more unpredictable. The appeal of the show, like the appeal of improvisational theater, was in wondering how the actors were going to cope with whatever unexpected curve the baby had just thrown at them. Like vomiting down daddy's back, which Little Leo once did on camera during the "Leo Grasso Show." Big Leo put on a sappy, phony smile of love and forgiveness, laid the baby down carefully on the floor, hung his head over his wife's shoulder, and seemed to puke down *her* back.

Well, you had to be there. And millions of people were, or at least in the home audience. The scene was now part of a tape called "Life with Leo," a collection of magic moments from the original show. According to the Living Arts section in last week's *Boston Globe*, "Life with Leo" was the top-selling video in the country. Second was selected footage from "America's Funniest Home Videos," another show with improvisational elements to it. Maria

Soares was a fan of both shows, her nephew said. It made sense, when I thought about it. You didn't have to know much English to enjoy either one.

"Ask her where the cord came from," I told Tony.

"What do you mean, cord?"

"The extension cord around the guy's neck."

"Oh, yeah. The cord."

It turned out she had never seen the cord before, either in Kathy Poindexter's old bedroom or anywhere else in the mansion. It could have been hidden in the room somewhere all along, though; all she ever gave the place was a quick once-over. Or Mr. Limbach could have brought it with him in his briefcase.

Briefcase?

"She says his briefcase, the boss's, was lying on the bed when she come in. She knows it's his because she seen him with it plenty of times."

"How come it wasn't in the pictures the police took, ask her."

Tony conferred with Maria for a minute.

"Okay, what it is, the briefcase wasn't there when the cops come. What happened, the doctor took it off with him . . ."

The doctor was Mark Unger, the psychiatrist whose office was in the upstairs rear of the Poor Attitudes House. Maria had gone from the museum room up to the psychiatrist's office to get him, as the closest thing to a boss now that the real boss was dead. When Dr. Unger came down with her, he had put the back of his fingers on Limbach's forehead long enough to discover that the body was cold, and then gone back to his office to phone the police. He took along the briefcase that had been on the bed, open, when Maria unlocked the room. As far as she could tell, there were nothing but papers in the case. There would have been plenty of room in it for an extension cord, though, even a long one.

Maria had followed the psychiatrist to his office, which was on the top floor, rear. It had a separate entrance, so that to reach it they had to go outside first. Afterward they both went back to the first-floor bedroom and waited there with the body until the police came.

"Ask her if they locked the door behind them when they went to call the cops," I told Tony. She answered no. The doctor had left the door standing open, and she hadn't wanted to close it. He was in charge. Maybe he wanted it open. The two of them were upstairs in Unger's office perhaps five minutes, perhaps ten. Unger left the briefcase behind him when they went back downstairs to wait for the police. She never saw it again.

I couldn't think of anything else to ask, and I was about to thank her for her time when it occurred to me that I still knew next to nothing about the dead man.

"Ask her how she liked Mr. Limbach," I told Tony.

"She liked him okay," the boy reported back. "I don't exactly get what she's saying, but it's like he didn't know how to be an important person or something . . ."

"Talk to her a little, see what she means," I said. The whole translation process was like wading with socks on; I couldn't really get a good feel for what was down under there. After a certain amount of back and forth, Tony gave his report.

"She says like he don't know the way he's supposed to act, like. I mean like he's this rich guy I guess, okay? Only he don't know how to give orders? Like if he gives an order it's like he don't like to give the order?"

"I get the idea," I said, and maybe I did.

When I got up to leave, Maria Soares nodded politely but otherwise made no movement. A mound of black with a pale face on top of it. I nodded back and said to Tony,

"Tell her thanks and I'll probably be coming by again, if I think of something else to ask." I didn't plan on coming back, but I figured it would be good for the boy to think I might.

On the corner I found a neighborhood grocery with a pay phone. I learned from the yellow pages that the only religious goods store in Cambridge specialized in Wiccan Shamanistic Magickal Afrocaribbean Botanicals. That's Cambridge for you. So I went to a place in Dorchester instead. It was called Shaughnessy's Religious Goods, and it had a complete line of crucifixion statues. One of them was a beauty, in real ivory but what the hell, I couldn't bring the elephant back to life by not buying the thing. I paid to have it sent Federal Express. A FedExed crucifix was the second best thing I could think of to do for Maria Soares, now that it was too late to do the best thing. Which would have been to keep my macho in my pants in the first place.

— 3 —

THE POOR ATTITUDES HOUSE WAS THE SORT OF VICTORIAN pile that was common enough in Cambridge, although it was larger than most and sat on more land. Once the mansion would have dominated the neighborhood and stood higher than the young trees planted to shade it. By now, though, the trees topped the house by thirty or forty feet. They were in their solid, stately prime while the house itself had turned into an old derelict sitting at the feet of the high rises nearby on Massachusetts Avenue.

The grounds, maybe a quarter of a block square, were closed in by a six-foot-high fence. It was made of cast-iron spears, once painted black but now mostly rust colored. Bushes had grown into the spaces between the palings, winding and twining so that the fence had nearly disappeared into the wild hedge. The high grass and weeds in the yard didn't quite hide the litter nobody had policed up in years. The trash wasn't the kind you'd see in the yard of a slovenly family, though. No tires, busted appliances, construction junk, rusting auto parts, rotting garbage, old mattresses, that kind of thing. It was kid trash—pizza boxes, beer and soda cans, a cracked Frisbee, Styrofoam from McDonald's and Burger King. On the front porch were a couple of bicycle wheels without tires, and an old weight bench. The effect was Animal House, not ghetto.

From Rosson I had a set of keys to the place, but the front door was unlocked just the way Maria Soares had said it usually was. I knocked lightly, just to go through the proper motions. I waited. The bright October sun was strong enough to warm my back, although the air was cool. When nobody answered, I let myself in. The front hall had an untidy but institutional look, like an entry of a dorm in some progressive college. A phone sat on a heavy oak table. On the wall above, somebody had nailed up a large sheet of Beaver Board. Messages and lists and notices and business cards covered this. Junk mail, circulars, menus from Chinese takeouts, and old newspapers and magazines were strewn on the long table.

Nobody seemed to be around, which figured. It was only a little after eleven, and Maria had said that no one got up much before noon. I thought I might as well keep busy till then by hunting out the room where Morty Limbach had died, and having a look for myself. I had my hand on the big knob of the first door on the left, a double door, really, when I let go in surprise. Or, to be honest, fear.

The instant I touched the door a cry came from behind it, an awful, eerie sound. Half-human, half-animal. It was a sound of torment and despair, a moan or a groan, all mingled, one voice or a chorus, no way to tell which. It went on and on, rising and falling, now dying almost away and then starting again. I was ready to turn and sneak out quietly, but I got on top of my fear and made myself reach for one of the big brass doorknobs again. The door creaked as it swung open, but no one inside gave any sign of hearing it.

In the big room beyond, the awful noise had stopped. Now a group of young people were blubbering through their lips while at the same time making a sort of a nonstop zooooom sound. They took no notice of me, and so I sat down in a busted armchair, a rip in its worn-out leather held together with duct tape. When the troupe got through zooming, they held their hands up to heaven in the prayer position, then lowered them slowly down toward ankle level. All throughout they made the weird moaning noise again, following their hands down through the scale from keening to deep groans.

It still sounded frightening, even though its sources weren't. They were dressed in high style for their age, with jeans torn horizontally at the knees and skin showing through. Old army fatigue jackets that might once have been mine, for all I knew. Dirty sneakers with holes in the soles. A red bandanna on one of the women, worn Aunt Jemima-fashion. On one of the men a T-shirt decorated with a huge Rorschach blot. On a nearby table sat a tin G.I. Joe lunch box, and a hat in the pillbox style that women wore in the thirties, from some attic or Salvation Army store. A ratty fringe of chestnut-colored fur ran along the top rim of the hat.

The young guy wearing the Rorschach blot was acting as the leader. He cut off the moaning and got everybody to bending over, with their heads hanging down. From where I was sitting, it turned out to be a good way of finding out who dyed and who didn't. Of the three blond women, one had dark roots. The women were able to get down farther than the men, but nobody looked particularly supple. They seemed relieved to straighten up when the guy with the blot gave the signal. Then they began rubbing their palms in circles on their cheeks, all the time groaning.

I felt quietly superior, a tolerant, good-natured guy watching the antics of a bunch of nuts. I stopped feeling that way, though, when I thought about what I had been doing a little less than twenty-four hours before. The Harvard wrestling room, on the third floor of Malkin Athletic Center, that the students called the Mac. A dozen or so wrestlers, in for a voluntary, unofficial preseason workout with a volunteer unofficial assistant coach, me. Each one of them silent, self-absorbed, the only sounds the shuffling of feet on the foam rubber mat or the whomp of bodies hurling themselves onto it. People making slow, oriental movements or twisting themselves into weird shapes. People crouching and lunging at the legs of imaginary opponents. People bridging like inchworms, only their feet and the tops of their heads touching the ground, everything else up in the air like the golden arches. Bunch of nuts, basically, and no doubt weirder to watch than the folks in front of me.

"Hi. Can we help you?" the Rorschach man asked when the troupe had finished its warm-up.

"I don't want to interrupt," I said. "Tom Bethany. I'm working with Morty Limbach's attorney."

"Oh, sure, Professor Rosson. Well . . ."

"I could come back."

"You're welcome to wait if you want to. Only thing is we might be an hour or so."

"If you don't mind, I don't."

And I didn't, either. It was interesting, actually. I had been to improvisational theater once or twice, when they had it upstairs over a jazz club on Porter Square. It struck me as kind of a trick, like presidential debating. In my days as a bodyguard and pilot for candidates I had sat in on debate prep, back in the '80 primaries. The bright guys from the issues staff would make lists of the questions the press panel might ask, which was about as difficult a job as figuring out what the kids will ask when you drive past

Disneyland. Then the bright guys would help the candidate come up with sound-bite answers that would seem responsive to the question if you weren't really paying attention. Which most of us weren't, to judge by the election results.

The trick in improv was also to turn the audience's contributions into a skit that seemed spontaneous but was actually preplanned, or so I had figured. But from what I was seeing, there was less consumer fraud in the theater than in political debating. The Poor Attitudes seemed to welcome curveballs.

"I want to work three objects, with Harvey receiving clues," said Rorschach, whose real name had turned out to be Ned. So Harvey went past me on his way out of the room, to wait while the rest of them picked the three objects he was supposed to guess with the help of the audience. The girl with the dark roots to her hair would be giving him the clues, and the others would become the audience, snapping their fingers whenever Harvey's guesses got close. Once he was out of earshot, everyone suggested objects. All of them sounded sufficiently off-the-wall to me, but Ned wasn't impressed.

"I hate to use the mundane ones," he said. "But that's what we generally get from a real audience, too. Okay then, a Butterball turkey, unwaxed dental floss, and a flamenco dancer's skirt."

The girl with the dark roots was named Nora. When Harvey came back in, she pretended to be a librarian, while Harvey picked up on the situation and played a reader looking for books on Satanism. Nora worked him through Butterball with clues that mostly went right by me, which is why I always develop some other interest when the party degenerates into charades. Ned kept breaking in with what seemed to be good coaching, but to a game I didn't know.

"Freeze and hold! You had an excellent clue, Nora,

but you were so casual that he thought it was all environment . . .

"Watch the energy, Harv. All one energy is no energy. But when you varied it, it was great . . .

"No, no, no, careful on that. Whatever you do, don't show friction with another actor to the audience . . .

"Always reach toward burying the game within the scene . . .

"Freeze! When that happens, *immediately* let them know you screwed up, even if you have to break the fourth wall."

I have a lot of trouble with people who holler out orders, but Ned had a way of doing it that the players didn't seem to mind. They just nodded each time and went on with the skit. Once *Butterball* was out of the way, Harvey got the turkey part pretty quickly. *Unwaxed dental floss* was tougher, and I would have still been working on it when the five o'clock whistle blew. But Harvey got that one, too. My only chance to feel superior came when it became clear that he didn't know the word *flamenco*. So he stalled at "flamingo dancer's skirt" and there was no way to get him past it.

After the verbal charades, four of the other players worked on a skit about two young lovers on their third date, just getting serious enough to have brought their lawyers along for backup. A lot of stuff about precoital agreements and sexual histories. Then one on TV weathermen, and another involving two movie critics. In less than an hour the rehearsal wound down, and the Rorschach guy came over.

"Hi, I'm Ned Levine," he said. "Sorry to make you sit through it all, but once we get going, we hate to break the energy."

"I liked it," I said.

"We've had better sessions. Today was sort of uneven."

42

"Well, that's life. Sort of uneven."

"I guess. But Morty dying and all . . . Actually, your chair, normally that was the chair he'd be in."

"He wouldn't be up with you guys?"

"Normally not."

"I thought he was a performer himself."

"He was. Pretty good, actually. That wasn't the problem. What it was, we're pretty unstructured here but it was still his house, you know? I don't think he wanted it to look like he was throwing his weight around."

"Bullshit," said the dyed blonde, Nora. The whole company was standing around now. "Couldn't you tell the heart was cut out of him?"

"Who cut the heart out of him?" I asked.

"That son of a bitch Leo," Nora said. "Everybody knows that."

"Not me. Tell me about it."

"You see what we're like up there?" Nora said. "We're like a family, kind of. You got to count on everybody else. Somebody drops the ball and the whole troupe just dies out there, no place to hide. You get close to each other, is what I'm saying. It's not like an office or something. I don't know what it's like. Maybe like war."

"I can see that," I said, and I could. I didn't know about theater companies, but I knew about war, or at least the odd variety of it we had in Laos. I thought of evenings in the bar at Sky House in Long Cheng, the secret city the CIA built just below the Plain of Jars. Case officers and forward air controllers and maybe an Air America pilot like me, overnighting. If somebody went out the next day and dropped the ball, you could sure enough die out there, no place to hide.

"So along comes Leo, this genius," Nora went on, giving a nasty twist to "genius." "He stays around just long enough to marry the other genius you've got and get him-

JEROME DOOLITTLE

self some exposure. At that point there's basically five of
you onstage, carrying the whole operation, right? Leo and
Kathy and Willser and Golden and you. You being Morty,
okay? You get the picture? You're Morty now, and you're
part of this great team.''

''I get it, sure.''

''Then one morning Leo takes off for New York without
telling you. He takes Kathy, Willser, Golden, along with
him. Everybody with talent in the company. Everybody but
you, Morty, and a few other duds. You, you're left all alone
back in Cambridge with practically nobody to play with.
The cake's all gone, the ice cream's melting, and the popu-
lar kids went off to another party. How would you like it
if that happened to you?''

''It sort of did, once,'' I said. And in a funny way it had,
to me and a lot of other guys in Laos, after the war wound
down. Particularly after the peace accords were signed in
'73, although I was gone by then.

''Well, then you know,'' Nora said. ''That's how Leo cut
the heart out of him. By leaving, the big fucking star was
telling poor Morty the only reason the other kids let him
play with them at all was because he bought them ice
cream.'' It struck me that both Nora and Professor Rosson
had used the same children's party image to describe Morty
Limbach's troubles.

''That's pretty harsh on Leo,'' Ned said.

''Damned right it's harsh. But how else could Morty
have read it, poor bastard?''

''Maybe you're right,'' Ned said. ''Maybe it did destroy
his self-confidence. He used to be active in the old Poor
Attitudes, from what you hear. But he wasn't recently.
Since I've been here, he only stepped in if we were short-
handed.''

''And only if we specifically asked him, when you think
about it,'' the one called Harvey said.

44

"Was he seriously depressed?" I asked. "Suicidal?"

"His head was probably a little fucked up, okay?" Ned said. "But that's the way heads are around here. I mean, just take a look at the rest of us."

Harvey let his mouth go slack and his left cheek began to twitch. "Hey, comedy attracts happy campers," he said. "We even got an in-house shrink."

"Morty was one of Dr. Unger's patients, I understand?"

"Like most of us," Ned said.

"Not like me," said Nora.

"Dahling," said Harvey, doing a Noel Coward character, "there's nothing so tiresome as a reformed neurotic."

"Oh, shut up!" said Nora, sounding angry.

"Hey, I'm sorry, all right?"

But Nora hurried past me, out of the room. Harvey looked uncomfortable.

"What's going on?" I asked.

"I don't really know," Harvey said. "All I meant was she used to go to Unger herself."

I was confused but I let it go; later I'd talk directly to Nora about it, whatever it was. For now I asked the players about the circumstances surrounding Morty Limbach's death. Nobody knew anything special. Everybody had been asleep when Maria came to work and discovered the body. Nobody knew anything had happened until the police started waking everybody up a little before ten.

The medical examiner said that Morty Limbach had died sometime around noon on Sunday, but none of the troupe was awake at the time. "We had a situation here where everybody was slamming Z's most of Sunday," Ned said. Saturday night, it turned out, had stretched well into Sunday morning for the Poor Attitudes. The cast and crew of the "Little Leo Show" had been in Boston to tape an episode in which Kathy Poindexter drags Little Leo along on a walking tour of the Freedom Trail with hilarious results.

45

For old times' sake, Kathy had invited the Poor Attitudes company to join hers at Red Bones in Cambridge, where everybody ate ribs and catfish and cornbread and drank pitchers of beer until they couldn't get any more down.

"What about Morty?" I asked.

"He didn't have more than a beer or two," Harvey said. "He seldom did."

"He didn't need it, Harvey," said Ned. "He was like you, high on life."

"Get high on this," Harvey said, extending a finger.

There was no ill will in any of this. It was just that the Poor Attitudes seemed to be always performing, always on. Life was a nonstop Ping-Pong game played with words.

Mostly the words didn't seem to hurt, or to be intended to hurt, although some of them had driven Nora from the room. It would be useful to look into that a little more, but for the moment I had the others in front of me. From them I learned that no one seemed to have come downstairs before midafternoon Sunday. No one admitted to having got out of bed at all before that time, except for visits to one of the four bathrooms on the second and third floors of the mansion. No one had heard anything unusual. No one had thought anything of Morty's absence throughout the day and evening, since he lived in a Boston condo.

In the days and weeks before his death, Morty had just been typical Morty, which seemed to signify even-tempered, kindly, a little passive. He hadn't appeared either particularly depressed or particularly happy. This didn't mean a thing, of course. It was what the neighbors typically say about anyone who jumps off a bridge or exercises his constitutional rights by hosing down a schoolyard with his AK-47. I thanked everyone for their time, and asked Ned, the player-director, to point out the room where Morty Limbach had died.

*   *   *

I sat on what had been Kathy Poindexter's bed, unsure of just what to do now that I was in the death room. Perhaps something would flow into my head, some insight. Nothing did.

I took the police photographer's pictures out of their envelope to help me imagine the scene Maria Soares had found. Not much had changed, as I learned when I positioned myself where the camera had been and matched the photos with the room. Only the body, the articles of clothing, and the orange extension cord were missing.

I sat where the body had been and bent forward, imagining the pressure of the cord around my neck. Less than five pounds of force, I knew from the little bit of literature I had come across in Widener Library, would have closed off the jugular; a couple or three pounds more and the flow through the carotid arteries would start to be pinched off. Limbach would be keeping himself close to orgasm, presumably, while edging up to unconsciousness as well. Orgasm wins, but just barely. Morty passes out and slumps forward, the weight of his head and upper body held by the cord. I balanced myself like that, legs spread wide, and tried to imagine my brain shutting down for lack of oxygen. Entirely painless, even pleasant, or people wouldn't keep going right up to the edge of consciousness time after time. This time, by bad luck, the cord presses on the sensitive carotid sinus. Reflex cardiac death occurs in less than three seconds. And I sit right here, bowing politely from the waist, until the cops come and let me down.

This was the scenario the good guys preferred: Hope, Rosson, and myself. The bad guys at the insurance company saw it differently. They saw a Morty Limbach who was suicidally depressed, but not so depressed that he wouldn't get a kick out of bilking a giant insurance company. And so he rigged the scene and masturbated to ejaculation before asphyxiating himself. Sure enough, the medical examiner bought the resulting suicide as the accidental death it appeared to be.

Even making allowances for my natural bias, the insurance company's position looked weak to me. How would Limbach have known, for one thing, that the insurance policy wouldn't pay off in case of suicide? Most policies would have, after all, and even the ACLU officials were surprised to learn that this one didn't. Was it possible the company planned to argue that Morty had disguised his suicide as accidental to avoid embarrassing his family? Wouldn't seem to make much sense, since the disguise itself had to be at least as embarrassing as suicide. Or maybe the company would maintain that embarrassment was the whole point—that a rejected, hostile son took this last opportunity to humiliate his family before the world. This was a possibility, perhaps, but not one I'd like to stand up and defend in court. The insurance people must have had something more convincing to go on, and no doubt I'd learn soon enough what it was. I had an appointment after lunch with a man named Myron Cooper, a vice president in charge of claims for Pilgrim Mutual Life.

The Pilgrim Mutual Life Insurance Company had its own building on Hanover Street, or at least had its name on the building. This was in Boston's financial district, which you got to on the T unless you wanted to pay heavy tribute to the parking lot mob or the tow truck mob. Besides, I liked the T. Its prices were low enough to keep out the riffraff, like the people who worked in the big offices on Hanover Street.

If Cooper's office was one of the big ones, I never got a chance to find out. The room the receptionist took me to for my appointment with Mr. Cooper was a sort of waiting room, with a sofa, armchairs, and coffee tables. A small coffee urn sat on a larger table against the rear wall, along with paper cups, plastic spoons, and little envelopes of sugar, nonsugar sweetener, and nondairy creamer. The door was unusually solid for an office door, and was so close-fitting that it made a faint pneumatic sound when the receptionist closed it behind me. Not much noise would get through that door. The lighting was concealed, and hotel art hung on the walls. So did a good-size mirror with a semi-expensive stainless-steel frame. You don't see mirrors too often in office buildings.

In front of me was Myron Cooper, smiling.

The chief of claims investigations for Pilgrim Mutual had the kind of pig face that didn't look good in a smile. He had a pig body too, solid and thick through the middle. The hand he held out was short-fingered but wide, and felt like a broad paw when I took it. He turned out to be the sort of jerk who thinks shaking hands is a contest. I only resisted enough so that he wouldn't hurt me. "Some grip," I said, trying to sound wide-eyed at the wonder of him.

"I work on it," he said. "I do a lot of match shooting."

"Oh, yeah? Is a strong grip important?" Listen to the other fellow. Show interest in what interests him.

"Well, the way you got to think about it," Cooper said, "your hand is your shooting platform."

He waved me to one of the chairs and handed me a card. It identified him as a vice president and as Chief, Claims Adjudication Division, Pilgrim Mutual Life Insurance Company. "Chief" sounded military, which I figured was no accident. A lot of Cooper's blond hair had long since gone south, but what remained was cropped into a short crewcut. Cooper's crewcut and Cooper himself reminded me of a field first sergeant in my basic training company at Fort Dix. I had taken an instant dislike to the sergeant, too.

"What can we do you for, Tom?" Cooper said, all hearty.

49

I explained that, as he no doubt knew, I was employed by Jerome Rosson to investigate the circumstances of the death of Professor Rosson's client Morton Limbach III.

"Why?" Cooper said, which was actually a pretty good question.

"Because Pilgrim doesn't want to pay off on his policy."

"Yeah, but what I mean is why would Rosson give a shit one way or the other? He wouldn't get the money. Not even the estate would get the money."

"He wants his client's wishes carried out."

"Why, though? This is my business, Bethany. I know what's normal, what isn't normal."

"What are you getting at?"

"What I'm getting at is who are you working for?"

"Rosson."

"Come on. Don't try to shit an old shitter. I think you're working for the ACLU."

"Not really. The ACLU and me are just good friends."

"Funny friends you got. I'll tell you the truth, Bethany, you come through that door I said to myself, This isn't the right guy. Guys like him don't work for the ACLU, for Rosson neither. Wrong guy, I said. This is a good guy. Then it came to me, why shouldn't a good guy be doing work for Rosson, you come right down to it? I mean, it's probably just a job, right? I'd probably do the same, his position. Take their money and fuck 'em, go your own way, am I right? Laugh all the way to the bank. How much is Rosson paying you?"

"Probably you should ask him."

"Whatever it is, the estate is wasting it. This guy killed himself."

"I don't know what happened yet," I said, "but the last thing it looks like is suicide."

"First thing, buddy boy. First thing."

I had a lot of trouble with "buddy boy," but I didn't say

anything about it. What I said instead was: "You must have come across something we don't know about, then. Why not just tell me about it, and then we can go away and not bother you?"

"That's exactly what the boss wants to do, is tell you about it," Cooper said. "Come on. He made ten minutes on his schedule for you."

— 4 —

THE BOSS TURNED OUT TO BE NOT JUST SOME LITTLE BOSS, but the big enchilada himself, Warren W. Westfall. I had run him through the *Boston Globe* index after my initial talk with Hope and now had a general fix on him. He had started out selling vacuum cleaners door-to-door, back in the fifties. A *Globe* reporter had tracked down a fellow salesman who recalled that the great man's nickname in those days had been Hocker.

Not long after Westfall got his foot in the door, evidently, he would ask where Mr. Clancy, or Mr. Donovan, or Mr. O'Malley worked, anyway? Oh, really, down the car barns, huh? They got any niggers working down there, where he works? Yeah, I thought I heard that. Nice rug you got there, Mrs. Clancy. The little guys crawl around on it some-times, playing? Reason I ask, what I want you to think about is some buck nigger down to the car barns, he's working alongside of Mr. Clancy. Probably the nigger's got a little of this, a little of that, you know how they are. TB, polio, maybe even one of them diseases we don't talk

52

about, who knows? So this nigger hocks up this big lunger and your good husband, he could step in it easy and never even notice, am I right? So back home he comes after work, he don't know he's carrying possibly death on his feet, and there's the little guy down on the rug . . .

"Now, Mrs. Clancy, did you happen to know that the Electrolux is a medically approved antiseptic device? True fact. This machine actually lifts germs right up out of your carpet and wraps 'em up for you so you never touch 'em and so doesn't the little guy, neither . . ."

After a while, though, Hocker Westfall evidently found the world of vacuum cleaners too confining. Realistically you could only expect to sell one per home, sometimes not even that. And some people didn't even have homes. But everybody is afraid of the Big C, so Hocker went into the cancer insurance dodge. For only twenty-five cents a day, the quarter part of a dollar, he flogged policies to anybody in the black neighborhoods of Roxbury, Dorchester, and Mattapan who was capable of making their mark on the bottom of an ironclad contract. The trick was to talk fast enough so the suckers didn't have time to remember that their regular health insurance already covered cancer. Pretty soon Westfall had his own agency, which pretty soon grew into his own little insurance company, which was bought by a bigger insurance company, Pilgrim. Westfall came with the deal, and soon became executive vice president.

Then during the Reagan-Bush years, all sorts of bottom growth was encouraged to break free and rise to the top of the pond, stimulated by social engineers like Simon, Boesky, Icahn, and Milken. The resulting scum began to appear in *Forbes* and *Fortune*. There they were profiled as workaholics with Midas touches, as charismatic big-picture men or tough, driving, hands-on operators. Risk-taking wheeler-dealers or managerial geniuses immersed in every detail of their operation. Some were low-key, some were high profile. Often they were philosopher-kings, who thought deep thoughts such as, "Cash flow is the name of the game."

The Hocker said that very thing to the writer from *Forbes,* in fact, when the magazine made him its cover boy five years ago. He was being honored for having just swallowed up an insurance company three times the size of Pilgrim. He had done this by conspiring with the management of the bigger company to take it over with its own money, and then forcing out his co-conspirators. "Tough-minded realist," *Forbes* said. Results-oriented. Eye on the bottom line.

Not just tough-minded, either. Really tough. I knew it by the servile sound of Cooper's voice when he announced me to his boss. I knew it by the way Warren W. Westfall stayed right where he was in his big leather chair behind the big, ugly glass table that served him for a desk, not bothering to get to his feet for an insignificant thing like me. Evidently I was expected to stand, since he didn't invite me to sit. Westfall was probably in his late fifties, still a good-looking man if you like the Tony Curtis type. Westfall's handsome head, like the actor's, seemed to belong with a much more rugged body than the one it was attached to. His voice was tougher than his body, too: angry and dead serious.

"So you're the son of a bitch thinks he can cheat me out of a quarter-million bucks, huh?" Westfall said.

"That's the son of a bitch I am, all right," I said. "Thanks, I *will* sit down."

Cooper remained standing. He looked uneasy, as if he expected to be blamed for my bad manners. "Hey, hey," he said. "Mr. Westfall, you want me to—"

"Take a walk, Myron," his boss said. When the door had closed behind Myron, Westfall's manner changed the

way it must have in the old vacuum cleaner days when
the first approach didn't seem to be working. He selected
a nice smile, one that just invited you to be his friend.

"Don't take any shit, do you, son?" he said. "I like that."
He kept on smiling.

"Do me a favor, okay?" I said. "You don't call me son,
I won't call you shithead."

"Shithead?"

"That's what I called my father, unless he was sober
enough to catch me."

"He drank, huh? That's rough on a kid. Now they got
support groups for that, I was reading the other day. Adult
children of alcoholics. I could have my girl look it up, send
you the address."

I was feeling like Reagan with Gorbachev. You just can't
keep a Cold War going with a guy who's decided he
doesn't want to fight anymore. So I gave it up.

"Your guy Myron," I said, "he said you had something
you wanted to tell me."

"Well, that's right. Couple things. First thing, you understand this business over Limbach's policy is a grudge
match, don't you?"

"No, I don't."

"Sure it is. This ACLU lawyer, Edwards, she calls herself
now, she used to work for me. You know that?"

"I know she had a summer job with the company, during law school."

"She tell you about her and me?"

I shook my head. Her and him would have been a natural, though. Like Ralph Nader and Nancy Reagan.

"Oh, yeah. Not that I ever let it come to anything, of
course, but she had a thing for me. Or maybe she was
angling for a regular staff job when she got out of law
school. Who knows, with the split-tails? Anyway, she had
been kind of coming on to me, you know, and finally one

day she comes right out with it. How about we drive up to Portland, somewhere like that, spend the weekend in this little place she knows? Normally why not, am I right? Not too bad of a looker.

"But she worked for me, okay? First thing I learned in business, never shit where you eat. I tried to let her down easy, not hurt her feelings, but lots of luck, right? I don't have to tell you how they are, you say no to them. She run around hollering like she was Snow White and I was trying to rip her little panties off, rape her or something. You fucking imagine? I had to let her go, naturally. So that's what's behind this whole thing."

"You're lucky," I said. "Nowadays she probably would have sued your ass for sexual harassment."

"Hey, it happens, don't think it doesn't. What a world, huh?"

In my head, I had the son of a bitch down on the floor. I had my knee in his face and was shifting my weight onto it until the thin bones splintered and his nose went flat. I never did anything harder than make myself stay where I was, in the chair I had helped myself to.

"What I'm telling you here," Westfall went on, "your boss is trying to break it off in me for old times' sake."

"Let me get this straight," I said, in pretty good control of myself by now. "You're telling me she got this guy to jack off before he killed himself so it would look accidental? Why didn't he just blow his brains out like normal people?"

"That one, you'd have to ask a shrink on. All I'm saying is the guy committed suicide and your boss from the ACLU is trying to collect because she still wants to break it off in me after all these years."

"How do you know he committed suicide? That's the point."

"For now, let's just say this guy's got a family, all right?

A family which I happen to know from some of my charity work, various charities. And the family happens to know from many years back that this guy is suicidal."

"What've they got? Papers? Notes? Letters? Medical records?"

"This thing goes to court, I wouldn't be surprised to see documents like that show up, no. I wouldn't be the least bit surprised."

"Surprise me now."

"Hey, I'd like nothing more. But the lawyers are tying my hands, you know? Once those pricks get in it, you can't talk man to man no more."

We went around a little bit on it, but he wouldn't tell me anything else. When I got up to leave, he got up, too, and started around the desk as if he wanted to shake. But I didn't know if I could control myself once I had my hands on him, so I made it to the door before he could make it to me. Myron Cooper was waiting outside for me.

On the way down in the elevator, he said, "Some guy, huh?"

"Yeah, some guy, all right."

"I was afraid he'd blow up when you sat down like that, but I think it tickled him. With Mr. W., you can never tell. He likes to keep people guessing."

We got off at the fourth floor, and Cooper led the way back into the peculiar waiting room we had been in before. He waved me to a chair, and took one himself. He clasped his hands behind his head, leaned back, and gave me a long look.

"Nam?" he asked.

"A couple times as a courier. Couple more times just across the border in the Highlands. Mostly I was in Laos, though."

"The company, huh?"

"No, the army and then the embassy."

"Sure, right. The *em*bassy. Sure." I had done a tour as an enlisted man with the army attaché's office, and then stayed on as a pilot for Air America, but let him think I had been a spook, if he wanted. "I thought it was something like that," he said. "You got the look."

"You got the look, too," I said. "MPs? Saigon?"

"Pretty close. Bien Hoa. I was in the air force. APs."

And so we talked for a while about the good old days when we still had a neo-empire and didn't have to make do with little dipshit places like Grenada and Panama. I was getting to be friends with Cooper, and friends share. What the hell, it was worth a try, anyway.

"Mr. Westfall talked about the family having proof that Limbach was suicidal," I said. "What's that all about?"

"Hey, I'd like to tell you," he said. "But I can't." So much for sharing.

"Yeah, well . . ." I said. "The lawyers, I guess."

"Yeah, I suppose it'll all come out in time."

"One of the lawyers is this Hope Edwards woman. Mr. Westfall knew her from way back, huh?"

"Yeah, you believe that shit? Actually, she's not too bad-looking a cunt either."

"No too bad looking a cunt, huh?"

"You've seen her, haven't you?"

"Actually I have, yeah."

"She can sit on my face anytime."

"You like that, Myron? You like people sitting on your face?"

"Hey, it's just a manner of speaking. No offense."

"I'm asking you, Myron. You like people sitting on your face?"

"Just who do you think you're talking to, fella?"

"A fat prick that I'm gonna sit on his face."

I stood up and started toward him, to see what he would do. I wasn't really sure what I would do, either. Maybe really sit on his face. Maybe he thought so, too, because he reached inside his jacket. I got to his hand before it could get to wherever it was going and used it to twist him around in his chair. I found a pistol in a quick-draw holster under his arm about the same time he found his voice.

"Hey, what the fuck do you think you're doing?" he said, as well as he could with his face jammed into the upholstery of the chair.

"I'm taking your gun away, dickhead." I threw it on the sofa behind me, so that he'd have to go through me to get it back.

I let him go, and he got up. He was over being surprised. Now he was outraged. "You son of a bitch," he said. "You'll be sorry."

And he charged, maybe 230 pounds of enraged porker. I grabbed his leading arm and let all that weight work for me as he rotated over my hip and down hard on his back. Before he could catch his breath I hauled him by the same arm back to where he had started. In a moment he was able to get to his feet again.

"Go get your gun, Myron," I said. "It's still on the sofa."

There wasn't any point in his getting it, of course. He wasn't going to shoot me in an office with hundreds of people around, or probably anywhere else, either. But I suspected he'd try for it again, anyway. Myron, I figured, was the NRA. Prickless when gunless.

This time he remembered his hour or two of unarmed combat training for the air police, and shot out a kick at my knee. The idea is to tear all the cartilage apart and give your opponent at least an instant trick knee, if you don't quite succeed in crippling him for good. But, like most of those hand-to-hand combat moves, it only works if you're quicker than the other guy and if he doesn't expect it. My knee wasn't where he had figured it would be when his foot arrived, but my hand was. I guided his kick up over his head, and he fell heavily on his back again. He gave sort of a squealing scream this time, which probably meant he had landed on the handcuffs I had noticed on his right hip when I was searching for his gun.

"What are you doing?" he said, once he had rolled over and scrabbled out of range. "Are you crazy?" Fair question, now that there was a pause and I could think about it. Certainly I wasn't acting completely rational. I had managed to keep myself from going after Westfall, and so now I was kicking his dog instead. Which may not have been exactly crazy, but was certainly pointless. While I was at it, though, I might as well see if I could get anything out of the dog.

"Sit in that chair, Myron," I said. "I want to talk to you."

"Fuck you."

"Hey, whatever, Myron."

I grabbed one of his arms and bent it so that the thing would break if he didn't get up off the floor, and then I made him sit down like a good boy where I wanted him to.

"Now, Myron," I said. I liked calling him Now Myron. "Now, Myron, tell me just exactly what makes you think Mr. Limbach committed suicide."

Cooper said nothing.

"Now, Myron, what we've got here is something you're probably not real used to. You're used to having the air force or a big company behind you while you push people around. You're used to having your little gun and your little handcuffs. You've asskissed your way to a little title, and you're used to having people scared of you because you're bigger and fatter than they are."

"Fuck you."

"Now, Myron, what you got to understand here is that I just turned into your superior officer. This time you're not the one who makes other people scared, you're the one who gets scared. That's because I can hurt you, Myron. Actually, the more important thing is that I *will* hurt you if you don't tell me what paper you've got on Limbach."

"Fuck you."

"Right." I got behind his chair, locked his head with my left arm, and forced the second knuckle of my right hand, slow but hard, into the bundle of nerves right below the ear. Cooper screamed, but we both knew that it wouldn't carry through that thick door.

"Now, Myron, what have you got?"

"Are you fucking crazy?"

I put my knuckle back in place, lightly. "Yeah, Myron, I am. What have you got?"

"Nothing. I mean, I swear to Christ, I don't know. Mr. Westfall knows the family and they let him into Limbach's condo."

"Why would they do that?"

"Because Mr. Westfall told them about the insurance policy, and they feel the same way about the ACLU that Mr. Westfall does."

"They don't want that money going to a bunch of damned Communists? That it, Myron?"

"Something like that. The other thing is the family didn't like the idea of how the guy was supposed to have died. The mother thought the guy must have killed himself, and maybe Mr. Westfall could find a note or something. The mother's got trouble with the idea her kid died jacking off."

"Better a suicide than a jerk-off, is that it?"

"Hey, I don't know. I'm just telling you what I hear. Supposedly she thinks he fixed things up to embarrass the family, then offed himself."

"So mummy lets her pal poke through her dead son's place so he can prove her son committed suicide? A boy's best friend is his mother, huh, Myron? Well, what did your boss find?''

''He didn't tell me what, exactly. But he said it was conclusive, what he found.''

''That was his word, 'conclusive'?''

''His exact word, and that's all he said. Honest to Christ. Really.''

''I believe you, Myron, account of you don't have the balls to lie to me. Your balls are over there on the sofa.''

I was right about that, because when I turned my back, I heard Cooper rising up out of his chair and coming for me. I turned in time to see him launching a tackle, which I didn't bother to avoid. As soon as we both hit the ground, I twisted on top of him and got him in control with a wristlock.

''Jesus, Myron,'' I said. ''You think you're back in high school? You think play stops when the runner's knee touches the ground? Come on, get up.''

He got up, since he could feel that the alternative was a broken wrist. I pushed him back into his chair. His eyes were shiny, about to overflow. Probably it was rage and frustration more than pain. I hadn't done any injury to him.

''You're crying, Myron. What would coach think?'' And sure enough, a tear did escape down his fat cheek. ''You ever make anybody cry back in Vietnam? *Answer me, shithead!*''

''Sometimes suspects.''

''What kind of suspects?''

''PX thieves, like that.''

''Men?'' He nodded.

''Women?'' He nodded.

''Kids?''

''Half of the kids were VC anyway,'' Cooper said.

"Everybody knew that." He wiped his wet cheeks with one of his broad, plump paws.

"How come you call him Mr. Westfall, Myron?" I asked.

"I got respect for a man like Mr. Westfall. He's done a lot with his life."

"You ever call him just Westfall?"

"I might sometimes."

"But not to his face?"

"Of course not. You were in the service. You wouldn't call an officer by just his name, to his face."

"Behind his back you might, huh? Ever call him Warren?"

"I don't remember."

"Who the fuck are you, you don't remember things? Reagan? I'm not some lawyer asking you about Ollie North, asshole. Me, you answer."

"Maybe I might have called him that. It's possible."

"Maybe when you were showing off to your rent-a-cops, or whoever the fuck works for you? Huh? Warren and me, we're like this. You ever call him by his nickname, Myron?"

"What nickname?"

"Say it, Myron. Say his nickname, you don't want me to go around with you again."

"I heard of people calling him Hocker."

"Don't whisper, Myron. Sing it right out."

"Hocker, I heard of."

"Tell me about this Hocker. What kind of guy he is."

And Cooper started talking about Westfall, what he really thought of his boss. Maybe he unlocked it all because I had become his new boss, at least for the moment. Or maybe he had been dying to tell somebody all along, and he knew it wouldn't get out of this room.

Anyway, it turned out that Myron was the kind of guy that busts his goddamned butt for the company and nobody gives a shit. Christ, you'd think he'd get a little recognition at least. Westfall would be nothing without Cooper, might even be in bankruptcy court or even jail. But did Westfall give a rat's ass? Hell, no. Wouldn't even approve a lousy little request for two more investigators. What did the cheap son of a bitch think, Myron was going to pocket their salaries himself? It was for the good of the company, for Christ's sake. And how about the time the bastard killed the Orlando trip? How was a guy supposed to keep up on law enforcement techniques if he couldn't go to law enforcement conferences, Myron would like to know? Disney World wasn't the fucking point. He didn't give a good goddamn whether he went to Disney fucking World or not. As it just so happened, Myron had already been to Disneyfucking*land!* Twice!

Once he had said enough for my purposes, I took the gun from the sofa and went over to examine the mirror. Myron didn't bother to ask why. The look on his face showed that he knew. The mirror was held on the wall by screws with decorative caps that I was able to pry off with my penknife. But I couldn't budge the screws themselves until I thought of the clip in Myron's gun. I went to work backing out the screws with the little lip at the bottom of the ammunition clip.

"You're scratching my gun," Cooper got up the courage to say.

"Don't worry about it, Myron. It's my gun now."

Cooper didn't answer, probably because he knew that my taking down the mirror meant his ass was forever mine. As I suspected and he knew, the mirror turned out to hide a hole in the wall. And a camcorder on a tripod looked through the hole. It made a soft noise as it ran.

I reached through the hole and took the tape out of the camcorder. The tape made a bulge in one of my side pockets and the gun in the other. I didn't like the way the bulges spoiled the lines in my J. Press jacket, which had cost me twenty dollars nearly new at Keezer's. But it couldn't be helped.

"You fixed this place like the customer room in a car dealership or one of those time-share scams, didn't you, Myron?" I said. "Somebody comes in and wants to talk about a disputed claim, maybe with their wife or their lawyer. So you sit them down in this nice waiting room, help them to some coffee and doughnuts, then you got to go do something for a few minutes. Soon as they think they're alone, maybe they'll be dumb enough to open up and you've got it all down on tape. That the way it works, Myron?"

He said nothing till I nudged his leg with my foot. Then he nodded.

"Only this time I'm the one that's got it on tape. Think the Hocker would like to see that tape? Think he'd like to see what a stand-up guy he's got working for him?"

Myron didn't look good.

"You can have the tape right now, Myron. Just tell me exactly what Westfall's got that makes him think Morty Limbach killed himself."

"I swear to Christ I don't know. Whatever it is, Mr. Westfall didn't show it to me. What I told you is all I know, swear to Christ."

"Actually I believed you before, Myron. Now I believe you even more."

"It's the truth. I swear it." Cooper held out his hand for the tape.

"Forget it, Myron. I'm keeping it."

"But you said—"

"No, I didn't. You have to listen, Myron. You didn't tell me what Westfall's got. You told me you didn't know what he's got. When you find out, you call me and I'll give you the tape back. Now come here."

Cooper didn't want to give me his keys, and he didn't want me to handcuff him to the elbow of piping that ran into the enclosed radiator under the window, either. But there wasn't a thing in the world he could do about it. I examined him sitting there and thought of a way I could improve the picture.

"Hey, what're you doing?" Myron asked.

"Same shit you used to do to the little kids at school. I'm de-pantsing you."

"Please," Cooper said. "For Christ's sake, please . . ." For some reason, the idea seemed to scare him more than anything that had happened so far. In a moment I saw why.

"Snappy, Myron," I said when I saw the red nylon bikini he wore, almost buried out of sight under his belly fat. "Very, very snappy." I had meant to leave him naked from the waist down, but I liked him this way even better. Cooper's hands were cuffed behind him, leaving him facing the door so that he couldn't hide his fashion statement from anyone coming in. His pants lay in a heap where I had pulled them over his shoes.

"Why?" Cooper said. "Why are you doing this to me?"

I might have said because of the starving kids he had made cry in Bien Hoa, or because he had put a picture in my head of Hope sitting on his face, or because I saw a little bit of myself in him. But I figured he wouldn't understand anymore than I did. I closed the heavy door behind me, leaving his keys in the lock. On my way out of the building, I stopped at the guard station in the lobby.

"You might want to check room four-oh-nine," I told the guy. "There's some kind of weird odor coming out of it. Smelled like shit to me."

Back at my office, which was Harvard Square when the weather was good and a Harvard Square coffee shop called the Tasty when it wasn't, I called Jerome Rosson from a sidewalk pay phone.

"I've got a sort of a report," I told the lawyer. "I'm just over in the Square. Want me to come by and tell you about it?"

"Why don't I come by instead?" my new employer said. "I ride the T home, so I've got to come to the Square anyway."

I told him I'd be on the terrace of Au Bon Pain. Since he said he was practically on his way out the door and would be there in ten minutes, I walked over to Herrell's to get us a couple pints of ice cream. With Rosson's energy level, he couldn't have a weight problem. As for myself, I'd have to eat the stuff by the quart to replace the calories I lost on the wrestling mat. I helped out with the coaching partly because I liked the sport. But it also forced me into regular, hard exercise, and without that I'd balloon up into a porker like Myron Cooper. I knew, because it had happened to me during my bush pilot days in Alaska. You don't get much exercise either flying or drinking, which were the two main things I was doing at the time.

I detoured a little on the way to the ice cream parlor, to visit several different trash cans and dumpsters. In each one I buried a different part of Myron's fancy chrome-plated gun, which I had earlier taken to pieces in the men's room in the basement of Boylston Hall, next to the language lab. The Tasty had no public rest room, but most of a person's little daily needs can be taken care of in or around Harvard Square, if the person just knows where to look. The last part of the gun was the bolt, which I dropped through a subway grating to rust away forever. I figured Myron wasn't the kind of a man who ought to be running around with a handgun on him, and neither was anybody else. If the politicians wouldn't do anything about the problem, I would.

I bought a pint of hazelnut cream and a pint of vanilla and got back to the Au Bon Pain terrace with them just as Rosson crossed the Square. He couldn't make himself wait for a hole in the traffic and darted right into the flow instead, showing nice change of pace and the ability to cut both ways. He came bustling up to the table and dove right into the hazelnut. "Damn, I love ice cream," he had said while getting the top off the carton. But after that he had no time for talking. He ate like what I had figured he was— a man in a state of permanent calorie debt.

I wasn't too far behind him. When we were both finished, I told him what I had found out. He was interested in the same things I was. Why had Nora, the woman in the improv troupe, run out of the room? Why had Limbach's mother let Warren Westfall visit Limbach's apartment, and what proof of suicide had Westfall found there?

"We could force it out of them on discovery," Rosson said. "But there's nothing before the court to base a discovery motion on yet. All they've done is tell us orally that they hope to stiff us."

"What the hell are Limbach's parents doing in this, anyway?" I asked. "Do they have any right to let their kid's insurance company into his apartment?"

"Maybe, or you could argue maybe not. But it's done now. Probably it's too late, but it might be a good idea for you to take a look around the place yourself."

"You think Morty's parents would let me in? They're Westfall's buddies, according to Cooper."

"I'll let you in."

"You've got the key?"

"Actually, you do. It's with the keys to the Poor Attitudes House. Dumb son of a bitch that I am, it never occurred to me to look through Morty's condo myself. The family was handling the funeral arrangements, and this problem with the insurance came up later. No reason at the time to check out the apartment. Yeah, right, no reason. Brilliant me, huh? And now that son of a bitch Westfall has got whatever it is he's got."

Professor Rosson must have driven his grade school teachers nuts. Even now, probably in his late forties, he had trouble sitting still. "I'll take a look at the place," I said. "Right now I got to run." This set him free to run himself, which he did. This time he was into and out of the Mass. Ave. traffic so quickly the drivers hardly had time to hit the brakes before he was disappearing down the T steps. I sat for a little while longer, trying to enjoy the perfect fall weather but failing. I was stewing over imagined wrongs, the worst kind.

At last I got up and walked down Brattle Street and over toward the Charles Hotel. I hadn't expected Hope to be back yet from her day downtown, and she wasn't. When she didn't answer my knock, I let myself in the room and settled down to wait. On the tube there was a battle of the titans, Dan Rather trying to read George Bush's lips. Television just doesn't get any better, except maybe for Barbara Walters interviewing Nancy Reagan. I turned it off and went back to brooding. The phone rang, and of course I let it ring until the caller got tired. It wasn't my phone. It might have been Hope's husband, or one of her kids, or any of the many other people who would be surprised to hear a male voice answer. I always have to slip around. . . . The old irritation of not being able to answer gave me something else to brood about. At last Hope's key turned in the lock.

"Hi, honey," Hope said when she saw me. "I'm home."

So what, I thought. She heard me think it.

"What's wrong?" she asked.

"Nothing." I sounded like my ex-wife used to sound, when I would do something like come to our little daughter's birthday party drunk.

69

"Sounds like something."

"It's all right." My ex-wife used to do that, too: every-thing she said would mean its opposite.

Hope sat down on the bed beside me and took one of my hands between two of hers. I let it lie there, dead. She squeezed once, lightly, and then just kept her hands on mine. Unoffended, waiting. She knew what to do; she was used to dealing with children. She waited and waited, until I said, "I've been thinking about going to law school."

"Law school?"

"Sure. What's wrong with that?"

"Nothing. You can afford it. It's been a long time since you took tests, so you might want to take the Kaplan course before you took the LSATs. My guess is you'd do very well on them. Maybe extremely well. You might max the test. You couldn't get into the first rank of law schools because you blew off your undergraduate courses back at Iowa. But you'd make it into the next rank. BC, BU, Northeastern, assuming you want to stay in the Boston area. If you decided to be at the top of your class, you would be. Your photographic memory alone would make it a cinch. You'd be a little old to get the eighty-five thousand–dollar offers from the big firms, but you wouldn't want to do that kind of work anyway. Lots of other kinds of law, though. You'd be a terrific lawyer."

She was leaning against the headboard. I was lying flat on the bed, with my head on the pillow. I was looking at the ceiling; she was looking down at me. "Now what is this all about?" Hope said.

"Nothing," I said. Again she waited.

"Let's just forget it," I said.

"Okay."

"I worked it out with Rosson, the money thing, so that's all right. I'm charging him a dollar."

"A dollar? There's something like thirty million dollars in that estate, Bethany."

"Yeah, well, it wouldn't come from the estate as a whole, would it?"

"Not the estate as a whole, no."

"Actually from the ACLU's quarter million?"

"That's right."

"But we were hoping I wouldn't notice."

"Who's we?"

"It's what Rosson told me. Direct quote. 'We were hoping you wouldn't notice.'"

"Oh, shit. Now I see what's going on. We lawyers, huh?"

I lay there without answering, all wounded dignity. Hope looked down at me for a long minute, and then bent down to put her lips to my ear. "How would you like to fuck a lawyer, Bethany?" she whispered. "Everyone says we're good at fucking people."

As I say, she knew how to deal with children. Of all ages. She began to undo my belt.

Later, afterward, she put her lips to my ear again, and whispered, "I'm sorry, Bethany. You know that, don't you?"

"Hey, hey. You don't have to apologize."

"Yeah, I do, actually. As soon as I finished talking to Rosson about the estate hiring you, I knew it was a dumb, condescending trick to try. I should have called him back, and I didn't."

"Okay, okay. Really."

"Okay, then. Now let me say that the ACLU *should* be paying for your services, and both Rosson and I truly believe that, and we didn't regard it as charity in any way, shape, or form. And let me further say, however, that I know perfectly well it's bad manners to turn down gifts. Which is what we were conspiring to do, since you had

71

already offered to work for nothing. And let me further say that none of this changes the fact that you're a stiff-necked, thin-skinned son of a bitch, Bethany.''

"Hey, it's not my fault," I said. "I was abused as a child." My idea was to be funny, but as soon as I said it I realized it might have been true. The abuse part was certainly true, although I didn't think of it as child abuse at the time. Where I grew up, in the lower reaches of Port Henry, New York, kids expected the old man to slap the shit out of them after he got through with mom. We'd brag to each other about the beatings we soaked up.

"Actually, you probably wouldn't let yourself off the hook by believing that," Hope said. "But actually, it's probably true." I said nothing, didn't have to. In an odd way, it was comforting to be in love with somebody that you couldn't bullshit on any level. Somebody who knew you at least as well as you knew yourself, and put up with you anyway. So I pushed ahead with the other thing I was mad about.

"While we're on it," I said, "why didn't you tell me about the trouble between you and Westfall?"

"Oh, shit. Well, there I don't feel so guilty. I didn't tell you because I didn't want you to tear the bastard's arm off and beat him to death with it. Truly I did want you to do that, of course. But it would be wrong."

"What happened between you?"

"What did he say?"

"Said you were trying to peddle your ass to him for a job with the company after you got out of law school. You tried to get him to go to Portland for a hot weekend, but he turned you down. Nothing personal, but his policy is not to screw the help. Your feelings were so hurt you hollered rape, and he had to fire you."

"Not rape exactly, but I certainly hollered. After he groped me in the elevator."

"Groped you how?"

"You don't need to hear this, Tom."

"Tell me anyway."

"He put his hand up my skirt."

"And he touched you?"

"He was working his fingers around, trying to . . . Jesus, is there any point going through this?"

"No. I'm sorry."

"Why not, though? You may as well have the whole picture, otherwise you'll be making up worse ones in your head. He stopped the elevator between floors and said he was thinking about giving me a real job after I got out of law school. So how about going with him to Portland over the weekend to talk it over? And he kissed me, which was worse than the other stuff, oddly enough. It seemed more personal and disgusting, somehow. He had breath like a sewer. Then up under my dress, and here, too."

She touched her breast.

"Which hand did he use?"

"Huh? Probably his right. I think he had his left arm around me, holding me. Why?"

"Just trying to get the picture. Go ahead."

"Well, at first I was too surprised and scared to do anything, but then I remembered something I read in a magazine, so I tried it. I told him I was about to throw up, and he let me go. I pressed the elevator button and then stood in front of it so he couldn't get to it. We only had one floor to go, and when it opened I ran out into the lobby, crying. That's the thing that makes me most ashamed, remembering it. That I let him make me cry. I didn't go to the police, because back then there wouldn't have been any sense bothering. Our consciousness hadn't really been raised yet, on sexual harassment in the workplace anyway. All I could think of to do was spend the rest of the day telling everybody exactly what happened. Naturally I never came back to the office. But I only had a week left before leaving for school anyway."

I just held her. I didn't make any tough noises about Westfall, because I knew she'd only say forget it, it was a long time ago. And I didn't want her to know that I had no intention of forgetting it. I held her until the tension in her back muscles went away, and then I asked a question that I hadn't come up with any remotely plausible answer to.

"Is there any possible link you can think of between Limbach's death and this business all those years ago with Westfall?"

"Nothing that makes the slightest sense to me, no. His type would have rationalized the whole thing in his mind long since. And from what he told you, that's just what he's done. He's turned himself into the victim."

"Could he have been carrying it around with him all these years, waiting to get back at you?" I asked.

"Not likely. It probably had more of an impact on me than it did on him. These things aren't likely to be single occurrences. If he grabbed me, he grabbed plenty of others. You win some, you lose some, I guess. He wouldn't be that upset about any single strikeout, would you think?"

"Most of the others probably kept their mouths shut about it, though."

"Probably. But let's suppose he's still mad at me after all these years. He finds out I work for the ACLU. He hates the ACLU anyway. His company is writing all these policies to our benefit. He picks out the biggest of them, which Limbach's was, incidentally. Already we've got a lot of ifs, but what then?"

"I don't know."

"I don't, either. All I could come up with was that he says, okay, here's my chance. I'll kill this guy Morty Limbach and make it look like suicide. That way I won't have to pay those Commie bastards all that money in case the guy would ever be hit by a truck, and that stuck-up college bitch will be sorry she ever messed with Hocker Westfall."

"Which is a hypothesis with certain problems," I said.

"Yeah, such as being absurd."

"On the other hand, Westfall is a friend of Limbach's parents, or at least a friend of his mother. She let him into Limbach's condo. Whatever he found there is supposed to be what gave him the idea Limbach killed himself."

"Westfall won't say what he found?"

"No. Just that it's conclusive. His exact word, apparently."

"We'll find it out on discovery eventually."

"That's what Rosson said, too. Actually, we might be able to find it out earlier. I've got a guy working on it."

"Who's that?"

"Guy named Cooper, Westfall's chief of security and claims investigations. Former remf from Vietnam."

"What's a rem?"

"Remf, with an *f*. Rear Echelon Motherfucker."

"Oh, sure, *remf*. Of course. Look, Bethany, setting aside this guy's war record for a minute, how come he's finding out stuff for you if he's working for Westfall?"

"Well, we came to kind of an understanding."

"Is this the kind of understanding I probably don't want to know anything about?"

"Probably it is, yeah."

— 5 —

NEXT MORNING I HEADED FOR MORTY LIMBACH'S CONDO. It turned out to be an expensive unit in an expensive mews lined on both sides with what used to be called row houses. A mews is what used to be called a dead-end alley. Fourteen Charterhouse Mews was halfway down the alley on the right. Like all the others, it had a red door with brass numbers and a brass mail slot and a brass-fitted light off to one side, made to look like a gaslight. The brass work was shiny—standing tall, as the dummy sergeants in basic used to say. But from the intimate knowledge of brass the dummies had given me, I knew that this stuff had never been polished. It was so new the lacquer hadn't worn off yet, that was all.

Just as Rosson had said, the key was one of the ones in the key case I had used at Poor Attitudes House. When I eventually found the right one, it produced the solid, satisfying click of a new, well-fitted dead-bolt lock. The little entry hall was bare of furniture except for an old golden oak hat rack that tipped off-center under a collection of sweat suits, jackets, and rain gear. A yellow oilskin foul weather hat sat on top of the mound. Apart from that, nothing—not even a doormat or a rug on the floor, or a picture on the wall.

I had pushed a pretty fair pile of mail aside when I opened the door. I knelt down to take a look, but there was nothing but bills, statements from banks and brokerages, and the kind of junk mail that this kind of address attracted: fund-raising letters from the Republican Party and other lobbyists for the rich, appeals from museums and symphonies, catalogs from Neiman Marcus, Orvis, the Sharper Image, Hammacher Schlemmer, L. L. Bean, and Land's End. I pushed the front door closed behind me and went exploring.

There were two bedrooms and a bath, a kitchen-dining area, a living room, and plenty of closet space. In this part of town, it added up to probably half a million bucks' worth of shelter from the elements. The rooms weren't bare, like the hall, but what furniture there was didn't match very well. A modern beanbag-type of chair, a little like the stuff in Rosson's office but not as expensive, sat next to an upholstered chair with a floral slipcover. Facing them was a sofa with a slipcover in the same pattern. A couple of tubular steel chairs were along the walls, along with a Chippendale or something like that. The kind of chair, anyway, that breaks and costs you a lot of money if you make the mistake of thinking the thing is supposed to be sat on. Probably plenty of people had made that mistake already, since there was only the one chair left, of what had no doubt been a set. Limbach's bedroom held a couple of wood-and-canvas director's chairs, a bed with no headboard or footboard, and a dressing table that had escaped from some aunt's or grandmother's boudoir. The table was shaped something like a kidney bean, with a glass top. It had a ruffled apricot-colored skirt. The only other furniture was a carved-oak Victorian dresser with a marble top and an adjustable mirror standing above it on supports.

Limbach had used the other bedroom as an office. He had made a large desk from a couple of two-drawer filing cabinets that supported a door laid flat between them. On it was a Macintosh SE, the same machine I had at home. Pushed back under the desk was a nylon carrying case, which was something I was thinking of getting for my own Mac. I pulled it out to take a look. On the inside of the cover were little pouches to hold the mouse, and the cables, and floppy disks. All these pouches were empty except for the one made to hold floppy disks, which bulged slightly in a way that didn't suggest floppies. Floppy disks, at least the ones the Mac uses, aren't floppy. They come in flat, stiff, little plastic squares.

What turned out to be bulging the pouch was $1,800, in hundred-dollar bills. Presumably it had been Morty's petty-cash box. I put the money in my pocket, because who would ever know? Well, shit, I would. This was a dumb thought to have—un-American really, in the Reagan-Bush era—but I couldn't seem to help myself. I knew I'd have to give the money to Rosson, who would drop it into the estate, where it would disappear like a spoonful into an ocean.

The phone rang. Now that I wasn't in Hope's hotel room, I could answer phones again. And so I did.

"Morty?" the voice said, sounding confused. "Uh, is Morty there?"

"Afraid not," I said. "Can I help you?"

"Well, yeah. Sure. Could you tell him Don Heiny called and he'll call again later? I just got in from Jordan."

"So you didn't hear about the accident?"

"What accident?"

I told him more or less what had happened, although I fuzzed up the exact details of Limbach's death.

"My God, that's awful," Heiny said at the end. "Sally must be devastated."

"Sally?"

"His mother. You don't know Mrs. Limbach?" And so I explained that I was working for the estate, and he hung up before I got around to asking what the hell he had been doing in Jordan. It beat going to Iraq, maybe, but not by much.

I started looking for whatever I was looking for by searching the files in the cabinets that held up the desk top. The files mostly contained business and tax records of no interest that I could see, so that I was able to spend only enough time on each document to make sure that it had nothing to do with suicidal inclinations. But Limbach's business affairs were extensive and complicated, so that even a fast check wound up taking nearly two hours.

Next I looked through Limbach's disk files, and booted up the computer. I checked out every data disk he had, which only turned out to be six. The best bet seemed to be the disk named Personal, and so I began with that one. I started in on Morty's mail. I had read two of his letters without coming across anything of interest and had just called the third up on the screen when I heard the noise. It was the same click of a dead-bolt I had made with the key myself, coming in. Only I hadn't locked the door behind me. I made myself think for a second. Someone must have come in through the unlocked door and then locked the door behind him. Why hadn't the someone called out when he came in through an open door that should have been locked?

I punched the printer on and sent Limbach's letter to it, hoping the noise from the printer would make it seem that I was busy at the desk. Instead I moved across the room and positioned myself behind the office door. If the visitor knocked, or even opened the door without knocking and stood there, fine. We could talk. If he came in fast, we wouldn't talk just yet.

He came in fast.

I got behind him and took him down, using his own momentum so that he hit hard. Too late, I saw that there was another man behind him. His kick got me full force, on the side of the face. There was no pain, not yet. Just the heavy blow, like a rock, and the knowledge I had to have been hurt. Without thought I did what I had to, what I had done before when the odds turned against me. I disabled the one I had my hands on. Since his arm was already up between his shoulder blades, I broke it at the elbow.

The second man hadn't quite got his balance back from the kick, and so I went for the leg that still had most of his weight on it. He fell on his partner, with me on top of them both. The one on the bottom was hollering in pain, but the second man wasn't hurt. He was strong and he was frantic, and I didn't dare let him loose. I put a carotid choke hold on him instead. In a few seconds, just the way it must have been for Limbach, he lost consciousness. I let go to see what I had.

They were two black men—boys, really, not more than nineteen or twenty. The one with the broken elbow had stopped screaming, now that the weight of two struggling bodies was off him. I hadn't seen the gun when I jumped him from the rear, and he must have lost track of it in the scramble. I put the thing in my pants pocket. It felt heavy, bulky, and awkward, the way a gun in your pocket always does. Worse than that, carrying the thing on a regular basis has harmful side effects. You turn into an asshole.

I ran my hands over both of them and took a knife off each kid. In the kitchen I found some strapping tape and used it to tie up the unconscious partner, who would be dangerous again any minute. Then I did the same for the one with the broken elbow.

"Ow, motherfucker, hey, man that fucking hurts," he hollered.

All this time I had been swallowing blood, and the adrenaline had worn off so that the pain in my mouth was reaching a peak. Two of my back teeth were loose, as I learned when I tested them with my tongue.

"Sorry about that," I said, and pulled the tape a little tighter. Maybe his hands would fall off. His partner, meanwhile, had regained consciousness but was keeping quiet. He would be disoriented for a little while yet.

I worked at my two molars once again with my tongue and one of them came loose. I spat it out like an olive pit and there it was in my palm, with little red chunks still sticking to the roots. A filling in the tooth made me think about happier days, when the molar had been part of me, to be repaired and kept around for my old age. Maybe hockey players and boxers took this kind of thing in stride, but wrestlers don't get their teeth knocked out very often. I was proud of my teeth. They were in good shape and up till now I had had all of them. I was abnormally, unreasonably mad at the punks. I put the molar away in my shirt pocket.

"How you feel, tough guy?" I said to the one I had choked into unconsciousness.

"Fuck you, motherfucker," he said. Evidently he felt normal again.

"Yeah, right. Well, I'm going in the kitchen now, see if I can find some pliers."

"What you want with pliers?" the one with the broken elbow asked. I thought it might do him good to wonder about that, so I didn't answer.

Out in the kitchen I found pliers in Limbach's tool drawer and weighed them in my hand while I thought about ways of using them. It was a pretty close thing, but in a few moments I had hold of myself again. These two muggers were going to wind up in Walpole soon enough anyway, just in the normal order of things. The one I really had a quarrel with was whoever sent them, and I thought I had a way to find out who he was without pliers.

I rummaged through the tool drawer but couldn't find the rope or cord I was looking for. The closest thing was a heavy-duty orange extension cord, of the same kind that had been around Limbach's neck. Maybe he kept one handy everywhere he spent time. Maybe they were essential to his private ritual. But the cord was no good for my purposes, since knots made with it would be easy to undo. I cut the rubber insulation with one of my new knives and pulled loose a couple of long lengths of the sixteen-gauge wire inside. I snipped the wires free with the pliers and went out to arrange the scene I had planned. So the two would-be hit men could see what a good job I was doing. I worked in front of them. I made two slip nooses in the ends of my wires, using complicated knots that I pulled tight with the pliers. Even if my prisoners were able to reach the knots with their bound hands, they'd never be able to work them loose with bare fingertips. The nooses went over their heads. The free ends went to a heavy window catch at about shoulder height, where I attached them with more fancy knots, pulled tight. At the end, the two could stand up or sit down, but they couldn't get away without strangling themselves.

"Where you going, man?" the one with the broken arm said when I headed for the door.

"I'm going to get a friend that used to interrogate prisoners in Vietnam. He's going to make you tell me who sent you."

"Ain't nobody sent us, man."

"Then you won't be able to tell him, will you? Too bad

for you, because he'll just keep on asking. He likes that shit."

"You crazy, man?"

"Not me, him. I can't even stand to watch."

I shut down Limbach's computer system and put the dust covers back on everything. My two prisoners watched, presumably without a clue, as I slipped Limbach's data disks into my pocket. My guess was all they knew about computers came from playing Space Invaders in the arcades. Then I left them there.

After I shut the office door behind me, I walked with a normal amount of noise to the front door. I made sure that it was still unlocked, and shut it loudly to give the impression I had gone out. Then I sneaked back across the living room toward the office. At first I couldn't hear anything from the two. But after a few minutes, they must have become convinced I was gone. I could hear their voices, although I couldn't make out the words. Maybe you didn't get much floor space for a half-million bucks, but at least you got solid doors.

It took much longer than I thought before they figured out the best of the few possibilities open to them. But at last I heard the sound I had been waiting for—the jangling crash of a phone hitting the floor. It had finally occurred to them to make the long stretch to the phone jack just within reach and use the wire to pull the phone off the desk and over to them. After the crash there was a considerable period of silence. I was afraid they might have snagged the phone or the receiver on something, but eventually I heard the pattern of phone conversation, speech alternating with silence. And then, after the phone call was over, the back-and-forth of voices as the two captives talked to each other. I quietly carried a chair over to the coat closet beside the front door. I made a space for the chair among the hanging coats and sat down to wait for whoever was coming.

It wouldn't have seemed like much of a wait, except for the throbbing in my jaw. Actually it only lasted a little less than half an hour from the time my two attackers had doped out a way to call their version of 911. I was nearly certain who would come running to the rescue, but I wanted to be a hundred percent sure. And I wanted to talk to the man, too. The longer I sat in the closet, hurting, the more I wanted to talk to him.

Through the crack I had left open in the closet door, I saw the front door open slowly and soundlessly. A hand appeared, with a gun in it. A German Luger, which figured.

"You guys in here?" a voice called out.

Another voice answered from the office, but you couldn't make out the words. Myron Cooper followed his Luger into the room, trying to get near enough to hear.

"Ronald? William?" he called. "You guys alone?"

As soon as the answer started to come, I left my closet and walked as light as I could up behind Cooper. He was so busy listening to his help that he didn't know I was there until I had his hand bent back between both of mine so that the Luger was pointed at his belly. There was a chance the gun could go off, of course, but it was a chance I could live with. The gun didn't go off, though. He had to let it fall to the rug, to save his wrist from getting broken.

"Oh, Jesus," Myron said, in the scared voice of a kid who knew he shouldn't have tried such a dumb trick in the first place.

"You got that right, Myron," I said, picking up the gun and pocketing it. I was getting to feel as loaded down and clumsy as a scuba diver waddling around with a tank and thirty pounds of weight belt. Not that I needed to be particularly agile, with Myron. We had already established the pecking order between us, back in his upscale surveillance room, and I had hardly bothered to keep an eye on him when I bent for the gun.

"Let me show you something, Myron," I said, taking my molar out of my shirt pocket. "This is my tooth. One of your hired hands kicked it out."

"I'm sorry . . ."

"Sorry is shit, Myron. How would you like to eat this tooth?"

"Eat it?"

"Right, Myron. Eat the tooth."

"No! I mean, listen . . . The dentist could put it back in. I heard they can do that now."

"Let's not fuck around here, Myron," I said, grabbing his face and squeezing his cheeks till he looked like a catfish. "Open your mouth and close your eyes and you will get a big surprise." I poked the tooth in, took hold of his hand again, and bent it into position.

"What I'm going to do," I told him, "I'm going to bust fingers till you swallow the son of a bitch."

I put pressure on a finger, and he swallowed desperately. But apparently the tooth didn't go down too easy, dry. I held on to the finger while he kept swallowing. Finally he finished, but I kept the pressure on his finger, just enough to almost break it but not quite. Although if I happened to press a little too hard, I wouldn't really give a rat's ass, either. Cooper seemed to sense this. Maybe making him eat the tooth had helped.

"Was this jerk-off hit squad your idea, Myron?" I asked, forcefully. "Or the Hocker's?"

"It was his idea."

"Bullshit, you thought it up yourself, didn't you?" I asked, a little more forcefully.

"Jesus, okay, all right. It was my idea."

JEROME DOOLITTLE

That was the problem with force, of course. Myron
would have confessed to killing both Kennedys.

"Actually, it probably *was* your idea, wasn't it, you fat
fuck? This guy Heiny, this family friend or whatever, he
calls here for Morty Limbach. I answer and tell him Morty's
dead, and he calls up Mommy, and Mommy calls who?
Myron Cooper? Shit, she doesn't know Myron Cooper
from third base. She calls the Hocker, and the Hocker calls
Myron. That's the way it had to be, am I right?"

Myron nodded.

"The thing is, what would the Hocker have against me?
A guy he never even heard of before yesterday? So proba-
bly he just said get your ass over there, Myron, tell the guy
Mommy said he should leave. Something like that."

This time Myron didn't nod. He could see where I was
going.

"But you're the one who had something against me,
aren't you, Myron? I humiliated you, I made a movie of
you. Best way to make sure Westfall never sees that movie,
your best shot is to make sure I never see Westfall. So you
send over a couple of bloods for me, maybe it'll look like
I walked in on a burglary and got killed. Am I warm,
Myron? You remember how to play that game, don't you?
I'm red hot, right?"

Myron said nothing, and I didn't try to make him. He
was too dumb to come up with a workable lie on the spot,
and he was scared enough to tell the truth if it would have
saved him. So him saying nothing meant that I had guessed
close enough. If the Hocker had been behind it, Cooper
would have told me so to get himself off the hook.

"Myron, Myron. What are we going to do with you,
you sorry fat fuck? Tell me, Myron, how come you got a
Luger?"

Myron looked puzzled. "They're a good gun," he said.

86

"There's a lot of good guns. How come this particular kind?"

"I'm a World War II collector."

"That right? You got a Colt .45, too?"

"They're not collectible."

"Sure, they are. But I bet what you collect is Nazi shit, isn't it, Myron? I bet you got an SS dagger, right? Come on, Myron. I'm asking you a question here."

"Edged weapons is a different field."

"I didn't ask you what kind of a fucking field it was. I asked you did you have one."

"Not a real good one, no."

"You're kind of cute, Myron, you know it? You even look a little bit like Göring. Probably he wore a little red bikini, too. You got your bikini on today, Myron? Answer me, you fuck."

Myron shook his head.

"I'm a collector too, Myron. I collect guns from assholes. I got two of yours now. You bring your handcuffs with you again, Myron?"

Myron nodded.

"Good," I said.

I took Myron's company car, because I didn't want him to get a look at the plates on mine. My license plate would only have led to a counterman named Joey Neary at a Harvard Square lunch counter named the Tasty, but I didn't want Myron to get even that close to who I was and where I lived. I used to have the car in my own name, and I still pay the registration, insurance, and all expenses. But now Joey was the owner of record. In return for his name, Joey got to use the car on his vacations, and any weekends when I didn't need it.

The arrangement wrapped up the last loose end I could think of that might lead a bureaucrat to me. Years ago I had decided that the best way to keep unwanted people out of my life was to get myself out of everybody's computers, to lay down no paper trail. I moved out of my old place in Allston and rented an apartment in Cambridge under a new identity, which was fully documented. My new neighbors know me as Tom Carpenter, who does some vague sort of consulting work. Carpenter pays his rent and his phone bill by postal money order. He has no credit cards, and consequently no credit history to be checked. He gets junk mail and the phone bill at his Ware Street address, a block and a half from Harvard Square. Any other mail, which isn't much, he gets people to send to a box in the Brattle Street post office that is rented in still another name.

A long time ago, I had played along with the government, doing things like registering with the Selective Service when our high school principal said you should. All it got me was drafted and taxed, and on a lot of mailing lists and in a lot of data bases, and so I finally said the hell with it. Now I'm like the Stealth bomber, invisible to radar. Actually neither one of us is really invisible, probably, but at least you'd have to be looking pretty hard to spot us on the screen. And if the government couldn't track me down easily, neither could Myron Cooper or William and Ronald.

I hadn't bothered to tell Cooper where we were headed in his company car. After a while, though, we got close enough so he could figure out that I was taking him back to his office. "What are you going to do?" he asked. Actually he had already asked this once or twice, after I had handcuffed him with one hand in front of him and the other behind him, the short chain running between his legs so that he had to walk bent over. But this time I answered him.

"Okay, Myron, here's what I'm going to do. While I left you handcuffed to your two pals back there, I went out and got your movie from my car. What happens now is we give the movie to the Hocker."

"Jesus, please don't do that, Bethany. I almost lost my job last time, for Christ's sake. What do you want? Just let me know and maybe we can work it out."

"Actually, Myron, what I want is for you to lose your job."

"Why, for God's sake? You never met me before, and right off you start fucking me up with my boss."

"The first time it was just because you pissed me off," I lied. Actually Westfall was the one who had pissed me off, more than pissed me off, when he said his filth about Hope. Cooper was just caught in the fallout.

"This time it's because you tried to kill me and I don't want you to try it again, so this is what I'm doing. The only balls you got, Myron, you borrow them. Used to be from the air force, now from a big insurance company. So I'm taking you away from your balls. That way I won't have to worry about you anymore."

"Listen, Bethany, please. I can—"

"Oh, shut up, Myron."

We parked in the garage under the Pilgrim Mutual building. Cooper's space was only two away from the one marked "Mr. Westfall, Pres." I made a mental note of the special low number on Westfall's Jaguar, a big-shot number. Cooper's slot was marked "Mr. Cooper, V.P." There were a half-dozen or so other V.P. slots around, but still, Myron had done pretty well for himself in the company. He even had a key to the executive elevator, so we took it up to the twenty-second floor, where Mr. Westfall, Pres., had his office. Cooper drew some stares, walking down the hall all hunched over, with his hands apparently clasped between his legs. But nobody said anything. My guess was that people in the company were scared of Myron.

On my earlier visit there had been two secretaries or

89

receptionists or whatever in Westfall's outer office. One was middle-aged and plain, obviously for service. The other was a young and pretty Asian-American woman, obviously for show. Only the older woman was at her desk this time.

"Good heavens, Mr. Cooper," she said. "Did you hurt your back?"

Then she spotted the handcuffs, and said, "Oh. Oh, my heavens."

"The boss in?" I asked.

"He's in conference," she said, which I figured meant he was in, all right. So I started Cooper, half-stumbling, toward the mahogany door.

"You can't go in there," the woman said, real fear in her voice when she saw where we were heading. But we went in anyway. Westfall was sitting behind his huge, ugly glass-topped desk. The young receptionist was kneeling in front of him, between his legs. He pushed her away and swiveled around in his big leather chair so his back was to us while he made himself decent.

"What the hell do you think you're doing?" he hollered. Tough.

The girl, left to fend for herself, got up and ran from the room.

"I brought Myron back to you," I said.

"Just what the fuck is going on here, Cooper?"

"He'll tell you after I leave," I said, "but he'll be lying. You want to find out what's actually going on, find out for yourself. Drag his ass over to Morty Limbach's old place. You know where it is. You've been there. I left two guys for you there, all tied up. Ask them what Myron used your money to hire them for. You got a VCR in here?"

Information was coming too fast for Westfall to deal with. "VCR?" he said. "What are you talking, VCR?"

"Well, you got a big TV over there, Mr. Westfall," I said. The "Mr." was to show respect. I had thought about it on the way over, and decided that respect was called for, at this stage of what I had in mind for him. "I was just asking if you had a VCR that went with it."

"Yeah, I got a VCR."

I took out the tape that showed Myron whining about his boss and put it on the glass table. "Play this on your VCR before you let Myron here say anything," I said. "Just play it, Mr. Westfall."

As I was closing the door behind me, I heard Myron say, "Mr. Westfall, I can—"

And I heard the Hocker say, "Shut up, asshole."

— 6 —

When I called Jerome Rosson, Hope happened to be in his office. She said she'd wait until I could get my car back from Limbach's place and drive to Harvard Law School. "Oh, Tom," she said when she saw me. The "Tom" was because the side of my face looked so bad. Usually she called me Bethany. "Tom, that's *awful.*"

"Well, it doesn't hurt any worse than when I had that damned impacted wisdom tooth out a couple years back. Of course, I guess this was an extraction, too."

"You lost a tooth?"

"Yeah, one."

"Sometimes they can put them back, you know."

"I didn't think about keeping it."

"What happened, anyway?" Rosson asked.

"Well, first off I've got eighteen hundred dollars for you. For the estate, anyway . . ."

I didn't tell them all the details, of course. I told them everything that had happened to me, all right, but I left out the part about busting in on Westfall as his secretary was tending to him. And I left out certain specifics of what had happened to the two boys and their boss, Myron.

"You think there might be something on the disks?" Rosson asked when I was done.

"It's worth a shot. Westfall evidently searched the place himself, and a guy like him, he's probably too important to bother learning anything about computers. If he grabbed anything, it was likely to be something on paper. If it was handwritten, we lose. If it was something printed out, it'd probably be on one of the disks I took."

"Well, we'll get it eventually, whatever it is," Rosson said. "But it'd be nice to have it now, just to know exactly what they've got their hands on."

"I'll check his files," I said. "I've got a Mac at home, the same machine Limbach had."

"Fine," Rosson said.

"Something else, though," I said. "A guy like Westfall, up from peddling vacuum cleaners and cancer insurance door-to-door, how come he knows somebody like Morty Limbach's mother?"

"I thought you said it was through charity work."

"Yeah, but does the Hocker really strike you as one of the thousand points of light?"

"You could call Toby Ingersoll," Hope said. "He probably knows the Limbachs."

Ingersoll, the director of the ACLU's Boston office, knew all the old money within a hundred miles of Boston and had a lot of it himself. He had grown up at cotillions, clubs, and regattas. His people were what the Kennedys tried to be and moved to New York because they couldn't. Hope knew the number, and I called it.

Ingersoll turned out to know about the Limbachs, sure enough. Particularly about Morty's mother, Sally.

"Turns out that in the old days, the Hocker was vacuum

cleaner salesman to the stars," I reported when Toby had hung up. "Westfall and Sally go way back."

"That certainly adds an element, doesn't it?" Rosson said.

"If the gossip is right, yeah. This is all stuff Toby sort of dimly remembers his mother talking about with her bridge friends. Kind of stuff where they'd shut up when they noticed he was listening."

"The good stuff," Hope said.

"Exactly. Anyway, apparently the Hocker knocked on her door one day and wound up demonstrating his machine, and presumably one demonstration led to another. Nobody really knew about that part, of course, but that didn't stop them guessing. Mainly because she started touting him and his vacuum cleaners to all her pals. Back then she's in her late thirties, something like that. Wealthy young matron neglected by her husband . . ."

"Was Morty born yet?" Hope asked.

"Toby isn't too clear on the time sequence, but his impression is that Morty was a young boy. The father was away a lot. Apparently he liked sailing and Sally got seasick."

"So she's at home, bored, and along comes this slick-talking traveling salesman," Hope said. "But Westfall! My God."

"Different strokes," I said. "He looked a little bit like Tony Curtis to me."

"I always thought Tony Curtis looked vaguely repellent," Rosson said.

"He was good in *The Boston Strangler*," I said.

"Exactly."

"How about all those women who opened their doors to him?" I said. "They didn't think he looked vaguely repellent."

"Come back down to earth, Bethany," Hope said. "It

94

was only a movie. Still, you're right. The point is that plenty of women could and did find Westfall attractive, and probably still do. He was handsome in an obvious kind of way, and he was charming in the same way. The charm was so phony that you'd think anybody would see through it, but they mostly didn't. The pathetic truth was that plenty of the secretaries in the office would fight for him to notice them."

"And he was a young guy when Sally Limbach met him," I said, "and probably he *was* slick-talking. And of course we don't know what she was like, herself."

"I do," Rosson said. "Or at least I can imagine, working back from what she's like now. Average looks, maybe a little on the plain side. No charm, no humor. Takes herself seriously. Not quick at all. Comes across as a little slow, actually."

"Probably essentially defenseless against a clever sociopath like Westfall," Hope said.

"He certainly would have seemed different to her, anyway," I said. "According to Toby she's the daughter of some Boston Brahmin guy without much money who used to run the Museum of Science. She dropped out of Pine Manor to marry Limbach."

"Let's get back to the dirt," Hope said. "She and Westfall have an affair. Then what?"

"Possible affair," I said. "Apparently there was talk, but not enough talk so it would get back to the husband . . ."

"Off on his yacht," Hope said.

"Off on his yacht, dumb and happy. The talk dies down for years. The ladies at the bridge club or whatever, they figure she got smart and dumped him. Which maybe she did, but years later the Hocker and his little company somehow put together a huge takeover bid and pull it off. Amazement in the financial district. Who's behind this masked stranger? Nobody knows, but some of the ladies at the bridge club, they're a lot older now, they start to talk again when Westfall shows up on some advisory board of the Harvard Divinity School and Sally Limbach is the one who pushed him for it."

"Let's just hold on a minute here," Hope said. *"The Harvard Divinity School?"*

"It's possible," Rosson said. "Principal product at Harvard is status. We don't just sell it to the students, either. Meese swapped government research money for a medal from the JFK School. Boesky bought his way onto the board of the School of Public Health."

"Hear that?" I said to Hope. "Why not the Hocker? What the hell, he's no rottener than those guys, and he's got big donor potential."

"You're right," Hope said. "I just wasn't thinking."

"But where does all this get us?" Rosson asked. It was the right question. We had some old rumors. Even if they were true, all they amounted to was a connection between Westfall and Morty's mother. And we already knew there was a connection between them, because Westfall himself had told us there was.

"Doesn't get us anywhere," I said.

"It's interesting that there might have been Limbach money behind Westfall's takeover bid," Hope said. "But even if there had been something between them years before, how would that translate into a business partnership?"

"Maybe Westfall has pictures," I said.

"Pictures?" Rosson asked. "What pictures?" Hope didn't have to ask. She had been around politics long enough to know.

"Pictures means you've got something on somebody," I said. "Pictures of the candidate in a sleeping bag with a Boy Scout. Documents, tapes. That kind of thing. In this case, hard proof that she had slept with him."

"My God, anything he'd have would be something like thirty years old," Rosson said. "It ain't much."

"It could work a lot of different ways," I said. "Old man Limbach could be staying married just because it costs so much for a rich guy to get divorced. Wouldn't cost so much if he could prove adultery."

"It could be that Westfall and Mrs. Limbach actually feel something for each other, too," Hope said. "The Hocker might be the big erotic memory of her life, although it's a difficult concept for me to grasp."

"I guess she might have been a magic moment for him, too," I said. "The commoner who screws the princess. Or maybe the Hocker was really screwing the husband. Or what the husband stood for."

"That certainly adds a new and sickening dimension," Hope said. "Imagine screwing the New York Yacht Club."

"Imagine the Limbachs are the secret owners of Pilgrim Mutual while you're at it," Professor Rosson said. "You still haven't explained why Pilgrim is fighting this claim."

"I know it," I said. "I'm going by to talk to the shrink this afternoon. This Mark Unger. See what he's got to say about suicidal tendencies and weird autoerotic tendencies."

"Oh, no, you're not, Bethany," Hope said. "You're going home and I'm going with you to make sure you get there and don't go wandering off. You look like one of those pictures they take of the loser after a prizefight."

Actually, she didn't take me home. She took me to her hotel instead, on the theory that what I needed was a place with room service. It seemed to me like a sound theory. Hope had me stretch out on top of the bed while she closed the drapes out of consideration for the invalid. It still didn't look much like a sick room. She sat down beside me and called room service.

"Well, I'd suggest a drugstore, if the hotel doesn't have an ice bag. Specifically I'd suggest the RIX drugstore on

JFK Street, two blocks away. If they don't have an ice bag, walk another block to the CVS on the Square. And don't forget the ice to go in it . . . I know there is, but the tray in it only has about six of those little tiny cubes. I want a bucketful. Now give me the kitchen . . . I know you're room service, I understand that, but I want to talk to the kitchen . . . No, I want the people who actually prepare the food . . .

"Custard, right. Just regular baked custard. Eggs, milk, sugar, vanilla . . . Yeah, right, exactly. Like flan, only without the caramel. Grate some nutmeg on top instead. . . . No, not the little cup things. Big Pyrex baking dishes, quart and a half or two quarts. Make two dishes, we'll put one in the refrigerator. Right, right . . ."

When she was through bossing around the staff, I went into more detail about my encounters with Cooper than I had back in Rosson's office. But I still didn't tell her every single little thing. For instance, I didn't make a big point over exactly what had happened to my molar. Or any point at all. There was enough on my charge sheet already.

As it was, when I finished she asked me, "How smart was all of that? I don't mean you could have predicted he'd send people to kill you, but why infuriate him when you didn't really have to?"

"It was a mistake," I said. "Dumb. I managed to hold on while Westfall talked about you, but then I lost it when Cooper started in. Besides, he's the kind of *Soldier of Fortune* asshole that turns me into a *Soldier of Fortune* asshole, too."

"You don't have to protect me, you know," she said. "The business with Westfall was a long time ago. It was unpleasant, but it truly wasn't that big a deal in my young life. It was just one of the normal hazards of growing up female in those days. Happened to all women."

"Still does," I said, "only not all of them know how to

deal with it." I told her about Westfall's pretty, diminutive secretary.

"Poor thing," Hope said. "Imagine the contempt he must feel, not just for her but for the other secretary, not even bothering to lock the door." I hadn't thought of that.

A knock sounded, and Hope went to answer it. It was the room service waiter. When he had gone, Hope filled the ice bag he had brought and propped it against my cheek with pillows. "Maybe at least the swelling will go down," she said. "Then all you'll have will be a huge, disgusting purple bruise."

She couldn't carry her lightness of tone through to the end of the sentence. I turned my head to look up at her, and she was crying.

"Damn you, Bethany," she said. "Damn you, damn you, damn you anyway. You could have got yourself killed, you know."

I put the ice bag to one side and lifted myself to a sitting position, so that I could take her in my arms. "I'm sorry," I said. "I really am. I'm sorry." As I held her, feeling her shake with the crying, I remembered what I had told Cooper earlier. Sorry is shit.

She got herself to stop crying after a minute or two, and then waited a minute or two more before she spoke. "I don't know what got into me," she said. "You're the one who got hurt, and I'm the one who's crying."

She got to her feet, so brisk and determined and self-controlled it was almost convincing, and headed for the bathroom. She closed the door and I heard the water running. She came out ten minutes later, wearing a bathrobe over nothing. But I knew she wasn't going to stay, because her hair was still up.

"How do you feel?" she asked.

"The side of my face hurts like hell and I feel tired."

"Too tired?"

"Nearly, but not quite."

"You lie there. Don't move at all. I'll do everything. No, no, don't move. Close your eyes."

"I can't watch?"

"Oh, all right, you can keep them open. You sicko."

She slipped off my shoes and then my socks, putting them out of sight on the floor. She undid my pants and worked them off me, leaving them in a pile down by my feet. She worked my shorts off me, too, putting them on top of the pants. I lay still, the way she had told me to, as she moved my legs apart to make room for herself.

The thin gold chain she wore around her neck kept getting in her way, and she kept moving it out of the way with her free hand. After a time I didn't notice anymore, didn't notice that and didn't notice the pain in my jaw either.

When I began to notice things again, she was on her way to the bathroom to dress. "Sleep," she said when she came out. My eyes were almost closed. Through my lashes she looked blurred as she bent over to kiss me. "I'll be back by dinnertime," she said. "Don't worry about keeping the ice bag on. Don't worry about anything. Just sleep."

I did, and only woke up enough to mumble and roll over when she came back in later that night. And so I wasted one of our too-few nights together. But for some reason pain tires you out. Presumably the body is hard at work, putting things back together again.

"I've got to go," Hope said when I finally came awake the next morning.

"I know. You said already." She had to go back to Washington today. Rosson and I could handle things, and she felt uncomfortable when she was away from the kids for more than a couple of days. Guilty.

One solution would be for me to move down to Washington, and I had thought about it more than once. I never

100

talked about it with Hope, though. I was afraid of the chance I'd be taking, by moving near her. Everything might be fine, but who could know? Maybe the value in what we had came from scarcity and would grow less the more we saw of each other. Or maybe it would strengthen so that we had to see each other more and more, and eventually all the time. That way her very decent husband and her three fine, bright, happy kids would suffer, and therefore so would she, and therefore so would I. And who could say where that road led?

The way things were at present might not have been perfect, but our occasional sadnesses were no worse than we could bear. And I doubted that anybody's good times got any happier than ours were. It could even be that the bittersweet was what made them that way. I was scared of poking at things for fear of knocking them out of balance. Since Hope never poked at our arrangement, either, she was probably scared of the same thing. There was no way I could be sure, of course. Short of poking.

Instead, I said, "I thought your flight didn't leave till noon."

"It doesn't, but I've got some things to go over with Toby at his office. You can stay here till checkout time. Watch 'Donahue.' Use that ice bag the way I told you to, or you'll grow up with a lopsided face. I should have made you sleep with it on. I'm not strict enough with you, Bethany."

"If it makes you feel better, you could tie me up."

"I should. A little discipline never hurt anybody."

"Come here, okay?"

She came. Into the soft hollow of her neck, I murmured, "Been too long, Hope. Too long. Find a way to come back up, okay?"

"You know I'll try," she murmured into my ear.

After she left I did what she said, although I was able to

tolerate the ice bag a lot longer than "Donahue." My idea of a match made in heaven was the time when Phil Donahue interviewed Billy Carter.

I was out of the Charles at noon, carrying my new ice bag. I hadn't bothered to clean up at the hotel, since I had to change clothes at home anyway. Once home, I stayed in the shower till my fingertips got shriveled. The skin on the side of my face still felt stretched and tender, so that I used a light touch in shaving it. But the swelling, sure enough, had gone down some. And the edges of the bruise were starting to turn the color of Chinese mustard. In two or three days it would be gone. Even though dull pain still radiated from the jawbone itself, it didn't hurt when I explored the tooth socket with my tongue. Didn't even hurt when I stuck my little finger back there. The mouth had an amazing capacity to heal itself, but it couldn't grow new teeth. I was still mad at Cooper, even though I had gotten back at him. Or presumably I had. I picked up the phone and dialed Pilgrim Mutual.

"Myron Cooper, please," I said.

"I'm sorry, sir, but Mr. Cooper is no longer employed by this firm. May I connect you with someone else in his department?"

"No, thanks. He's the one I was after."

I got a pint of Ben & Jerry's Heath Bar Crunch from the freezer, figuring it would be sort of a halfway house between custard and real food. The ice cream went down fine, as long as I confined action to the left side of my mouth and let the chunks of Heath Bar thaw a little.

The ache in my jaw would go away just as fast if I kept busy as if I lay down, so I headed over to the Poor Attitudes House on foot. My appointment with Dr. Mark Unger, the psychiatrist, wasn't till four-thirty. But I figured I might catch Nora Dawson, the trouper who had run out of the room during my first visit to Poor Attitudes House. If she wasn't in, it was another perfect day just to find a park bench somewhere and sit in the mild autumn sun.

But it turned out Nora was in, and Ned hollered up the stairs for her. The actor-director wore a new T-shirt today. Instead of a Rorschach blot, this one said CATS ARE SERIAL KILLERS. A guy who hated cats couldn't be all bad.

Nora came down wearing a mismatched sweat suit. The shirt was standard gray, but the pants were crimson, with HARVARD UNIVERSITY running down the outsides of the legs. This high-concept jock stuff always looks a little silly with the Harvard name on it, although no doubt the Harvards don't think so. But the combination always makes me think of Harvard's own Henry Kissinger defending the *Mayaguez* idiocy on TV. "We are not going around looking for opportunities to prove our manhood," he told all of us lesser mortals, glancing down to make sure his little wiener was still attached. Or maybe I just imagined the glance.

"Could you spare a few minutes?" I asked Nora when she appeared on the stairs.

"Jeez, I'd have to check my dance card," she said. "Yeah, looks like I can fit you in, all right. I'm not down for anything till Christmas."

"I got something at four-thirty myself," I said.

"Just time for a quickie," said Nora. "About twenty-five quickies, actually, the way *my* boyfriend is." She looked like she had just got up, but already she was on stage. Nora led me first to the kitchen, where she poured us both some coffee from an office coffee maker, and then to the big downstairs room in which I had watched the Poor Attitudes rehearsing. The way took us past Kathy Poindexter's old room, the room where Limbach had died.

"I always feel funny when I go past that room," she said, when we had closed the door to the rehearsal room behind us. "Poor Morty."

"Were you pretty close to him?"

"Yeah, I guess I was close to him. Anyway we were fucking. Is that what you mean by close?"

"Is that what you mean?"

"A question for a question, huh? That's what that prick Unger used to do."

"Is he a prick?"

"I don't know. I don't know anymore who's a prick and who isn't. Most people think he's a saint."

"But he was a prick to you?"

"My opinion is a minority opinion."

"What did Morty think of him?"

"Morty said he helped him a lot."

"Were you Unger's patient, too?"

"For a while, yeah."

"Did he help you?"

"He called it help."

"What was it?"

"Hey, can we get off of Unger?"

"I'm sorry. Can we talk about Morty, though?"

"Can we talk?" Nora said, leaning toward me and sounding like Joan Rivers. "Sure, why not?"

She had met him in the only place their paths would be likely to cross, being that he was a millionaire and she was the daughter of a dead rummy cop. He summered in Bar Harbor. She summered in Dorchester, clerking in a 7-Eleven. He drifted through Bard and she struggled through a couple of work-study years at Northeastern on whatever her mother could spare from a policeman's pension. Nora was studying drama but gave it up when a friend took her to an audition at the Poor Attitudes House. There she met Morty Limbach and became part of the troupe.

"It wasn't a casting couch deal," Nora said. "That wasn't Morty's kind of a thing at all. It was months before we fell in . . . well, shit, before we started fucking. All right?"

"All right with me."

104

"What I mean is there was nothing *wrong* about it. We weren't *exploiting* each other. I was just *depressed*, okay?"

"Sounds okay to me. Who didn't think it was?"

"His mother wasn't too pleased."

"Was that what you were depressed about?"

"Shit, no. That isn't the kind of thing you get depressed about."

"Then what?"

"Isn't everybody always depressed about the same thing? Lack of love. Morty understood about that."

"Who didn't love him?"

"He didn't love himself. He told me once about how he was walking along with a cousin one time, some jerk he couldn't stand. They had just come from an ice cream place and the guy said something that really ticked Morty off. 'I was so damned mad'—this is Morty talking now—'so damned mad I threw my cone right down on the sidewalk.'

"You see what I mean?" Nora asked.

"Maybe, but tell me."

"Well, Morty didn't think there was anything weird about that story at all. He just told it to me to show me how much he hated this cousin. He was surprised when I asked him why he didn't throw the *cousin's* cone on the sidewalk. All those years since, the thought never once occurred to him. I mean, even *I'm* not as fucked up that way as Morty was."

Then she thought about that.

"Well, maybe I am," she said after a moment. "There isn't a healthy ego in this whole goddamned place except maybe for Ned. Maybe that's why he isn't very funny. He *knows* funny, but he can't *be* funny."

"Leo Grasso always looked like he had a pretty healthy ego."

"Well, I didn't know him but I heard a lot about him. I wouldn't say healthy. I'd say inflamed."

Actually that sounded like a plausible diagnosis, now that I thought about the loud, domineering, unstable, insensitive character Leo had created on TV.

"Leo was kind of a monster," Nora went on. "A monster genius, like Sid Caesar, John Belushi. They don't just throw their cones into the gutter, those guys. They throw their whole lives."

"Is there a chance Morty did that? Threw his life away?"

"Jesus, I hope not. I guess I think not, too. I mean, I don't want to lay all that Love of a Good Woman shit on you, but we were doing okay, in our own little way."

Then why did he keep a room as a shrine to Kathy Poindexter? I wondered. And why did he choose it to die in?

"What about the weird way they found him?" I asked instead.

"I just don't believe it."

"Don't believe they found him that way?"

"I don't believe he was into that kind of stuff. I mean, I understand that it isn't the kind of thing you'd tell anybody about, even somebody you . . . especially somebody you . . . But I still don't believe it."

"Can you give me an idea why?"

"Well, he was . . . Shit, I don't know how to put this. All right. Morty wasn't very imaginative that way. Nothing wrong with him, I don't mean that. But new things, different things made him *uneasy*, you know? I'm not explaining this so good, am I?"

"If you're saying straight missionary position, you're doing fine."

"Not quite that dull maybe, but not too far off," Nora said. "Morty was very sweet, but he wasn't a real sexual kind of person. I mean, you know, some people have a feel for it, make it so it's never the same way twice . . ."

She sounded uncomfortable in spite of all her tough talk

earlier about how she and Morty were fucking, all right? It might be better to find a woman to finish out this particular line of questioning for me. Maybe Gladys Williams would do it.

"I see what you mean," I said, although her reasoning didn't strike me as convincing. It seemed possible that somebody who was basically shy might seem unimaginative with women and still be totally bizarre in his private fantasies. It even seemed likely. I was there to learn, though, not to debate. I asked her instead whether Morty had talent.

"He was okay," Nora said. "Maybe a little better than okay, even. But he didn't have that edge, you know? Like you listen to a guy like Cuomo and you feel there's an edge to him, you listen to Bush and it's just not there. It's hard to describe, but do you know what I mean by an edge?"

"I think so." Toughness, skepticism, a hint of bitterness underneath, I figured she meant. Quick-witted, an instinctive counterpuncher . . .

"Like Morty might have dyed his hair," she said, "but he wouldn't've let it grow in."

"Now you've lost me."

"It was just something I was thinking about last night, the hair," she said. "Okay, I've got dark roots, right? I had it dyed a while back, big pain in the ass. They have to strip the old color out, which in my case it's kind of a mouse shit brown, I always think of it. Then they slap the dye on and you're a blonde, you're ready to go out there and have more fun.

"Only you don't, so piss on being blonde. Besides, going in for a new dye job every few weeks is a major pain in the ass. So let's be a brunette again. You're a man, you go down to the barber's and get a butch. You're a woman, you don't really have that option unless you're seriously

107

weird. So two things you can do. If you're like most girls you go to the beauty parlor, order up another dye job only this time in your original color. Hi, Doris, how ya doing? You got something nice in a mouse shit today?

"Or you can do like I'm doing. Let it grow out over the next year or so. The two-tone option. You look ridiculous, but so what? Hey, you don't like it, fella, up your nose.

"Anyway," Nora went on, "what I was thinking about last night was that Morty would dye his hair probably, but he'd never go two-tone for months. It sounds stupid when you say it, but that's what I thought when you asked me did he have talent. He did, but he didn't have the edge to go two-tone. He was better as a straight man, second banana . . ."

"Did he know it?"

"Oh, sure. If there was anything bad to be known about Morty, he knew it by heart. It was the good things he never seemed to pick up on."

"What were they?"

"He was kind. 'I'm a born sucker' was naturally the way he put it. Well, he was. Kind people *are* born suckers, that's the truth of it. He was generous. Morty figured since he hadn't done anything to earn all that money, he didn't have any real right to it. So the best thing was to do good with it. That's what he was doing in a small way here, with the Poor Attitudes. You could say he was doing it for himself, buying his way into show business because he couldn't make it any other way. Maybe it was like that, a little bit. But ask anybody here. Morty never made himself the pitcher just because it was his ball. Morty gave a shit about all of us. To give you a for instance, you think he had to pay the shrink bills for half the company? I mean, that's above and beyond, isn't it?"

"Unger doesn't volunteer his services, huh?"

"Shit, no, he's a doctor. Doctors don't volunteer."

"They always talk about it," I said.

"I know they do, but my sister's a nurse at Mt. Auburn and she says when doctors quote volunteer they mean something different from you and me. Maybe they come down to the hospital one night a week and stitch a few people up or something, but the hospital pays them for it."

"Who does Unger see?"

"The ones who are in analysis now? Only Bob and Harvey. But before there were plenty of others. Leo Grasso and Kathy, I know, except Leo only went a few times. Emily Golden, Hugh Levanter. Probably half a dozen others, over the years. The ones before I came, I wouldn't know their names."

"It adds up to a lot of money, huh?"

"Try three times a week at a hundred bucks an hour."

"No discount for artists?"

"Unger doesn't give discounts, he gets 'em. He pays two hundred bucks a month for his office upstairs. Someplace else he'd probably have to pay a thousand bucks for that much space. In an okay neighborhood like this? Shit, at least a thousand."

"Did Morty know that?"

"Sure he knew it. But he thought Unger walked on water. Dr. Feelgood was the only thing Morty and me ever fought about."

"Feelgood, huh? He gives pills?"

"He hates pills. With him, it's all the talking cure."

"Why Dr. Feelgood, then?"

"Hey, let's stick to Morty, all right?"

She had been the one to bring Unger back into the conversation, which I of course didn't point out. The psychiatrist was the only sore spot I had poked at so far, but it seemed to be one she herself couldn't stop scratching.

"How about you and Morty, then? Was anything serious going on there?"

"I told you. We were—"

"Right, but aside from that. Like were you engaged, or were you going to move into his place?"

"He wanted me to move in, and I wouldn't."

"Why not?"

"Well, his idea was I would move in and maybe after a while I would change my mind and marry him."

"Why was that such a bad idea?"

"Same reason I wouldn't marry him. The money."

"People would think you were after his money?"

"His mother certainly would. Did. She thought the same thing about Kathy."

"Kathy Poindexter?"

"You didn't know about Kathy? Her and Morty were together a long time."

"And Mrs. Limbach broke them up?"

"She tried, all right. Kathy's mother was a secretary, I think. Not in the Social Register, anyway. Probably lucky to make the phone book."

"You say she tried to break them up. She didn't, though?"

"No, what really broke them up was Leo. When Leo showed up, it was like Nichols and May right from the start. They played off each other absolutely perfect. He was a shit, but maybe she was after a shit, who knows? Maybe that's why she dumped Morty. Morty's your basic nonshit."

"Look, Nora, let me ask you something that's none of my damned business, but it occurs to me. You think maybe you dumped Morty because he's a nonshit, too?"

"I didn't dump him."

"Not exactly dump him, maybe. But you wouldn't marry him and you wouldn't move in with him."

"I just thought that was better."

"Why?"

"That way, he wouldn't have to wonder if his mother wasn't maybe right, that I was after his money."

"Did you tell Morty that?"

"Once or twice. Maybe a million times."

"He wasn't convinced, huh?"

"He couldn't see it, no."

Neither could I.

"Look," I said, "in my experience pretty near always when you have two people that are in love, one of them's more in love than the other. You know?"

"You mean it's not like in the movies?"

"Come on, Nora."

"Listen, Bethany, I really want to help you. But I just don't feel comfortable talking about this kind of shit, you know?"

"Actually I don't either. How about those Red Sox, huh?"

— 7 —

THE ENTRANCE TO MARK UNGER'S OFFICE WAS AROUND THE building, in back. The small sign on the door said MARK UNGER, M.D. BY APPOINTMENT ONLY. RING FOR ENTRANCE. While I still had my finger on the doorbell, the buzzer sounded to let me in. The door opened onto a narrow, windowless staircase up to the top floor. Presumably this had been the servants' entry once.

Dr. Mark Unger was waiting at the head of the stairs. He looked nothing at all like my idea of a psychoanalyst. He was about my height, just short of six feet. Probably he weighed ten pounds less, which would put him at about 170. Within a couple of years of forty, one way or another. He had sandy-colored hair worn just over the ears. He wore tan slacks, loafers, and a black-and-red-striped rugby shirt with the sleeves pushed up on his muscular forearms. He had a fading tan from the summer, and appeared fit. Unger was a little short of being handsome, but he looked friendly and clever.

"Mark Unger," he said, sticking out his hand. "Come

on in, come on in. It's four-thirty, so you must be Tom Bethany." He put an arm lightly around my shoulders and guided me over to an armchair upholstered in yellow. Generally I can do without strangers touching me, but he was so easy and natural about it that I didn't mind. Unger sat down facing me, in an armchair that was downscale from mine, comfortable but with more of a Salvation Army look. A copy of Kirk Douglas's autobiography lay facedown on the table alongside the chair. There were no diplomas on the wall, or shelves full of professional books and journals. The only thing that marked the place as a psychiatrist's office was a black tufted-leather couch against the wall, between Unger and me. It looked just like the couches in the cartoons. The raised end with the headrest was over by Unger, so that the patient couldn't see the analyst, again like the cartoons.

"Did you see me out the window?" I asked. "You buzzed me in practically before I rang the doorbell."

Unger fished up a buzzer from down somewhere in his chair, with the kind of linoleum-brown cord that you used to see looped on hospital beds, when hospital beds had high iron frames painted white. The kind of buzzer you'd ring and the nurse wouldn't come till she finished her crossword puzzle, or at least that's the way it worked in the American infirmary in Vientiane. I once spent a few days there after I crash-landed my Porter Pilatus just south of the Plain of Jars.

"I liberated it from Mass. General when I was interning there," Unger said, smiling. He shoved the buzzer back down between the cushions. "Heat you up some coffee?" he said, gesturing toward the windowsill, where a pot sat on a hot plate with little legs. Both the pot and the hot plate looked as if they came from the Salvation Army, too. Like his chair, they weren't dirty or shabby. Just old.

"I'm fine," I said, and gestured at his coffee-making rig. "You look like you go to yard sales."

"It's worse than that," Dr. Unger said. "I go around the neighborhood every Tuesday night when the trash is out. Like a raccoon working his territory. I got in the habit when I was in medical training and busted."

"I do the same thing. The only thing in my apartment I bought new is the electronic stuff. Well, yeah, my La-Z-Boy, too."

"You've got a La-Z-Boy? That's my dream, to find one out on the sidewalk some night, not in too bad shape."

"Yeah, well, I finally gave up looking and bought one at the George Washington Day sales. Cambridge is no good for recliners. You want a busted Barcelona chair, then you're in the right place. Spend the rest of your life wriggling around in the goddamn thing, trying to get comfortable . . ."

And so on, talking together about the scavenging life until I figured maybe his time was limited. "No," Unger said. "My regular four o'clock is out of town, and he would have been my last for the day."

"Well, anyway, I don't want to tie you up too long. I just wanted to know, is there an ethical problem with what I want to talk about? Whether Morty Limbach was suicidal?"

"It's a gray area, frankly, when the patient is deceased. If it were a question of talking to the press or testifying in court, I'd want to check with the Massachusetts Medical Society and the Psychological Association. But you're retained by Morty's estate, and I guess if anybody represents his interests, you and Professor Rosson do. I don't see any problem talking with you informally, no."

"Well, was he, then? Suicidal?"

"There's no real yes or no answer to that. An analyst seldom deals with happy people. Certainly Morty wasn't a person who was predominantly happy. At times he was very depressed. If you asked me the question in court, I'd say that I had no evidence that he was suicidal. In the course of his analysis, the notion of suicide never came up, and I'd remember it if it had."

"Supposing I asked you in court whether you remembered everything that every one of your patients said?"

"I'd say of course not, but that this is something I'd absolutely remember. It's the first thing you ask about when a patient comes to you suffering from depression. For a psychoanalyst, a depressed patient committing suicide is what you have your nightmares about."

"If he had mentioned suicide, would you have dated notes or any other kind of record of it?"

"Absolutely. Anything of real significance I make a note of after the session."

"So the absence of notes would mean he never made that kind of threat?"

"Threats to commit suicide? Not a word. Not even suicidal thoughts."

"Doesn't everybody have suicidal thoughts?"

"Everybody? Probably not. *Practically* everybody, at one time or another? Probably so. It's a question of degree. If Morty had said something like, 'Sometimes you wonder whether it's all worth it,' would that have been suicidal? I wouldn't think so. How about, 'Sometimes *I* wonder whether it's all worth it?' Still not much to worry about. How about, 'I think about suicide all the time'? Now you've got trouble."

"Couldn't a patient be thinking about suicide all the time but not telling you?"

"Possible but unlikely. A suicidal patient is a severely depressed patient, almost by definition. Depression is a big part of what we'd be dealing with in our sessions. And suicidal thoughts would be a big part of that."

"So if Morty didn't talk about suicidal tendencies, it's a good bet he didn't have them?"

"Not a sure bet, but a good bet."

"What about if he had weird autoerotic tendencies? Would those come out in therapy?"

"Good question. I just don't know. I know they *didn't* come out in therapy. But it's entirely possible that he just hadn't surfaced it yet. Or that he didn't see it as a problem that he needed help with."

"Is it a problem?"

"My tendency would be to say no. Or at least probably not. It could indicate a problem, be a symptom of something underlying. Particularly if it were carried out in a highly risky way, or were part of some pretended suicide ritual. But if it were just an effort to enhance the sensation of orgasm, then I'd say no."

"But it *is* highly risky, isn't it?"

"Personally I doubt it. Look, nobody knows how many people do it. The only solid number you have is how many people die doing it, and that's only a very few. If only a few do it and most of them die, then it's highly risky. If lots of people do it and most of them don't die, then it isn't very risky. Which I suspect is in fact the case."

"So for every person that had an accident, there could be plenty of others who never do?"

"Seems likely to me," Unger said. "Often even the victim's parents or wife don't have any idea what's going on until they come home one day and find the guy dead."

"Wife? Is that common?"

"It's not unknown. Plenty of married men masturbate. Plenty of men who masturbate do it in pretty weird ways. Practically none of them advertise it. What I'm saying here is that this is an area where we just don't know. There just aren't any reliable data."

"Can you kind of walk me through what happened from

the time the cleaning lady came up to get you, till the cops took over?"

"Well, I went down with Maria and I saw there had been an accident . . ."

"You thought right away it was an accident?"

"No question."

"Why?"

"The way he was. If you wanted to hang yourself, you wouldn't sit down on the floor and tie the rope to a curtain rod. It was a classic autoerotic fatality-type situation. I made sure he was dead, and then—"

"Let me back up for a minute, okay. I want to kind of visualize it. How did you make sure he was dead? Took his pulse?"

"No need to. I just put the backs of my fingers to his forehead. The temperature tells you."

"Okay, now he's dead. Then what?"

"I guess I looked around for a minute."

"Anything strike you as odd? Unfamiliar? Out of place? Knocked over?"

"Hard to say. I didn't know the room, so I couldn't say if anything was out of place or unfamiliar. Didn't look like anything was. Certainly nothing knocked over. Well, I shouldn't say certainly. I didn't notice anything knocked over. No signs of struggle. Is that what you mean?"

"I don't really know. I just want to see what you saw."

"Just what the police saw, I guess. Then we went back upstairs, Maria and I, and I called 911. They came fast, I'll say that for them."

"Did they come to your office?"

"No, I told them to come straight to the front door and come on in, I'd be waiting in the room."

"Why not meet them at the door?"

"I had some idea we should guard the crime scene."

"You said you thought it was an accident."

"I meant like in mysteries. Guard the crime scene."

"And the cops came quickly. How quickly?"

"I didn't really time it, but I'd say that we were in the room less than five minutes before I heard the siren outside and then the policeman hollered from the front door."

"Then what?"

"I told them to come on down the hall, him and his partner. They came in, and then more cops and emergency personnel came. We told them what little we knew, or I did, anyway. Maria knows more English than she lets on, I imagine, but she doesn't like to speak it. After a while they told us we could go, and that was it."

"Did the cops ask you if you touched anything?"

"I'm pretty sure they did. Yes."

"What did you say?"

"I said no."

"How about the briefcase?"

"Who told you about the briefcase?" Unger didn't sound defensive. Just curious. "Oh, Maria," he said. "Of course."

"Why didn't you tell the police about it?"

"Well, there wasn't anything in it that would have been any use to them."

"Yeah, well, still . . ."

"I guess I grabbed the briefcase because of mysteries, too," he said. "You always read about cops pocketing any valuables they find at a crime scene, and so I took it away for safekeeping."

"Did it look like it had valuables in it?"

"No, but I just thought of what if it was me, would I want the police pawing through my briefcase? So I took it back up here."

"What was in it?"

"A paperback book. Parking ticket. Credit card receipts. A couple of letters, looked like business letters. Professor Rosson would know exactly."

"How would he know?"

"I gave the briefcase to him. I figured it was part of the estate."

"I was thinking on the way over here what it was like," I said to Jerome Rosson, who was still for the moment, looking out the window of his office. And listening to me get hot.

"Know what I came up with?" I was saying. "What I came up with was it was like when the marines hit the beach at Danang back when, '65 or something? Anyway, when that asshole Johnson sent the first combat troops in. Anyway, all these dumb skinheads charge up onto the beach ready to kill Cong and what do they find? There's a bunch of bar girls waiting for them with flowers."

"I'm sorry," Rosson said.

"Sure, okay. But you've got to tell me these things. There I am lying in the weeds getting ready to jump out and sandbag this guy with a briefcase, and it turns out you had the damned thing all along."

"I never even thought of it," Rosson said, back in motion now. He crossed from the window and sat down at his desk, but then got up, as if the chair were red hot. As he paced, he said, "I truly forgot it. I went through the stuff inside it in case there might be something I should know about, something that would affect the estate. The only things that did were a parking ticket and a bill from Visa. I paid both of them out of estate funds, and I haven't thought about it again until you walked in here all mad."

"What about the cops? Why didn't you turn it over to them?"

"No reason to. The medical examiner ruled it accidental death. Nothing in the briefcase bore on the circumstances of his death. No criminal investigation was involved. No investigation at all would have been involved if Pilgrim hadn't tried to stiff the beneficiary of Morty's policy."

"Suppose there was a suicide note in the briefcase and Unger gave it to Westfall?"

"Why would he do that?"

"Shit, I don't know. He was Morty's shrink. Maybe he knew about the policy. Maybe he hates the ACLU. Who the hell knows? Maybe he sold the damned note to Westfall."

"Or maybe there wasn't any note."

"Probably there wasn't, but the point is we don't know."

"Nor would we know if I had told the police. By then Unger could have taken anything at all out of the briefcase."

Rosson was right, of course. He had had no particular reason to mention the briefcase either to me or to the cops. I had no reason to think that Unger had taken anything from it, and no way of finding out if he had. Neither did the police. Probably my feelings would get over being hurt, and certainly there was no point blaming Rosson for something that wasn't his fault.

"I'm sorry," I said. "I shouldn't have got hot."

"I'm sorry, too," the professor said. "It should have occurred to me."

"Yeah, well, it should have occurred to me that it wouldn't occur to you. You want your dollar back?"

"Hell, no. You want to give it back?"

"Hell, no. You still got the briefcase?"

Rosson pointed to a corner of his office, and there it was on the floor. I had assumed it was his. I went through the stuff in it. As both Unger and Rosson had said, there was nothing that signified. The paperback was *A Streetcar Named Desire.*

"Well, shit," I said. "Where do we go from here?"

"You tell me," said Rosson.

"Nowhere much. Whatever this paper is that Westfall

has, you say the ACLU can get it from his lawyers as soon as the company refuses in writing to pay the claim?''

"That's right."

"Well, till then we won't know exactly what we're facing. So I'll just keep poking around in the dark. See if I can get a woman friend of mine to talk some more to one of the kids in the Poor Attitudes. The kid was sleeping with Morty, and I got the feeling she might open up more with a woman. I'll go over to the medical school library and try to find out something about autoerotic fatalities. Your library here had a little bit on it, but most of the good forensic medicine stuff is over there in Countway."

The Francis A. Countway Library of Medicine was open evenings, but it was way over in Boston with the rest of Harvard's medical school, and consequently the hell with it. Instead I went out Mass. Ave. to a Mexican restaurant called the Forest Café. A lot of Mexican food hits the belly like a sack of BBs, but at the Forest you can avoid getting a plate full of cement mix by sticking to the excellent appetizers. I had fried squid rings and broiled mushroom caps, and a couple of glasses of iced tea. The place hasn't got a liquor license, which would have ruled it out in my heavy drinking days. Now that I had cut way down it was still a drawback, but one I could live with.

After supper I walked across Harvard Yard toward home, loafing along in no particular hurry. Stopping to look at the notices on the campus bulletin boards. Sitting for a while on the steps of Widener, watching the students go by. One of the guys I wrestle with claims that the admissions office won't let a girl into Harvard if she wears anything bigger than a 36C cup. Nothing I saw proved him wrong, although aside from that one little feature there were plenty of good-looking girls. Watching, I wondered why so many grown men were attracted to girls this age.

I'd take a good-looking woman in her thirties or forties over nearly any nineteen-year-old who ever lived. Or I think I would. Even in the mail-order catalogs, the ones who catch my eye are the ones of a certain age. Right around Hope's age, come to think of it.

And so after a while I got up and walked on back home, untempted. There I poured myself the beer I had missed at the dry restaurant and sat down at my Macintosh to go through Morty's disks. Thank God Morty didn't have a hard drive with forty megabytes of information on it, in maybe hundreds of different files and folders and folders within folders. The single floppy disk I was starting out with had forty-six different documents on it. Most of them didn't look very promising, but Morty might have given misleading names to files he didn't want anybody to look at, for all I knew. To a file containing a suicide note, for instance. The only way to do the job right was to call up every file on every disk, and check it off on a list before moving on.

I went through thank-you notes, business correspondence, efforts at blank verse that struck me as pretty bad, personal letters, a sort of a hypochondriac's diary in which he had listed years' worth of small ailments as they cropped up. The fact that he kept it at all was mildly interesting, but the truth was that his health seemed to have been pretty good. Nobody dies of hemorrhoids or tendonitis. And on I went, calling up file after file, scrolling through each one so that I wouldn't miss anything significant that might be in the middle. It took me forty-five minutes to get through the first disk.

At the end of it I had more of a feel for what Morty had been like than before. He had a way of taking a run at things with great enthusiasm, it seemed, and then letting them drop when something else struck him. I came across lots of beginnings and fragments—of stories, poems, skits, some scraps that looked as if they might have set out to be plays. But there was no hint of secret autoerotic hobbies in any of the material, although some of it—the poetry in particular—was pretty personal.

I ejected the first disk and slid in the second one. The fifth file I called up was named Downdump 1. It was the first of a series that ended with Downdump 16. I realized as soon as I started reading that Downdump was his shorthand for down in the dumps. The files seemed to have been run off at top speed. They were full of uncorrected typos and other errors, as if the purpose wasn't to communicate, even to himself, but to unload. The Downdumps seemed to be an attempt at catharsis, an effort to let all the black stuff out of his head. They amounted to a sort of diary, but a diary of emotions rather than events. The main emotions were despair, self-disgust, and sadness. The first one started out.

what is depression well m;ight you ask my friend it is a habit which better people than i know doubt cd break and no doubt do. does mummy idear does she ever get deapressed shit i dont knw, she doesnt seemt to. inl the magazine what was it one of them anyway i ran actross at the mansion, nyorker maybe, there was a thing about tgennessee williams somebody asked him how about it tennessee what is happiness and te poor guy said i dont know i guess its insensitivity and there it is, thats what iit is all right, tennessee had that one right why the lfuck should i be born with no skin whereas for example dad dear dad hs skin like a rhino so it cant be gneenetic, can it? dont seem like being skinless comes from mums neither but maybe it doesindeed since she hqs a secret softspot yes her do. we are tallking here aftr all about a person that keeps a picture of ahuman toad behind her wedding picutre of dddayddy dear because i babydear found it ohyes he didtoo babybear when yong ;of age perhaps 10 or so at annyrate too yng to wonder abt what is that picture doing hidden there givn the sancltitty of theold marriage vows. later the yng lad going back for a more mature look he decidees this is some old flame no doubt altho seemsm odd to have a toadflame do it not? nontheless ole mr. toade it be with inscription on back so that toadname later proves fmailiar when lad all grown and name nowseen all over business pages as hero of our times we live in some times huh. bakc to the cnetral point here which is nature vs nurture. facts are poppydear and mommy dear got stainlessteel skin the both of em so score stans at nurture two nature zip bottom of ninth, jesus, why didn't i get her skin sted of her eyes youve got your mother's eyes dear, great, thanks a lot, wish i cd see thru them . . .

And on and on, one cry of pain after another until I had got through the sixteen numbered files. Then I called up the next file, which was named Downdump endit. And right away I was pretty sure I knew what Hocker Westfall had found in Morty's apartment. When I called up the file after that, Downdump endit-A, I was absolutely sure.

Before going to bed I set the alarm. I wanted to get up early enough to reach Professor Rosson before he took off for whatever he did Saturday mornings.

"First you've got the sixteen Downdump files," I told Rosson, who met me in his office, in tennis clothes. He was on his way to the Radcliffe courts, out Garden Street. His reservation was for nine, but he had left home a half an hour earlier than he needed to. This gave me time to show him Morty's suicide note before I myself took off to spend a beautiful Saturday in the medical library.

"What those are is kind of stream-of-consciousness stuff dated over the last couple of years," I said. "Mostly they're about his love life, which looked to him like a total disaster. Actually it was probably about par for the course.

We're talking about two women here, to judge by the dates, context, so forth.''

"No names?" Professor Rosson asked.

"No names. Both of them seemed to have been in emotional trouble when he took up with them. No specifics given, but he talks about them kind of like they were distressed merchandise. His take is that nobody who wasn't all fucked up would bother with a guy like him. The first woman left him. The second one didn't, but he keeps thinking she's about to. So the second one practically has to be a girl in the Poor Attitudes named Nora. She tells me she was sleeping with him.''

"Of course he could have been sleeping with someone else, too," Rosson said.

"Not a chance. Read the stuff and you'll see. Comes to women, Morty had tunnel vision. Anyway, it's a pretty good guess that the first of the women he talks about was Kathy Poindexter. Nora said he had an affair with her that ended when Leo Grasso showed up and married her.''

"I never knew that," Rosson said. "No reason I would have, though. We never talked about his personal life.''

"You'll know about it now," I said. "Twenty-one pages of it, single spaced. I printed it out for you last night. Well, actually, you won't really know about his personal life. What this is, is like background music. You don't get the plot, just the mood. Tough stuff to read. The feeling you get is here's this poor bastard who's just basically too decent for this particular world. He's always turning the other cheek, and what he winds up with is two slapped cheeks.''

"Some people enjoy that, I suppose," said Rosson. "At least so the psychiatrists say.''

"Yeah, well, I've never been convinced. Plenty of people get slapped that never asked for it. Fact is, you got a lot of slappers out there. That's where the real problem is.''

I removed a stack of printouts from the briefcase I was taking to the medical library. "These are your copies," I said. "No need to look at the thick file right away. That's the Downdump series I was just telling you about. But probably you ought to check the one called Downdump endit-A."

I glanced over my own copy while he read his. It said:

Maybe give form to some of downdump. Employ it to be the foundation of a story that ends in suicide perhaps; uti-liqzing the eecummings where is your blueyed boy mr death poem. the person, man, young man, would leave a note behind and in the note would be something from the poem, watersmooth silver stallion whatever it is, anyway the detectives would colme and the parents would be all broken up and nobody, the detectives nor the parents ouwld recognize the quote until narrator came and knew but wouldn't tell them. idea being they the parents wouldn't understand the poem, anyh more than they understood their son or what was going on in him, so whyl tell the parents? anyway tone the important thing here. spare prose. stripped down, flat, etc. understated. note itself would be only cry of anguish in the story, so important to get right. use real material torn out of own guts, etc., pitiful downdump guts as abobve. shit. well anyway do it, don't just sit on your ass forever and never get started.

okay the hnote: i leave this note not to whoever (whom-ever?) it may concern but to whoever may understand, whoever can see into me as if transparent. surely someone can, or is it that X-ray eyes (the X-Ray I? maybe) can only see inward into the flesh of the possessor (possessed?) But it may be that there is another cursed with similiar vision and it is for him or her I write (maybe best not her?) (here quote from cummings poem, look up). Wlhat has kept me from this step all these years is the fear that there would be those still living who might be harmed, however slightly,

126

by my act. Tlhis being no longer so, here if your blueyed
boy now, Mr. Death. Along those lines, anyway. Polish. /s/

Rosson put his copy down, and said, "Not much there,
legally speaking."

"No," I said. "Now read the one marked Downdump
endit-D. It's his fourth draft."

Version D was free from typos, unlike the three earlier
ones. He seemed to have been satisfied with it at last, and
to have put it into final form.

I leave this note not to whomever it may concern, for no
one will be concerned much or long about my death, but
to whomever may share my X-ray I with its power to see
with clarity through skin, flesh, and bone to the underlying
comic insignificance which I am about to end. Clowns cry;
clowns die. Jesus he was a loathsome man and what i want
to know is how do you like your myeyed boy Mister Death.

Underneath the text, Limbach had typed a series of equal
signs, so as to make a centered double line long enough
to write a signature on.

"Shit," Rosson said when he had finished reading. "I
bet that *is* what Westfall took out of the apartment. Morty
must have printed the damned thing out. And signed it
too, God knows why. But if it weren't signed, Pilgrim's
lawyers would have told Westfall he didn't have anything.
Shit, shit, shit. We could have trouble with this."

"But not serious trouble, right? Doesn't the sequence
make it perfectly clear that he wasn't writing a real suicide
note?"

"Sure, but sometimes the law is an ass. All the court
will have in front of it is a sheet of paper. A signed sheet
of paper, probably. We say, look, your honor, here are
three documents which we have caused to be printed from

a disk which we believe but cannot prove was once in the possession of the deceased and has since been in the possession, at least potentially, of an unknown number of unknown individuals, some of whom may be interested parties in the case. Opposing counsel jumps up. Mr. Rosson, do you have any notion of how many Macintoshes have been sold in the Boston area alone? Would you stipulate to tens of thousands? Would you further stipulate to the existence of thousands of owners of those machines who must know how to use them? Is it not true, Mr. Rosson, that any one of those thousands would be fully capable of creating documents on just such a disk as this and causing it to be brought before this court today without a shred of, and so forth and et cetera . . ."

"Okay, okay," I said. "We could have trouble with this."

"On the other hand, we're not completely shot down in flames," Rosson said and began to drum his fingers on the table as he organized the problem. "Why would Morty stage such a weird death? Because of his documented view of himself as a pathetic clown, the insurance company would argue. Classic self-hatred. It's right there in the note. But why set a stage that carefully, and then leave a signed suicide note back in his apartment, where Mr. Westfall found it? Harder to answer. They'd say no one can ever know what goes through the mind of a man about to kill himself. All right, I say, but why isn't there a date on it? They'd say, why should there be? We're not dealing with a formal legal document, here. We're dealing with a testament to his state of mind. Maybe he prepared it days, weeks, months in advance. Pre-need, like a cemetery plot."

Rosson stopped drumming his fingers, jumped to his feet, and started pacing instead. "At least we're a little smarter now than we were, though. We know it isn't entirely a grudge thing on Westfall's part, although maybe that's part of it. Not having seen the draft versions in the computer, he could reasonably assume from the note he presumably found that his company didn't owe the money. Well, well . . ."

He picked up his tennis racket and started hitting it against the heel of his left hand. "Anyway, we know now what we're going to be up against," he said. "Onward and upward. Me to play tennis."

"Me to the med school library."

"What's over there?"

"Well, we've got two things Morty could have died of. Suicide by hanging or accidental autoerotic fatality. I thought I'd look into both, and there goes my Saturday. Sunday's looking better. Picnic down by the river with a couple of women."

"Sounds like fun."

Of course medical libraries are fun, too. By closing time at Countway Library I had run down most of what I wanted, in periodicals with names like the *American Journal of Forensic Medicine* and *Trauma*. It was slow work because along the way I kept coming across things that demanded attention. The profile shot of the drowned man whose face had been eaten off by snapping turtles, for example. The man who finally died after ten minutes of trying to commit suicide by sawing his chest open with a Homelite chain saw. The airline pilot whose personal idea of fun was to rig his Volkswagen to run around in circles while he trotted along behind it on a chain that went around his neck, down his back, and out between his legs. During one session the chain got caught around the rear axle, reeled him in, and that was that.

Countway is over in Boston with the rest of the medical school. The end of the line for the return shuttle bus is where Harvard Street runs into Mass. Ave., which is only a block from my apartment, on Ware Street. But I headed the other way, toward the gym, and only remembered when I was practically there that the place was closed Saturday evenings. So I turned around and walked back past my apartment to Barsamian's, a yuppie supermarket on Mass. Ave. It's the place to go if you want to buy overpriced stuff for a picnic. And that's what I wanted to do, since I didn't feel like buying the materials for less money at the Broadway Supermarket and putting them together myself.

— 8 —

NEXT MORNING AT ELEVEN, GLADYS WILLIAMS AND I WERE sitting on the same patch of grass we had used for our picnic the week before, between the Anderson Bridge and the Radcliffe women's boat house. There were small puffs of clouds high up, moving along fast. But down where we were, the wind was only a breeze that ruffled the surface of the Charles.

"I told Nora eleven-thirty, so we could talk first," I said to Gladys. I told her what Nora had told me about her relationship with Morty Limbach, and about her reluctance to tell me why she didn't like their mutual analyst, Mark Unger. "Mainly, though," I said, "I'm interested in what she can say about Morty's sex life. Apparently you can be into this weird shit on the side and your wife or girlfriend might never know. But maybe there would be hints. Mild bondage activities, something or other. And what about the room he died in? Did she know that Morty kept it like some kind of shrine, and he'd lock himself in there sometimes? Did she know what for?"

"Wouldn't she tell you?"

"The whole area of sex, she seemed nervous about. I thought maybe a little bit of just-between-us-girls . . ."

"What? What? You're asking me to betray my sex, Bethany? Well, okay, I'll do it. But I'll tell her I'm doing it on your behalf, to pass along to you. I'm not going to sandbag her by letting her think it really is just between us girls."

"That's fine. I didn't get the feeling she didn't want to cooperate. I just got the feeling she felt uncomfortable talking to a man about this stuff."

"Especially a monogamous pervert like you, huh? Which brings me to the question, when am I going to meet your main squeeze, Bethany? She was up here all week, wasn't she? Well?"

"Yeah, but I didn't think you'd want to watch."

"Think again, fella. Next time she's up, I want to meet her. Got that straight?"

"There's nobody I'd rather have her meet, Gladys. I feel confident you gals would get along real fine."

"Oh, blow it out your ass, Bethany. Just shut up and tell me about these problems you said you had with the death scene photos."

"Things were missing, mainly. The pictures didn't show any padding between the extension cord and his neck. Was there any?"

"No. Why would there be?"

"According to what I've been reading, most people who are into this stuff use some kind of padding to keep the ligature from leaving marks."

"Makes sense. Probably more comfortable, too. But there wasn't any."

"Couldn't have come loose and fallen down? Nothing on the floor he might have used for padding? A sock? Handkerchief? Anything like fur or lamb's wool?"

"No, nothing."

"Anything like a gag, blindfold, chains, belts, girdles?"

"A belt, but it was in his pants."

"Any injuries except to his neck?"

"Would have been in the report, although I've got to say we didn't look very hard."

"Nonfatal stuff, like small cigarette burns, marks from pins or needles?"

"Would have been in the report, too. Well, maybe not. Easy to miss a pin or needle mark. No burns, anyway."

"Any female clothing on or near him?"

"Nope. Plenty in the closet, of course."

"Mirrors, photographs?"

"Near him? No."

"Pornography, sexual devices?"

"Nope."

"Weird books?"

"No books at all, but what do you mean by weird?"

"Books on knots, extrasensory perception, Houdini, witchcraft, telepathy, masochism. You know, weird."

"Oh, I get it. You mean *weird*. This is all shit you're supposed to find, is that it?"

"Not all of it necessarily, but some of it. The FBI has kind of a checklist, what to look for, and only two of the things on it were present. Maybe only one thing. A self-rescue mechanism."

"I didn't see anything like that."

"The whole way he did it amounted to a self-rescue mechanism, the way they define it. Sometimes it's an elaborate releasing device, but in this case he didn't need one. To relieve the pressure, all he had to do was straighten up."

"What other thing was present?"

"Masturbatory activity, which was maybe going on but maybe it wasn't, too. Turns out the semen doesn't prove it. Evidently you find semen in all kinds of deaths."

133

"Actually that's right. One time we had this guy killed in a mugging, and I found seminal stains on his underwear. So what the hell's going on here anyway, I thought, so I looked it up. Turned out no matter how a guy dies, there can be spermatozoa in the urethra. In fact, there very often is."

"Exactly," I said. "Something else. Did you ever see a naked suicide?"

"No, you practically never see that. Except in jails, for some reason."

"You see it in autoerotic asphyxia, too."

"And Limbach wasn't completely naked, was he?"

"Not very naked at all. Just his shoes and pants off. Generally in these cases, if you find any clothing on the guy at all, it's supposed to be women's underwear."

"What you're saying here, Bethany, it goes both ways. Suicide, he'd be dressed. Autoerotic asphyxia, he'd be naked. The guy's neither one. He's half and half."

"Right."

"So what's left?" Gladys thought for a moment. "Let me see the pictures again," she said.

I took the manila envelope out of my gym bag and handed it to her. She went through the photos she had given me earlier, stopping now and then to examine one carefully.

"What's left is murder, I suppose," she said. "But I don't know. Checklist or no checklist, we've got a guy that just ejaculated here. This isn't spermatozoa in the urethra or a little seepage."

"Yeah," I said. "I keep coming back to that myself. But there's another thing that bothers me." I pointed to a shot that showed Limbach's whole body. "Anything strike you about that?"

"Nothing in particular," she said after a moment.

"Well, I happened to have pulled the pants off of a certain person not too long ago . . ."

"I'm not sure I want to hear about this, Studley."

"No, probably not," I said. So I didn't tell her about Myron Cooper's red bikini briefs. "Anyway, the point is that when I was finished, the pants were in the same position they are in that picture."

"Jesus, you're right. You take your pants off while you're sitting down on the ground, you draw your legs up, don't you? You wouldn't normally leave them down by your feet, would you? Nor your shoes."

"Not normally, no," I said. "Although you could, I guess."

"Still, it do make you wonder."

I saw Nora coming down the slope past the boat house and stuffed the glossies back into their envelope so she wouldn't see what they were. She didn't need a photo exhibit. I did the introducing, which was followed by a little bit of the sniffing around that people of the same sex and age tend to do when they first meet. Stiff, polite, suspicious, ready to fight or flee. "Tom tells me you . . ." "That must be very interesting . . ." "I've heard so much about . . ." That kind of thing.

"Listen," I said after a minute, "maybe I didn't introduce you two right. Nora Dawson, this is Gladys Williams. Gladys, this is Nora. Nora, Gladys is called Gladys, so you've both got dorky names that you hate your mother for giving you. Also what Gladys does for a living is comb out the pubic hair on corpses. So you two girls should have a lot to talk about."

"Fuck you, sexist pig," Gladys said.

"See?" I pointed out to Nora. "You're both sewer mouths, too. Now what I'm asking Gladys to do is just to probe into your love life and your psychoanalysis. You don't have any problem with that, do you? No, I thought not."

All the time, I was taking off my own shoes and pants. I had running shorts underneath, and got my running shoes out of the gym bag.

"While you're doing all that," I went on, "I'm going to run the loop up to Arsenal Bridge and back. Should take about a half an hour. Then I'll grab my bag and swing by the gym to shower, and then we can eat. Before I get up, though, I want you to notice where my shoes and pants are."

They were close at hand, right where I had taken them off and not down by where my feet were, now that I had stretched my legs out again. A natural conversational ice-breaker, I figured.

When I got back from my run the two of them weren't exactly picking lice out of each other's hair, but they were friends, anyway. I opened up the basket and set out my half-dozen containers of fancy stuff. The deli at Barsamian's went in for saffron-yellow rice, and pasta in complicated shapes. Some of the pasta was regular macaroni color, but most of it was in dull, ugly shades of green and pale red. Probably this meant that the coloring agents were organic, natural, biodegradable, and cancer free. Spinach and beet juice, maybe. We eat a lot of that kind of thing in Cambridge, to make up for the carcinogens in the tap water.

"You better like it," I said. "It cost seven bucks a pound." For myself I pulled a bottle of India Pale Ale out of the ice in the cooler, to replace the vital fluids I had lost during my run. Pink pasta could come later.

After our meal, Gladys said, "We've been talking it over, me and Nora, and we think you're right."

"Right about what?"

"That it couldn't have been an accidental autoerotic fatality. Or a staged suicide, either."

"Because of the things we talked about?"

"Other stuff, too. The stains. Okay if I tell him, Nora?"

"Go ahead."

"Okay, the semen stains were on his underpants and on the floor in front of him. You can't really see in the pictures, but I was there and that's the way it was."

"I know. The cleaning lady told me the same thing."

"Both on his shorts and on the rug, six or eight inches away, okay?"

"Okay, except I don't get it."

"Well, Nora never fooled around with anybody but Morty, of course . . ."

"Yeah, sure," said Nora.

"But I did, over the years, and some guys are squirters and some guys aren't, if you know what I mean."

"Sure I know."

"That's interesting. Don't you think that's interesting, Nora? Exactly how do you know?"

"In junior high a bunch of us used to go to this old barn and have contests. Fastest, farthest. Shit like that. One poor guy could never get any distance at all."

"Which guy was that, Bethany?"

"I was hoping you wouldn't ask. Anyway, you're saying here that Morty . . ."

"Right," said Gladys. Nora nodded, but Gladys did the talking. "Morty had no range at all."

I tried to imagine the moments before Morty's death: the placement of his body, the physical possibilities. "He could have changed his position after he ejaculated," I said. "Particularly if he was setting up a scene, the way the insurance company says he was. But supposing he wasn't, then how could semen stains have got out there? . . . Jesus, there's one obvious way, isn't there?"

"Exactly," Gladys said.

"Easy enough to prove," I said. "Can't you run a DNA test to see if it's really his sperm?"

"My God, Bethany, where are you? Still back in the barn? Nobody's called it sperm for twenty, thirty years."

"Whatever. Can't you test it?"

"We can test it if we have it. Only we don't."

"You don't hold on to evidence?"

"Evidence of what? That was an accidental death, according to the idiot we got for an assistant medical examiner. To be fair, I thought it was, too."

"Couldn't you test his shorts?"

"The undertaker probably burned them or threw them out."

"How about the spots on the rug?"

"Too degraded by now. And even if you could still find traces, you couldn't prove they were the same ones."

"No, I guess you couldn't," I said, remembering what Maria Soares had said about the state of the bed sheets in Poor Attitudes House. "Shit."

"Still, I bet I'm right," Gladys said. "I bet somebody else set the scene."

"Play that out in your mind step by step," I said.

Gladys was quiet for a moment, imagining what the man must have done. "Jesus," she said then. "That is unbelievably sick, you know it?"

"You really think somebody killed him?" Nora said.

"I think it's a possibility," I said. "A lot of things point away from accidental death or suicide, and what's left?"

"God, I hope you're right."

"You sound like you don't think I am."

"It's just that I can't help thinking, what if I had said okay, cool, let's get married Monday? You know?"

"I can see where you can't help thinking it, but it's still

probably horseshit," Gladys said. "Besides, you didn't turn him down flat."

"Not exactly flat. In my mind I was sort of decided, but what I actually told him was let's go on the way we are for a couple of months, see how it goes, then we'll see."

"That doesn't sound like it would have pushed him over the edge," I said. "Sounds to me like it would have given him a reason to hold on."

"Well, maybe . . . I hope you guys are right."

"Sure we are," I said, and I did feel pretty sure. "Morty had to have been through worse than this when Kathy Poindexter dumped him. And he didn't kill himself then, did he?"

"But who would have wanted to kill him?" Nora said. "I mean, basically nobody."

"Nobody we know about, anyway. What I've got to start with is who *could* have killed him."

"Basically everybody," Gladys said.

"Everybody who was important in his life, anyway."

"Mostly that was us, in the Poor Attitudes," Nora said. "Is that who you mean?"

"The people from the 'Little Leo Show' were all around that weekend, too."

"In fact, anybody could have walked in off the street and done it," Gladys said. "The front door was open."

"Yeah, theoretically."

"But you think it's bullshit."

"Yeah, I guess I do."

"I guess I do, too," Gladys admitted.

"Unger could have done it," Nora said.

"Why do you say that?"

"He's a shit, that's why. The guy that killed Morty had to be a shit. Unger's a shit. Logical. Actually, I know it isn't."

139

"Got a little logic in it anyway," I said. "That mean you'll tell me about Unger now?"

"No. I mean, I want to help you out and maybe the shit really did it, in addition to being a shit. But I felt stupid enough telling Gladys about me and Marky-baby. Let her tell you. I can't face it twice." Nora got up to go. "Thanks for the picnic and everything," she said. "So I'll be seeing you this evening, Gladys, okay?"

"What's going on this evening?" I asked Gladys after Nora was gone.

"Harry and I are double-dating with her and this boy." Harry was one of the two men Gladys was currently seeing, as they say.

"What boy?"

"This computer nerd, Jimmy. Grad student at MIT. You wouldn't know him."

"Jesus, Gladys, getting information out of you is like pulling ticks off a collie. Is this Jimmy one of your discards or what?"

"We had a thing for a while, yeah. Once I got him broken in he turned out to have kind of a gift for it. Good hands."

"So why did you run him off?"

"I felt I had nothing more to teach him. We're still friends, naturally."

"Tell me something, how the fuck do you always manage to stay friends with the guys you dump?"

"The trick is to have them dump you."

"Come on, Gladys. Jesus, do I have to get the tweezers out?"

"If you have to know, in Jimmy's case, I began to develop certain unattractive personal habits. Grooming-wise. Washing-wise."

"I'm not sure I want to know the details."

"I am. You don't."

140

"But he still thinks of you as a friend, huh?"

"A dirty friend, yes. And now it's time for Jimmy to go off on his own, try out what old Mrs. Robinson taught him. I ask nothing for myself, Bethany. Only to leave the world a little better place than I found it."

As far as I could see, this made Gladys sort of a cross between Dr. Ruth Westheimer and Mother Theresa. And I would have said exactly that, except I only thought of it later. At the time, I just made a retching noise and changed the subject to Mark Unger.

"Old, old story," Gladys said. "Or at least I've heard it a couple of times before. Her shrink got Nora to talk herself into bed with him. Then he dumped her when he started screwing his three o'clock, too."

"How did she know about the three o'clock?"

"She followed him one night. He picked the other woman up at her apartment and took her to what Nora used to think of as their favorite restaurant. Some Indian dump out by Porter Square."

"But how did she know it was his three o'clock?"

"Because she was his two o'clock. They'd meet coming and going. Nora always thought the three o'clock looked kind of defeated and mousy. She used to feel sorry for her."

"That's got to hurt, huh?"

"Better believe it. Anyway, Nora stopped going to Unger, naturally. Man, she really, really hates him. It's more than just some guy that cheated on her."

"What else is it, then?"

"What's the right word? Betrayal, maybe? Not that he betrayed her with another woman, so much. Hey, everybody gets betrayed that way. You're knocked flat, sure, but you live to fuck another day."

"What was it, then?"

"More like you think you're the favorite daughter and

141

one day dad tells you, Oh, by the way, you're a stupid ugly pain-in-the-ass and you always bored the shit out of me."

"Plus you're adopted," I said.

"Yeah, like that. That's not a good example, I know. But what happened with her and Unger goes beyond being jilted. Sure he fucked her. Okay, right. But he mind-fucked her, too."

"In what way?"

"I don't know. She got kind of vague right in there. I'm just giving you the impression I got from her."

"You suppose he mind-fucked Morty, too?"

"How?"

"I don't know. Drove him to suicide? Drove him to auto-erotic asphyxia?"

"Yeah, that sounds good," Gladys said. "Take your mind off your troubles, why don't you, Morty? Give oxygen deprivation a try."

"All right, it's bullshit. But what isn't? Everything that suggests murder, you could explain it just as easily the way the insurance company does. Morty himself could have been the one who made all those mistakes setting the scene."

"Except for spraying semen all over."

"Even that's physically possible, I guess. But it's a little hard to figure why he'd bother, isn't it? It's a little easier to figure why somebody else would do it, not knowing anything about Morty's muzzle velocity. So if it walks like a duck . . ."

"Walks like a duck?"

"A thing guys would say over in Asia. If it walks like a duck and it quacks like a duck, it's probably a duck."

Monday morning I had time for the *Boston Globe* and a relaxed breakfast at the counter of the Tasty. I had the two eggs over light, the two slices of Wonder Bread toast, the grape jelly in the little plastic cup, the pat of butter on the little paper square, and the mug of generic tea. The sliver of lemon that came with my tea, on the other hand, was the equivalent of the slivers of lemon served in the finest restaurants in the land.

"The fuck you doing now, Bethany?" said the counterman, Joey Neary.

"Seeing if I can read the paper through my lemon."

"Can you?"

"Sort of, but it's a little fuzzy."

"You want, I could cut you a thinner one."

"That's okay, Joey. I'll put the fucking thing in my tea instead."

"Good move, Bethany. Julia Childs was in the other day and she done the exact same thing."

The pay phone rang and Joey answered it, interrupting our volley. "I'll see if he's here," Joey said. "Yeah, he's here."

It was Jerome Rosson, returning the call I had made to his office before ordering breakfast. He was just on his way to his first class, so I hurried through the doubts and speculations that Gladys and I had come up with.

"Actually, all of this could be helpful if this ever gets to court," Professor Rosson said. "Individually, nothing you've got is particularly convincing, but it's suggestive, isn't it? Gives us something to think about that we weren't thinking about before. Where do we go next?"

"I guess I'll start poking around again, this time trying to find out whether anybody had a reason to kill the poor bastard. Probably want to go back to the Poor Attitudes House. Talk to Unger again. Talk to Morty's parents, I guess."

"If they'll see you," Rosson said. "Don't bet on it."

"Maybe go down to New York, talk to the people at the 'Little Leo Show.' "

"Why them?"

"They all know the mansion, and they were in Boston filming the show that weekend. I guess any of them could have done it. If it was done. Do you have any other ideas about who to talk to?"

"Not really, no. My impression was that the Poor Attitudes were pretty much Morty's life. I don't think he knew too many other people."

"Would anybody make money out of killing him? What's in his will, for instance?"

"Million dollars to Bard College to endow a chair in drama. Quarter million to his old prep school, Putney. Two million to his mother. Remainder endows something called the Poor Attitudes Theater Foundation."

"How much are we talking about, the remainder?"

"After taxes, something like eighteen million."

"Not too shabby. Who runs the foundation?"

"Teddy Elliman, if he wants to. Maybe he'll be too busy, now that he's directing the hottest show on TV."

"I bet he could make room in his life for eighteen million bucks, don't you?"

— 9 —

I WENT BACK TO THE COUNTER AND FINISHED MY TEA. IT WAS no worse cold than it had been hot. Then I had Joey fish out my Boston phone directory from where he kept it under the counter.

"Joey, there's bagel crumbs all over this," I said, brushing them off onto his floor.

"Tell you what you could do, Bethany. You could carry the fucker around with you all day, keep it nice."

Both Morton Limbachs were in the book—Jr., on Brattle Street in Cambridge, and III, at the condo on Charterhouse Mews in Boston. A woman answered the Cambridge number. She told me that Mr. Limbach was off sailing and could she, Mrs. Limbach, help me? I told her thanks, no message, nothing important. I ordered another cup of hot water to go with my used tea bag, and thought about Mrs. Limbach. Professor Rosson was likely to be right about her being reluctant to see me. On the other hand, she couldn't be totally unapproachable. The Hocker had been able to sell her a vacuum cleaner, and so much more. I thought about the Hocker, the little I had seen of him and the good deal I had heard about him. How would Warren W. Westfall handle this little problem? Simple. The Hocker would lie.

The world is full of Westfalls. They are the promoters, the dealers, the lobbyists, the rainmakers, the image makers, the politicians, the fund-raisers. Their lies are obvious and transparent, like the lies of good old Bill Underwood, the financial services guy who had called me cold last week. But transparent and obvious generally works okay, or good old Bill wouldn't be able to make a living peddling securities he knows practically nothing about to suckers who know even less. It works because most people have trouble believing that somebody would just flat out look them in the face and lie.

The best liars are the ones who are simple enough to believe their own lies. If they're simple enough to deceive themselves totally, like Reagan, they're okay in our books. You've got to love a guy who's that sincere. Second best are liars like Johnson, who couldn't tell the difference between what was real and what wasn't. Third best are the tactical liars, like Nixon and the Hocker, who know the difference but don't care. If a lie will get the job done, then tell one.

Maybe I would never be world-class, like Ronald and Lyndon, but at least I could hope to get down to the Hocker's and the Trickster's level. So I headed over to Brattle Street for the walk out to the Morton Limbach Juniors'. It turned out to be not as handsome as the Longfellow House nearby, but somewhat larger. The hundred-year-old trees out front were so big that not enough sun got under them to grow decent grass, just sparse, wiry stuff that let the brown dirt show through. A low picket fence ran along the front of the grounds. I lifted the latch on the gate and started up the walk, ready to talk my way past the maid and to madame. As it happened, I didn't need to. Old money answers its own door, or did this time.

"Yes," said the gray-haired woman I saw through the screen. She couldn't be the maid, not wearing low-heeled brown leather shoes with fringed tongues. Either fringed tongues had come back, or she had owned the shoes since the forties.

"Mrs. Limbach?"

"Yes."

"Look, I'm sorry to bother you. I'm Tom Bethany." No recognition. "No reason you'd know the name, but I've been working on some problems connected with your son's estate—"

Now she remembered the name.

"I know exactly who you are," she said. "Whatever it is you want, you'll have to talk to our lawyers."

"It isn't any kind of a legal thing, Mrs. Limbach. It's more of a personal thing, something I wanted to say to you in person."

"Something personal?"

"Yeah. That I'm sorry."

She couldn't figure out what to say to that, so I picked up the ball myself. "I didn't know what the job was when I said I'd go to work for this guy Rosson," I said. "Do you know anything about Rosson? Reason I ask, I was in the army in Vietnam and a few things this guy says, they sound like Jane Fonda. Hanoi Jane, we used to call her. Listen, you mind if I come in . . ."

She let me sit down in a small parlor off to the right of the entrance hall. I clasped my hands between my knees and leaned a little bit forward, head bowed in what I hoped would look like penitence. I spoke to the floor.

"Mrs. Limbach, I tell you the truth, this thing worries me. Not so much this guy's politics, that's his own business whether I like it or not. It's what he wants me to do. It just isn't fair to the family, is the way I look at it."

"What does he want you to do?"

"This is the first time I worked for the guy, you understand. I didn't know I was getting into this kind of thing . . ."

"What kind of thing?"

"Well, he doesn't say to lie exactly, or phony up evidence. Just kind of shade things, overlook things . . ." I wrung my hands, something I had always wanted to try. Was I going too far? Apparently not.

"Overlook what things?"

"Well, Mrs. Limbach, my instinct is your son could have committed suicide."

"Of course he did."

"Only Professor Rosson doesn't want to hear that."

"Naturally not. His darling ACLU."

"ACLU? How does the ACLU fit into it?"

It turned out that Rosson was an ACLU fellow traveler, if not an actual card-carrying member, which wouldn't surprise her, either. I was amazed and horrified to learn it, and to learn that the ACLU would get its hands on a young fortune if Morty had died accidentally. That explained a lot.

"Well, I just do research, kind of a paralegal," I said. "I'm not a big-shot professor like this guy is, but I've still got my reputation to think of, you know? I wouldn't want him using my research report, my name on it, to pull off something that wasn't right."

By now I wasn't looking down at my hands anymore. I was looking with honest, worried eyes at Sally Limbach. She was a woman somewhere in her sixties, neither pretty nor plain. She would have been in the unmemorable middle of any freshman facebook. In a facebook for grandmothers, that's still where she would have been. Nothing

about her really stayed with you. Just another face, with
no signs of emotional wear on it. Just another aging figure,
neither fat nor thin, shapely nor shapeless.

"If I could get some idea of why he might have, you
know, taken his own life," I said. "Well it could maybe
help me to get a handle on this thing . . ." I let my voice
trail off, and waited.

"He was always a difficult child," Sally Limbach said.
"He would wander off somewhere, away from the others,
and he'd never come when you called. Used to drive his
father absolutely crazy. And of course he was the despair
of his teachers. He would test beautifully, and then get C's
and D's. Attitude, simple attitude. Stubborn as a mule. Got
it from his grandfather. Grandfather Limbach always had
to have his own way. He was a hard driver. He used to
say he didn't get ulcers, he gave them, and that's just
exactly what that grandson of his was doing when he killed
himself. He was giving *us* ulcers."

"That's awful, isn't it?" I said, thinking that it sure
enough was awful. "Hard to imagine anybody would do
that."

"Oh, people do it, all right. I'm not a doctor, but a very
dear friend of mine has looked into the matter very carefully and suicide is a very common way of getting back at
your parents."

"What would he be getting back at you for?"

"I'm sure I couldn't say. He never wanted for anything.
God knows why he was depressed in the first place."

"Depressed, huh? That would tie in with suicide, all
right."

"Oh, yes, depressed to the point that he was under psy-
chiatric care. Many psychiatrists. For years and years, not
that it ever seemed to do the slightest good. But we tried.
God knows, we tried everything for that boy."

"Mrs. Limbach, I hate to ask you this, but I just feel like

149

I ought to, and I hope you won't take it wrong. Let's assume it was suicide, okay, which probably it was. But what about the weird way he was found?"

"I don't know anything at all about that side of his life, and I'm sure I'm happier not knowing. He had a series of totally unsuitable female friends and God knows what he might have learned from them. A very dear friend of mine had one of them investigated and she was practically a prostitute. One of the little actresses he was always hiring."

"You don't suppose she had something to do with, you know, the way he was found?"

"I suppose it's possible, but he was fully capable of staging that little bit of make-believe all by himself. I don't suppose you ever saw any of the so-called skits his group puts on? Well, I can tell you that they could be very, very sophomoric and very, very unpleasant."

"You think it's possible that the *condition* he was in, you know what I mean, pardon me, Mrs. Limbach, but the condition of his clothes and like on the rug? You think he could have done that and then committed suicide?"

"He was perfectly capable of it. You'd have to know him."

"Well, I suggested to Professor Rosson that maybe something like that happened and the first thing he asks me is why? Why not just go ahead and commit suicide without all the weirdness, you know?"

"To hurt the ones who loved him. I already explained that. He was perfectly well aware of the impression he would be making, I'm sure. On us, the family. You'd understand if you knew Morty the way we do in the family. He used to collect snakes when he was a boy. His grandfather would say, My God, boy, all the animals in the world and you have to pick snakes. Why snakes? Well, of course I knew why snakes. Because everybody else thought snakes were perfectly disgusting."

"So what you're saying, if he wanted to commit suicide, he might very well have worked out a way to do it so that it wouldn't look like suicide, it would have looked like something . . ."

"Perfectly disgusting."

"That would explain a lot of things, all right. Like why he didn't leave a suicide note."

"Well, he just might not have been quite as smart as he thought he was on that one," Sally Limbach said.

"You mean he did leave a note?"

"Everything will come out in due time."

"Your friend has the note, huh?"

"What friend?"

"Well, the one you mentioned. The one who found out about Morty's girlfriend, the hooker or whatever."

"All in due time."

We talked for a while longer about this and that, but nothing substantive. She probably imagined that what she had told me at the start was nothing substantive, either. Like a child, she seemed to think that a secret was kept as long as you didn't say it straight out. She didn't grasp that the real world wasn't a courtroom; the real world was a place where sworn and direct testimony wasn't required. Where most information changed hands by hint, inflection, tone, indirection. By non-telling as often as by telling. I knew now that Westfall had possession of some sort of suicide note, and that he used his investigators to check up on Morty's love life. I could take that information to the bank, if not to court.

After Mrs. Limbach showed me out, I looked back from the front gate with the idea of waving good-bye. We had got to be pretty good friends, after all. But she had closed the door.

A thought struck me as I walked along replaying the conversation to myself. She had referred to Morty as "that boy," "he," or "the child," but she never used the word *son*. Poor Morty.

Poor Sally, too, although it was a harder reach for me. Like half the world she was of below-average intelligence, smart enough to figure out road maps and simple instructions. Then one day the genes pull a fast one on her and she's got a fairly smart kid on her hands. To her he must have looked like a really smart kid. Another woman might have been delighted, but she probably saw the child's quickness and curiosity as hostile, menacing, sullen. In the land of the blind, the one-eyed man isn't king. He's a freak. And it probably isn't fair to blame the blind for it.

But I did.

Back in Harvard Square, I took the inbound T to North Station and walked over to the Registry of Motor Vehicles. I wanted to find out where Warren W. Westfall lived, and he wasn't in the phone book. But I had spotted his license number in the company garage. It was one of the special plates with only numbers, no letters, that you can get in Massachusetts if you're politically wired. And from just a license plate number, Massachusetts lets you find out things about the automobile owner that his own mother doesn't know.

There wasn't even a line in the bare, bleak little office where a Hispanic woman and a woman who looked Vietnamese sat behind a counter ready to hook me into the Commonwealth's data base. I put Westfall's plate number down on a mimeographed application for registration information, the Hispanic woman keyed it into the computer, the printer whirred, and the woman handed me a printout headed Registration/Title Inquiry. Total elapsed time was something like thirty seconds. Now I knew the vehicle identification number, the title number, the style, and the color, as well as the number of cylinders and seats and doors in Westfall's new Jaguar. I knew the car had no

152

liens against it, was insured by Pilgrim Mutual, and was owned sure enough by Warren W. Westfall. I knew the number of Westfall's Massachusetts driver's license, and I knew his address. Which was on Beacon Hill, which figured. Where else?

By the time I showed up, a little before nine that evening, lights showed in most of the town houses in Westfall's absurdly expensive neighborhood. I wore a golf cap for my visit to Beacon Hill. Normally you'd have to staple a golf cap to my skull to get me to wear one, but my theory was that the thing would draw attention away from my features. It had cost me two bucks at Oona's used clothes. Two bucks more got me the knitted ski mask in my pocket, which would make my features totally irrelevant during the most dangerous part of my plan. I put the cap on and risked leaving the car in a no-parking zone for the few minutes it took me to inspect Westfall's three-story town house. Apart from a light over the door, the house was dark. And his Jaguar was nowhere around.

I didn't want to wait outdoors, since this was the kind of neighborhood where cops pay attention to people hanging around outdoors. So I found an illegal place and sat behind the wheel until a car left a legal one down the block. I just beat another guy to it. I locked up and scouted the rear of Westfall's house to see if his car was there. The house backed up on a wide alleyway with rear doors and even a few tiny yards on both sides. Instead of a backyard, Westfall's house had a garage with an automatic door. I had a long night ahead of me if the car was inside and Westfall was out for the evening or even out of town. I went back to my car, which was parked near enough so that nobody could drive into the alley without me seeing them. I sat on the passenger's side so it would look like I was waiting for a few minutes while the driver was away on some brief and no doubt legitimate business. Since I myself couldn't leave on brief and legitimate business without possibly missing Westfall, I had an empty mayonnaise jar stashed on the floor.

The third car that came down the narrow street was a Jaguar, but it didn't have Westfall's plates. And then for a long time nothing was a Jaguar. After a while I started to count the number of cars that came by in a minute—sometimes none—and then to play license tag poker with an imaginary opponent. By half past twelve I was forty-five bucks up on myself and starting to think this was a pretty stupid way to spend my late-night hours. About the best you could say for it was that it beat watching Ted Koppel being articulate at the expense of some other member of the Establishment.

And then along came the right Jaguar with the right plates.

I was out of the car and moving fast before the car even turned into the alleyway. As I hustled along I pulled the tan ski mask over my head and yanked the golf cap down. My aim was to be strolling innocently up behind him at just about the time he was activating his garage door.

And I was.

As I hoped, he had been too busy watching the door going up to notice the pedestrian to his rear. When the car started to move, I crouched down in Westfall's blind spot and ran right in after him. The garage door lowered behind me, and I heard Westfall getting out of his car. Since the light was on in the garage, I stayed bent over until the car door slammed. Once he was out of the car, though, it wouldn't matter whether he saw me. He couldn't possibly get back in it and lock the doors in time. I had covered half the distance to him before he heard me, and turned.

I gave a stupid-sounding martial arts cry as I gestured with my left hand to get him looking that way. Then I swung my right forearm like a club into the side of his neck. The idea is to produce a heavy, diffuse impact—the kind of effect you get from running somebody backward into a wall. You see it now and then on the football field, when a blocker blindsides a defenseman just right. If the guy manages to get to his feet at all, he totters around for a while in total confusion. And Westfall was no linebacker.

His legs gave way and he crumpled to the ground almost in slow motion. I was right on top of him, putting most of my weight on one knee, and that knee in his belly. I doubt if he felt it. His eyes were open, and his pupils were still jittering from the shock. I waited for a few seconds until his eyes quieted down and he was able to pay attention to things again.

Then I broke the second finger on his right hand, the finger I figured he used to grope with. As he was screaming over that, I did my own groping. I grabbed a handful between his legs and squeezed with all my force. The screaming turned into blubbering when I finally let go. I reached inside his coat for his wallet, and then hunted around in his car till I found the beeper that worked the garage door. The last I saw of him as I stood outside and watched the door come down, he was curled up on the oily garage floor in his twelve-hundred-dollar suit, holding his crushed nuts and crying. He looked good.

It was possible that neighbors had heard him screaming, or seen me on my way in or out of the garage, or even seen him lying there. But I walked away at normal speed, counting on the Kitty Genovese effect. Even if one of the rich neighbors had enough sense of civic duty to call the cops, and even if the cops came a lot quicker than normal, my best bet was walking instead of running. So I jammed my mask and cap inside my jacket and ambled along trying to look harmless. It was hard not to sprint for cover, though. The adrenaline high had worn off and now the fear was telling me to flee.

My anonymous old Datsun was parked out of sight from the alleyway, but I was still nervous about the dome light that went on when I got in. And I kept the headlights off till I was a couple blocks away. A couple of traffic-free blocks, at that time of night. When I was well away from Beacon Hill, I tossed the garage-opening device out, in an unaimed left-handed hook shot that sent it over the car and down a weed-grown embankment. Fighting the impulse to floor it, I kept my speed legal till I reached the parking lot of a fast-food joint on Huntington Avenue. I pulled over long enough to dump the cap and the mask into a trash receptacle.

Back in the car, I went through the Hocker's elegant wallet. It looked like alligator, but no doubt came from some South American crocodile on the endangered species list. The Hocker wouldn't be satisfied with less than the best. He had been carrying $420 in cash, which I would have switched to my own wallet, except that I stopped carrying wallets after my third one slipped out of my pocket at the movies during high school. Since then I've carried my cash loose, folded into my shirt pocket, and haven't lost a nickel. Even the time in Saigon when a half-dozen six- and seven-year-old pickpockets swarmed me outside of a Tu Do Street bar. They cleaned out the keys, penknife, and small change in my pants pockets, but they weren't tall enough to reach the paper money.

Aside from the $420, the major items of interest in West-fall's pocket were credit cards. He had a full collection of them. I didn't carry credit cards myself, and so it was pretty exciting to have all these gold and platinum beauties, each presumably backed by the generous lines of credit that banks extend to thieves and swindlers. All I had to do was figure out his private four-digit access number, which might be possible. I had a good deal to go on, actually. Most people pick a number easy to remember, and the Registry of Motor Vehicles had given me most of the numbers in Westfall's life that he would be liable to know by heart. I headed toward Cambridge, with the idea of stopping off at each of the money machines along the way. The worst the automatic tellers could do was say no.

And the first one did. When I tried 4-6-33, the Hocker's date of birth, the machine responded in an encouraging way, clicking and whirring after I told it I wanted five hundred dollars. But once the thing finished making noises, it flashed me the finger: "Your password is not correct," the screen said. "Please enter your correct password." The same thing happened when I tried the first four digits of his Social Security number. I wasn't sure if the machine ate your card after a certain number of wrong numbers, so I drove on to the next machine and tried another card on it. The number I punched in was Westfall's big-shot, politically connected, no-letter, four-digit license plate number, 1404, and it was a winner. When the whirring noises stopped this time, ten crisp fifties clanked out of the slot. I tried the first card again, using 1404 in case Westfall had simplified his life by getting all his credit card companies to assign him the same number. That's just what he had done, and I got another $500.

I drove on toward home, hitting every automatic teller around Kendall Square, and then around Porter Square. I tried the Cirrus, the Yankee 24, and the Plus systems. My magic number made them all work. Bank of Boston. Coolidge Cool Card. MasterCard. Visa. Everything worked. It was the damnedest experience. I felt like one of those experimental monkeys with the electrodes in the pleasure centers of their brains, the ones that hit the bliss button over and over until they die of starvation. All that saved me was the machines themselves, which ate all my cards one by one as I maxed them out, until at last I had nothing left. Except $12,500 in brand-new bills.

Lying in bed the next morning, I thought about all the things I could buy with the Hocker's money, starting with a new car and working down to a new VCR. Mine was a bottom-of-the-line Korean machine, picked up at Lechmere's for $189 during the George Washington Day sales, and all it would do was play movies. Everyone else had one that could record off the TV in case an emergency called you away from the set when "Knott's Landing" was on. On the other hand, I didn't watch "Knott's Landing," and my old Datsun got me the same places a new car would go.

I was feeling the same way I feel when I go to a mall with money in my pockets and the idea that I ought to buy something nice for myself. Looking over the stuff in Abercrombie & Fitch or Williams-Sonoma or Brooks Brothers, the most I manage to work up is a vague itch, easy not to scratch. I didn't have expensive toys for such a long time that the need for them has mostly died away. What I have instead is a swelled head over how I can get along just fine without fancy toys. This attitude problem left me with $12,500 in new bills, and no home for them. After a while, though, I worked out a solution.

But first came breakfast, which was a microwaved portion of the lamb stew I make in big batches whenever the fit comes over me and freeze in old pint containers. For a long time I favored the ones Stonyfield Farm uses for its yogurt, but a while ago I switched to the ones for Frusen Glädjé ice cream. More durable.

After breakfast I drove to the Star Market out Mt. Auburn Street and started to push a basket up and down the aisles. For a while I hung around a black woman with three small kids. To look natural, I put stuff in my basket from time to time as I looked her over. Her clothes were from J. C. Penney's or Bradlees. So were her kids' clothes. The smaller the kid, the more dilapidated the clothes got, which is the way it was in my family, too. Things were pretty beat up once they worked their way down to number four, which was me. The woman was going heavy on the junk foods—cookies and Twinkies and chocolate syrup, Kool-Aid and Froot Loops. The kids knew all the unhealthiest stuff by sight, and clamored for it, and she went along. One of the cute things the supermarkets do is put the worst of the crap for kids on the lower shelves, where they can get their hands on it.

"Put that back, you," she said to one of her little boys who had reached above the garbage meant for him and pulled down a box of gelatine. There was a picture of some disgusting red dessert on the box, which he probably figured was inside.

"I told you put that back, Clarence," she said when he didn't. "You do what your momma tells you or you'll wish you did." He was moving to put the box back, but not soon enough to suit her. He cried out in fear when she reached for him, and the fear changed to a scream of real pain when she jerked his arm hard enough that the kid was lucky she didn't dislocate it. She dragged him screaming down the aisle behind her. The box of gelatine lay where it had fallen on the floor, until I picked it up and replaced it.

Okay, she wasn't the one.

I picked up another one a few minutes later, this one also black and young, but with four kids instead of three. There were two boys and two girls, all preschool. She had the littlest one, a girl, in the basket. Both girls had ribbons in their hair. The kids' clothes were ragged, but they were as clean as you can reasonably expect kids' clothes to be. A rip in one of the boys' striped T-shirts had been sewn up. But the mother was no better a shopper than the first one, to judge by the contents of her cart.

"You cut that out, Tiffany," she said to her oldest child. "You know you ain't supposed to hit on your little brother. You done real good for a while, what you starting up for now?" The little girl stopped hitting, and her mother patted her on the head. "That's a girl," she said. "Now you keep on being a good girl, momma buy you some bubble gum."

I moved away, putting the stuff in my basket back on the shelves and generally killing time till momma was done. I went empty-handed to the express checkout and picked up four candy bars while I was in line. The woman, two lines over, was getting out her food stamps. Good. She was one of those welfare queens that Reagan must have loved, he created so many of them. After I paid, I went outside and waited in the parking lot until she came out with her kids. She headed out to the far end of the lot and then kept on going, pushing her cart down the sidewalk. I came walking up behind them and said, "Hey, Tiffany, want a candy bar?"

The little girl turned around at her name, spotted that there was a candy bar sure enough, and reached for it. Then she took her hand back and looked at her mother to see what to do.

"How you know her name?" the mother said, holding herself tensely. Good, solid maternal reaction.

"I heard you in the market," I said, holding out the rest of the candy bars to the other kids.

"What you giving them candy for?"

"They look like okay kids."

"What you want with us, anyway?" She pulled the shopping cart a little ways away from me, an action that seemed to suggest something to her. "It's okay if I take this home with me," she said. "I ax Mr. Henderson, he say he know me, know I always brings it back. You ax him, he tell you he done told me it's all right."

"How about if you got a nice wagon for the boy, here? He could pull the groceries home, then have the wagon to play with."

"Where I going to get the money to go buying wagons with?"

"Ask your husband."

"You ax him, can you find him."

"Gone, huh?" She looked at me as if I just got off the boat. Of course he was gone. "Well, then," I said, "take this."

"What you got in there?"

"Take a look."

"Money," she said in a whisper, when she saw the stack of bills inside the manila envelope I had given her. "Where you get all that money?"

"Doesn't matter," I said. "It's yours."

"What am I supposed to do with it?"

"Hell, I don't care. Only thing I'd suggest, don't buy cancer insurance with it."

— 10 —

NEXT DAY THE SKY WAS GRAY, THE FIRST DAY IN A WEEK OR so that had been less than perfect. Since the forecaster said things might get even more raw by the afternoon, I wore a heavy wool sweater under my suede jacket. Already there was enough chill in the air to have driven everybody off the Au Bon Pain terrace except the Chessmaster and a victim. They were playing thirty seconds to a move, and at intervals whoever had just moved would hit the bell on the timer to start the other guy's countdown. The Chessmaster, a Harvard man, was apparently pretty good. At least he seemed to win most of his games fast enough to make himself a living wage at two bucks a win.

Unlike him, I didn't need to be out in the weather to attract customers. Instead I sat inside Au Bon Pain to read my paper and drink my hot chocolate. The *Globe* had nothing about the brutal mugging of millionaire insurance mogul Warren W. Westfall. It would have happened too late for their deadline. But there was an article in the entertainment section on the Poor Attitudes, although the head-

line didn't mention them. It read: BOFFO BABY BOOKS
BOSTON BENEFIT, which wasn't too bad an effort for the
Globe. Their idea of a red-hot headline is generally some-
thing like LITTLE-KNOWN WOMEN POETS HONORED IN
PHILADELPHIA.

The story began, "Who says you can't go home again?
Kathy Poindexter, who used to play local club dates and
is now America's second-hottest TV star, is returning to the
Boston area with America's first-hottest TV star. Who is,
of course, her son. Who is Little Leo. Who is the all-time
premier box-office draw, diaper division, in the history of
the world. (The infant Jesus, as Leo's late dad liked to
point out, only drew a crowd of three.) Baby Leo and his
mom are slated to appear at a gala for mom's old troupe,
the Poor Attitudes."

I wondered why I hadn't heard of this. Probably because
I hadn't asked, and everybody figured I already knew.
Kathy and Little Leo and the show's other regulars, it
turned out, had agreed to appear with the new Poor Attitudes troupe at a gala show to benefit Boston-area community theater. The Boston Art Commission would distribute
whatever funds were raised to deserving theater groups. It
would be a variety show, with a mix of improvised and
prepared skits, songs, and monologues. And the real beneficiaries, I guessed, would be the Poor Attitudes. It didn't
seem likely that Kathy Poindexter and Co. would disrupt
their lives to give a hand to community theater, but the
exposure would certainly help out her struggling alma
mater. The benefit was scheduled for a week from Friday,
at the Prince Restaurant in Saugus.

I left my paper on the table for the next guy and headed
for the Poor Attitudes House. I had been planning on going
there anyway, to ask around a little more about Morty
Limbach. And the mansion was on my way to Central

Square, where I was going to have lunch with the assistant chief of Cambridge detectives, a friend of Gladys Williams.

I found Ned Levine, the actor-director of the Poor Attitudes, filling the coffee machine in the kitchen. No one else seemed to be up yet. "Oh, yeah," he said when I asked him about the gala. "Morty set that up with Kathy when they were here for their shoot. The weekend Morty . . . anyway, that weekend. Apparently after he died Kathy saw it as kind of a memorial for him, so she went ahead with everything on her own. Got her publicity people to make the arrangements. That's what we were rehearsing for, when you saw us last week. Not that you can rehearse this stuff, really. But you try to stay sharp."

"A gala should be good for business, huh?"

"Jesus, I hope so. That's part of the idea. My impression from what I hear, Leo Grasso walked off to New York and never looked back. But Kathy felt kind of guilty leaving. And it's been hard to get back up to where we were in terms of audience acceptance, so she was going to give us a boost. Get a really influential audience together for us, get the word of mouth going. Plus what Kathy hopes is that it'll help us turn into sort of a farm club for Kathy Productions."

"Presumably that's the company that does the 'Little Leo Show'?"

"Now, yes. But she wants to move out into producing other shows, too."

"What goes on at this gala? Are Kathy and the baby going to perform with you?"

"Not doing bits with us, not in that sense. We wouldn't be able to work together in advance, and you need to get used to each other. But she's going to emcee, and do either one or two things on her own. Not just her, I don't mean. Her with the baby, and some of the other people from the show."

164

"I was thinking of going down to New York sometime soon," I said. "Talk to her, maybe to Elliman."

"You'll like her. She's great."

"He's not so great?"

"Well, I didn't say that, but come to think of it, why didn't I? He's not so great, no."

"Why not?"

"Nothing specific. He's smart and he's talented, but there's just a kind of a weirdness there. Like he's trying to pass for an earthling, but he's not really the same species we are. Probably that's all a load of shit, of course, and he's just plain folks and the rest of us are the aliens. Probably I just don't like the way he walked out on us here and moved in on Kathy and had a giant success and had his picture in *People* taken lying beside his fucking pool in the fucking Hamptons. Probably I'm just jealous."

A couple other people had wandered downstairs by then and I got down to the business of the day, which was to find out if Morty had any enemies. Apparently not. Everybody liked Morty, which was unusual, since he was their benefactor. Nobody had even heard of anybody who disliked him. Nobody had a bad word to say about him, or had even heard one said.

I thought of all the pain and despair Morty had poured into the computer files he called Downdump. Did he know that he was universally liked, and maybe even loved, for the gentleness he thought was weakness? Did he know how rare it was to be able to help people without making them hate you? There were clues in the files that he did, actually. Little passing thoughts, that he raised only to dismiss: "everybodyh lthnks im great yeah big dieal. shit why not, everybody likes a beanbag too iguess, why not, what the fuck did a ggbeangag ever do to them. how do the beanbags feel aobut themsleves thogh?"

165

I tried another tack. "How about Morty himself?" I asked. "Was there anybody *he* didn't like?"

Well, no. That was one of the reasons everybody liked Morty: he seemed to like everybody else. Leo Grasso was evidently a prime son of a bitch, but nobody ever heard Morty say a word against him. Dump on Leo and Morty would just listen and nod, and explain the kind of strain it puts a man under, having a talent like Leo's. With a genius, you have to make allowances.

"We were going to have them make a floral display for Morty's funeral with a banner or something that said No More Mr. Nice Guy," Ned said. "Only then we figured maybe the family would think it was too flip, you know?"

"Which they would have," said Bob, one of the players who had just shown up. "They came to one of our shows this summer and they were totally baffled. When everybody else laughed, they'd smile. But they'd smile a little late, so you could tell they didn't really get it."

"Or maybe they got it and didn't like it," Ned said. "Either way, a fun couple."

I hadn't said why I was asking whether Morty had had any enemies, but of course I didn't have to. Ned took me aside as I was leaving.

"Do you think somebody killed Morty?" he asked.

"There's no evidence of that at all," I said, which was certainly true in the legal sense. And I didn't want it to get around that I thought he might have been murdered. Whoever did it, I didn't want to scare him into disappearing. "What I'm trying to do is just put together a picture of his life," I told Ned. "The insurance company claims he killed himself, but as far as I can make out he didn't have any reason to."

Of course he actually did. Chronic depression is one of the most common reasons of all, but it's not always fatal. Not even usually. Winston Churchill lived with it for ninety years or so. Morty had lived with it, too. He had worked out his ways of coping: pouring his pain into his analysis and into his computer, no doubt among other things.

"Well, Morty had his lows," Ned said.

"Yeah, but he was functioning," I said. "He had plans, things to live for. If nobody can point to any particular new development that might have pushed him over the edge, then what caused him to lose his balance?"

Nothing had, or at least that was the argument I was putting together for the assistant chief of Cambridge's detectives. Lieutenant William X. Curtin was a member of the small underground of intelligent people that exists within any bureaucracy, police or otherwise, if only you can find them. I got to Cambridge police headquarters after a ten-minute walk in light drizzle, and asked my way to Lieutenant Curtin's tiny office, off the big room where the lower-ranking detectives had their desks. It was the first time I had seen him on his home grounds. Curtin had two straight chairs for visitors. One was wood. The other had a tubular steel frame, starting to rust, with a seat and back made of plywood covered with red plastic. This was the one I took, on the theory that there might be an eighth of an inch of comfortable padding under the plastic. "Gladys says you got something on your mind," the detective said. And he listened without comment while I told him at some length why I thought somebody might have killed Morty. Even if I didn't have any real evidence of it, I said. Always end on a strong note.

"Naturally you wouldn't have any evidence if it didn't happen," he said. "If it was an accidental death for instance, which happens to be exactly the way we're carrying it."

"I think you may be carrying it wrong," I said.

"Well, fuck, we been wrong before," he said, pulling a paper bag out of his desk. In the bag were a little carton of milk, a sandwich wrapped in plastic, an apple, and a couple of graham crackers. A kid's lunch. "Want half the sandwich?" Curtin asked. It didn't sound as if he really wanted to share.

"No thanks."

"Okay. So tell me while I eat, why we're wrong."

I finished telling and he finished eating about the same time.

"I like that part about the come spots," Curtin said. "Of course it doesn't add up to jackshit, you understand."

"Of course not."

"Still, it's interesting, huh?"

"I could give you notes on all this stuff."

"Nah, it's not worth it. I'm not going to do anything with it. Although if I didn't have anything better to do, maybe I'd have somebody look into it."

"I don't have anything better to do."

"Yeah, I thought probably not."

"Because if it turns out to be murder then it can't very well be suicide. And then the insurance company has to pay off."

"Couldn't happen to a nicer guy than the Hocker."

"You know Westfall?"

"The Hocker and I go way back. I was a kid just out of the academy, my partner and me went on a domestic dispute call. It was a retard couple that met in the training school and they heard about getting married. Decided they wanted some of that shit. So they were evidently border-line, could kind of function, so the school says why not? No problem with kids, the guy's had a vasectomy. What the fuck, let the poor bastards give it a go. So they fixed him up with a job in the hospital laundry, Mt. Auburn I think, and she was in some sheltered workshop part time. Anyway, she was home when the Hocker comes by waving his big fucking Electrolux. She didn't look retarded the way most of them do, well, maybe a little bit she did. But she was kind of cute, really.

"Naturally you could tell what she was as soon as she opened her mouth, though. Dying to please. Did everything she was told, and she'd keep on doing it till somebody told her to stop. A guy like the Hocker, it was like giving a piano to Liberace.

"In about two minutes he had her signed up for the super-duper six-hundred-dollar model that whistles 'Dixie' and cures the clap while you wait. Two more minutes and he has her copping his joint in the living room. So that night the husband comes home and asks what kind of a day did you have, dear, and she says, Well, I bought this vacuum cleaner and then this nice man told me to suck his dick.

"Now the guy's not a retard to the point where he can't figure this one out, so he clips her and she doesn't know what she's done wrong so she sits down on the floor and starts crying, and he sits down on the floor and starts crying, too, and the neighbors call in about all the noise.

"I'm trying to sort the thing out, but unfortunately my partner is this stone asshole who starts to make jokes, figuring they can't understand. Only the husband flashes on it, and pokes him. So asshole has got to go and charge him with assaulting an officer, which technically is what the retard did all right. Upshot is the guy gets probation and goes back to the home, the girl can't hack it alone so she goes to another home, and the marriage is annulled."

"Pretty story," I said.

"Real pretty," Curtin said. "That's what we call justice, you fucking believe it?"

"What about the Hocker?"

"Nothing we could do. He denied touching her, and her testimony wouldn't have been worth shit. Maybe now it would have, possibly, but back then forget about it. Nothing I could do. Officially anyway."

"How about unofficially?"

"Yeah, well, not much there, either. I just happened to see him a couple days after the incident when I was off duty and happened to be following his ass around. I took him down to the basement of an apartment house he was knocking on the doors, and requested the subject to show me his dick. He didn't want to do it at first so I had to request him a little more politely before he would whip it out. Son of a bitch if he didn't turn out to have a chancre on it, just like the girl said he did. Actually what she told us was he had a boo-boo on his wee-wee."

"Jesus, that's cute."

"I thought so, too. I kept the fucker down in the basement for a little while, trying not to leave any marks. Then I told him any time I saw his car parked on my beat it was going to be parked illegally and I'd bust all the windows out and wait right beside it till the tow truck came."

"Well, I guess it's something," I said.

"Not much, though. Actually I was just moving him a few streets away, dumping my shit on the next guy, but you do what you can. All they gave me at the time was that one beat to be responsible for."

"Now you've got the whole city."

"Yeah, but the fucker's way up there beyond my reach now. Far as I know, he doesn't even live here. So go ahead and take his two hundred fifty K, you got my blessing."

"Could be twice as much, if we get lucky. When I mentioned murder, the lawyer said that would bring it under the double-indemnity clause. The company has to pay twice the face amount of the insurance if death is from bodily injury caused by external, violent, and accidental means."

"Half a million bucks, huh? Maybe the ACLU killed Limbach. Burned him down for the insurance money."

"Good an answer as anything I've got," I said. "Well, anyway, I just wanted you to know I was looking."

"Sure, look. No harm in that. I hear of anything you ought to be looking at, maybe I'll give you a call. What's your number?"

I gave him the number of the pay phone at the Tasty, and he started making out a Rolodex card on me. "What's your address?" he asked.

"I'm kind of between places."

"So give me both of them."

"Probably better if you just leave a message at that number." Curtin lost his friendliness at that point. No known address makes cops uneasy. They like everybody to be in the bureaucratic data base.

"It'd be a pain in the ass for everybody if I had to find out for myself," he said.

"Aw, shit," I said. "Let me tell you how it is, then. Nobody wants me, no warrants out for me, no charges outstanding, no judgments against me, no claims against me, no debts. Here or anywhere else. I just like my privacy, so I'm unlisted and I rent under another name."

"Is Tom Bethany your real name?"

"Yes, it is. But the name fell out of the computers years ago, before I moved to Cambridge." From right across the river in Allston, but I didn't say that.

"What does that mean, 'fell out'?"

"Means that one day I just wasn't there anymore. Mail came back marked No Forwarding Address. My credit cards were all paid up, but never used again. I wasn't in the phone book, or anybody's else's book. I showed up here with another name on the mailbox."

"What's the point? Draft dodging?"

"I had already done my service."

"Taxes?"

"At the time, I didn't make enough to pay taxes."

"At the time, huh?"

"Probably the feds and the state would want some now."

"Are you that rich, to go through all that shit to duck taxes?"

"That's not really the point, either. Although I do figure I can spend it better than Bush can. The point is partly to be hard to find if anybody comes after me. Same reason cops have unlisted phones."

"People come after you?"

"One or two might, if they knew where to come. But that's not the main point. The main point is I just like my privacy a lot. Really a lot. That may not make too much sense as a reason, but I can't explain it any better than that. Well, shit, I'll try, though. You ever ride the freights?"

"No."

"I did for a while, when I was a kid. You're going along in a boxcar, real slow. Summer evening, maybe, and you're rolling through a little town. You see people in their yards, poor people mostly, that live down by the tracks. You wave at them, they wave back. Off you go, not too fast, but fast enough so nobody can get on. You're in this boxcar and the people that waved are back in the town with keys and telephone numbers and checkbooks and bills and general chickenshit that you don't have any of. What you have is a boxcar with your legs hanging out of the door and not even the president of the United States can take that away from you. Not even the conductor can. Because they don't know you're on the train."

That was the best I could do, and Lieutenant Curtin thought it over for a minute. "That makes sense to you?" he asked.

"I don't know why, but yeah."

"Well, what the hell, I guess you're not hurting the train any."

"I pick up messages at that number I gave you. If you're in a real hurry, Gladys can always get through to me."

I was glad we were friends again. Curtin was the smartest man with any real rank in the Cambridge police department, according to Gladys. And Gladys would know, being smart herself. The intelligent people in any organization smell each other out pretty quickly. And are smelled out by the dummies who run things, too. Not too many of the best ones even get to the upper middle ranges, like Curtin. In the bureaucracies I've been in or close to, scum rises a lot faster than cream. The half-smart make lieutenant-general or general, the really smart stall out at lieutenant-colonel or colonel.

It was lucky for me that Curtin had made it as far as he did, because that was far enough to have saved me from a lot of embarrassing questions and possibly from criminal charges in a nasty business I got involved in not long ago. And it had saved somebody else from spending the rest of her life in jail for a killing that was probably justified in the eyes of the Lord, or at least an Old Testament kind of a Lord. Which seemed to be Curtin's kind of Lord, all right, to judge by the story he had just told me. Once the Hocker got out of that basement, I would bet he never gave a serious thought to selling a vacuum cleaner or anything else within the Cambridge city limits. Curtin was of average height and a little scrawny, the way mountain climbers and triathletes sometimes look a little scrawny. And he gave that same impression—that he was bred for hunting, not for show. Once he got his teeth into your ankle, you'd have to cut his head off to get loose.

"You read the business pages?" Curtin asked.

"Not much."

"Me neither. But every day when I go by the newsstand

I check the *Wall Street Journal,* that little index they run of all the companies they mention that day? Every so often they got something on Pilgrim Mutual and I buy the paper, clip the story for my files."

"I thought you said he was beyond your reach now."

"It's a long life," Curtin said. "Maybe someday he'll get back into it."

"He's a great man now. He's on the board of the Harvard Divinity School."

"He could be His Holiness himself, I wouldn't care. You can't shine shit."

The drizzle was still holding just short of rain as I walked back down toward the Poor Attitudes House. I hadn't made an appointment with Dr. Unger, but it was on my way and maybe I could catch him between patients. Then it struck me that between patients was probably right now, since it was a couple minutes past two. And if I waited much longer I probably couldn't reach him by phone, since he operated without a secretary. I stopped at a pay phone and called. He was between patients, free at the moment, but he had a full load the rest of the afternoon and would meet me after work at the Harvest. Beer was pretty high at the Harvest, but I still had the $420 I had stolen from Westfall's wallet. I headed down to the Malkin Athletic Center to see if there was anybody hanging around the wrestling room.

There wasn't, so I went at it alone for a couple of hours until I had reduced myself to a state of exhaustion. Then I collapsed on the rubber floor mat like a wet towel, and must have dropped off. Voices woke me up, and I heard one of them say, "I think you're supposed to feel for a pulse."

It was a sophomore 185-pounder I often work out with, and so I greeted him with a friendly, "Fuck you, Jeff."

"Shit, he's alive," the sophomore said to his 135-pound teammate. "But I doubt he can wrestle."

This meant I had to show him, which meant I didn't have time for a sauna before going to meet Mark Unger at six o'clock. He was sitting at the bar when I got there. We took a table. "I thought it was clearing up," he said, gesturing at my wet hair. "Has it started raining again?"

"I just came from the gym."

"Really? Which club do you go to?"

"The Harvard gym. I help out with the wrestling team."

"You must be pretty good."

"I used to be," I said, which was true enough. I had made the Olympic team that Carter refused to send to Moscow in 1980 because he was so mad at the Russians for invading Afghanistan. So the Soviets won eighty gold medals and we won zip. Carter had been sort of like Morty Limbach, when Morty got so mad at his cousin that he threw his own ice cream cone on the ground. Only this time I happened to be one of the cones. By 1984 I was too old for competition at the international level, and by 1988 I was even older, and so on and so forth.

Unger was interested to hear all this. He turned out to be a karate black belt himself, which didn't necessarily mean much. My understanding is that some academies give them out the way Harvard gives out cum laudes, so freely that they lose a lot of their meaning. But Unger's black belt probably did signify something, since he said he had made it to the semifinals in his division at last year's Boston International. He made that sound big time, although I wouldn't know. I always figured karate was essentially Mickey Mouse, but no doubt Chuck Norris thinks the same thing about wrestling.

Anyway, once we got to the second round of beer we had both, in a mature, civilized way, established our cre-

175

dentials as alpha males, jock division. And it was time to get down to business.

"Was Morty on any kind of medication?" I asked. The question didn't have anything to do with his death, I didn't think, but it had been on my mind ever since reading his tortured Downdump journals.

"Not that I know of," Unger said. "Certainly not from me."

"Don't they have pills for depression now?"

"Yes, they do. Prozac is the most fashionable one just now. Would it have relieved some of Morty's pain? Probably yes. Would it have cured him? Certainly not. I don't know if those were questions you were going to ask, but they're the ones I ask myself."

"I don't know that I was going to ask them, either, but I more or less had them in mind. Was analysis working for Morty?"

"Not yet, not much. It can take years. Sometimes it doesn't work, but when it does, it's the most wonderful thing in the world for an analyst. To help somebody expose the underlying structure of their problems, so they can rearrange their emotions into healthy patterns—I can't imagine anything more rewarding than that. And I honestly don't think you can get to that point if you mask those root causes with medication."

I still felt Morty would have been better off with a little chemical help to ease him through the long nights, but there was no point arguing doctrine with a Freudian. It was like arguing with a supply-sider or a cold warrior, or an astrologer. All the evidence in the world might be against them, but in the end it didn't come down to evidence. It came down to faith.

"What about Morty's relations with other people?" I asked.

"They were better than he thought," the psychiatrist

said. "It's a common pattern with people who had the sort of relationship with their parents that he did."

"What sort of relationship was that?"

"His father was largely absent, playing golf or off sailing all over the world. In effect he granted himself a divorce without going to the courts, which I suppose would have been a pretty expensive proposition in his case."

Unless he had proof his wife had committed adultery, I thought. With, for instance, the Hocker. "What about the mother?" I asked Dr. Unger.

"I've met Sally Limbach a couple of times, and nothing much stands out about her," the psychiatrist said. "She's not exactly self-effacing, but I imagine that's because people have been deferring to her money and social position all her life. Take that away, and she'd be sort of a dim personality, I suspect. Off on the edges of things."

"Of course she *was* off on the edges of things," I said. "At least as far as her husband was concerned. Would she try to build herself back up by finding another man, do you think?"

"Well, I'd be working from a toe bone and trying to figure out what the whole dinosaur looked like. All I really know about her is from what Morty said, and he never mentioned lovers."

"From the toe bone, though, what would you say?"

"I'd say she probably didn't have to build herself back up. Someone who isn't particularly sensitive or introspective tends to accept the world's judgment of herself. Her family and money command respect from most of the world, and she would have accepted that as her due. If her husband neglected her, she might have seen the problem as his, not hers. If she needed a man, she might have gone out and got one. Or she might not have. Or she might not have needed one. But the truth is that this kind of speculation is totally useless BS. I just don't have the data to work with."

"You have data on the relationship between Morty and his mother, though," I said. "What kind of picture comes out of that?"

"A fairly common one. She tended to blame the sins of the absent father on the son who was handy. A lot of divorced mothers do that, too. Since they can't get at the real object of their resentment, they take it out on his male offspring. Sally Limbach seems to have done the same thing. And then at other times she'd turn right around and try to enlist the boy as an ally against his father. It would be just mommy and little Morty against the cruel world, which was big Mort. So she'd either love her son to death or blame him for all her troubles. The point is there was no consistency. You can drive laboratory rats into withdrawal and apathy the same way. You baffle them by changing the rules randomly. One time the rat presses the lever he gets a piece of candy. Next time he gets an electric shock."

"Does it make the rats get mad and go around picking fights with other rats."

"No," Unger said. "Overcrowding is the way to do that." It sounded plausible. For instance, I was one of eight kids.

"So Morty wouldn't be likely to go around making enemies?"

"It wouldn't be in his pattern, no. People might take advantage of him, pick on him, and perhaps you could argue that his passivity was the cause of it. But those people would be users, not real enemies."

"From his point of view, couldn't they *seem* to be enemies?"

"Probably not. You'd have to push Morty very hard before he'd start to blame you instead of himself for whatever pain you were causing him. Actually I don't think you *could* have pushed him that hard. This is a man who . . . Well, let's put it this way. You could have stolen his best girl and ruined his business, and he'd never say a harsh word about you."

"You're talking about Leo Grasso?"

"I suppose there's no harm identifying him. Both men are dead."

"I know he used to make apologies for Grasso in public, but in private?"

"We'd talk about it, but I could never get him to surface any resentment against Leo. I knew it had to be there, but it was still too deeply buried."

"What about resentment toward you?"

"Well, there's always a certain amount of that in analysis. You're causing the patient to open up wounds that he's kept carefully concealed for a lifetime, and it's a painful process. Only natural to feel resentment toward the person you see as the immediate cause of that pain."

"I meant resentment over you and Nora Dawson."

Unger had been taking a sip of beer. He kept the glass up to his mouth after he finished swallowing and looked at me for a long beat. Then he put the glass back down.

"Nora," he said softly. "Poor thing."

"Tell me about it."

"Remember the other time we talked, and I told you an analyst's worst nightmare was a patient suicide? The second worst is what happened with Nora. You know what transference is?"

"Sort of, but tell me."

"It's the direction of your childhood emotions toward a new object, often the analyst."

"Nora fell in love with you?"

"Yes, she did. A perfectly normal stage for a patient in analysis to pass through. Nothing to worry about. The only way it can cause any lasting harm is if the analyst encourages the patient. You do not allow her to act out her emotional transference, not merely as a question of medical ethics, but as a matter of sound therapeutic practice."

"In other words, you don't sleep with the patient?"

"No, you don't. Not just because it's ethically questionable. More importantly, it undercuts the therapy. In the long run, sometimes even in the short run, it's more likely to harm the patient than to help her. So you don't do it. And I didn't."

"Nora, we're talking about here?"

"Nora, yes. Her transference was unusually strong, an obsession, really. Listen, I can't tell you what happened in her sessions. Morty is dead and the situation is different. But Nora isn't, and I can't break confidentiality any more than I have already. I've only gone this far because I have a pretty good idea what she told you. It's probably the same thing she's told me."

"She said you and she were having an affair until she found out you were seeing another woman."

"She's not lying. For her, that's exactly what happened. She couldn't deal with what she interpreted as my rejection of her, no doubt mirroring her perception of her father's rejection of her. And so when I rejected her, as she saw it—for both ethical and medical reasons—she dealt with that by transforming the episode in her mind. She became delusional. She convinced herself that we had entered into an affair. She went so far as to imagine a rival, and actually to follow me in the evenings. Pretty soon she caught me with another woman, which is normal enough. I see a lot of women. In fact I've got to leave pretty soon to pick one up at her apartment.

"The woman Nora saw me with was another patient, though. Which is moderately uncommon but not unheard of. I occasionally see a patient socially, if I feel he or she has got back on a pretty solid emotional footing and the therapeutic relationship won't be damaged by it. That wasn't the case with Nora, not by a long shot. Her delusion proved it. She had constructed a very clever scenario that recapitulated what her relationship with her father had been. Love on her part. Met with rejection, abandonment and betrayal on his. You may not be aware of it, but her father was an alcoholic who died when she was a girl.

"At our next session Nora demanded that I drop the other patient. I realized that matters had gone too far to be salvaged. I gave her the names of two good female psychiatrists and I terminated the therapy. I hated to do it, because she was still deeply disturbed. But I didn't feel I had any other choice, medically speaking."

"And then right away she took up with Morty," I said. "On the rebound, so to speak. At least it would look that way to her, I guess."

"It probably would, yes."

"Did you know about it?"

"Oh, yes. Morty talked about it in our sessions. At first I was uneasy, since both of them were so troubled. But then I came to feel it was a constructive relationship for both of them. It was helping Morty recover from his long-standing depression over losing Kathy. Maybe—I have no way of knowing, but it seems possible—maybe it was helping Nora cope with the breakup of her imaginary affair with me."

"It didn't bother Morty that his girlfriend had this delusion?"

"He didn't know about it. She was shrewd enough not to try her story out on him. Like everybody else in the Poor Attitudes, she knew that Morty and I go back a long way. Our personal and professional relationship was very solid, and I suspect she hesitated to challenge that with her story. It's even possible that she knew on a certain level that the story was untrue."

"And she wouldn't want to run any risk of alienating Morty," I said. "Not when she was getting close to that much money."

"I don't think that was it at all," Unger said. "I think her attraction to him was perfectly sincere. The money may even have seemed like an obstacle to her. Nora needs love, not money."

"That's the way she struck me, too."

"Why did you suggest she was a gold digger, then?"

"I just wanted to see how you'd handle it."

Unger's eyes narrowed a little bit, but then the beginning of a scowl went away and he grinned. "Who the hell am I to complain?" he said. "I provoke responses for a living myself."

— 11 —

Monday, Wednesday, and Friday mornings I go up and down, up and down on my bed, doing four hundred sit-ups. Once you've worked up to the point where you can do a hundred or so sit-ups, there's no limit. You can keep on doing them until boredom sets in, because exhaustion won't stop you. It's sub-aerobic, so the lactic acid doesn't build up any faster than the bloodstream can carry it away from the muscles. I stop at four hundred because if I go on much longer, the skin over my tail bone rubs raw.

The intellectual equivalent of doing sit-ups is watching the network morning shows, and so I graze among the three of them with my remote control while bobbing up and down on my bed like any other yo-yo. Zap, so much for our latest drug czar and here comes an actress who has just finished working with the most wonderful people on the most wonderful film and zap, so much for her and here comes Willard Scott. Maybe I'll live long enough for Willard to show my picture to the folks someday and call me a fine-looking old gentleman. If only I do enough sit-ups.

But I finished my four hundred anyway. It was Wednesday, and that's what I do Wednesday mornings. After that I took my shower and walked down to the Li'l Peach for a *Globe,* and took it back home to read it. Today my mugging of Warren W. Westfall had made the third page of the metro section, a one-column headline over a three-inch story. Plainly the story wouldn't have made the paper at all if some police reporter hadn't recognized the victim's name. The prominent business leader had been attacked in the garage of his home by a masked intruder who broke his finger and stole his wallet. No mention of the massage I had given him, or of the credit card withdrawals I had made. Maybe he hadn't heard about those yet.

So that was that. I had gotten clean away with my first mugging, although getting away with muggings wasn't much to brag about. Any moron can do it, to judge by Mike Tyson. Still I felt good about it. I wished I could have taken the *Globe*'s story straight to Hope and laid it at her feet, proud as a cat with a dead rat. But even Tyson wouldn't be that dumb.

I couldn't tell Jerome Rosson my news either, since he was another officer of the court. But as it turned out I didn't have to. "See what happened to our pal Westfall?" the lawyer asked when I called him to report that I hadn't learned anything much from my interviews the day before.

"I was just reading about it in the *Globe,*" I said. "I'm pretty broken up."

"Well, you don't wish something like that on anybody, of course . . ." Rosson said.

"I do. That bastard could be robbed every night of his life, and it still wouldn't be as much as he's stolen over the years."

"I suppose that's true, isn't it? Speaking of Westfall, I got a call yesterday from his claims adjustment man, what's his name . . . wait a minute, I've got it, right here . . ."

"Myron Cooper?"

"That's it. Here's my note. Wants you to call him on an urgent basis. His words. What do you suppose he wants?"

"I don't know," I said, and I damned sure didn't. Naturally my first thoughts were guilty ones, but I couldn't see any way he'd be onto me for my payback of Westfall. "Cooper doesn't even work for Westfall anymore. I called him at Pilgrim last week and they said he was no longer employed by the company."

"Maybe this is his home number, then."

The number he read was a Newton exchange. After Rosson hung up I called and a woman answered, which surprised me. I had never considered that there might be a Mrs. Myron Cooper, although why not? Cooper was an asshole, true enough, but for every man there's a mate.

"I'll see if Mr. Cooper is available," the mate said, as if he might have been in conference. Maybe he had got her from the secretarial pool. Mr. Cooper did turn out to be available, because he came on the line and I heard the click as his wife hung up.

"Tom," he said, old pals. "Boy, you're a hard man to find."

"Yeah, well, you did it. What do you want?"

"I want to get you together with the old man, actually."

"What old man?"

"Mr. Westfall."

"How come you're in charge of his schedule, Myron? He fired your ass."

"Oh, shit, didn't you ever have a CO like that? He gets mad and fires you one day, the next day he forgets all about it."

"How come I'm calling you at home, then?"

"Taking a few days off. Listen, what it is, he's been thinking about this material he has, on the Limbach thing. He's decided the hell with the lawyers, why not turn it over to you now? Your people are going to have to see it anyway, soon as legal paper gets filed in this thing. So why not now, huh?"

"Why not? Have him messenger it over to Rosson."

"He took a liking to you, Tom. Wants to deal directly with you. Can you see him at eleven tonight?"

"The Hocker does business at eleven?"

"It's the earliest he can get to it. He's tied up all day and he has some charity thing this evening, but he'll be finished by eleven."

"Where do we meet, Myron? In the graveyard?"

"Graveyard? No, he wants to do it in the Public Garden."

"Naturally you're bullshitting me, right, Myron?"

"No, that's where he wants to do it. There's a big tree over by the lake where they got the swan boats. Only tree with a bench under it. You know the one?"

"I could probably find it."

"That's where, then. Eleven, okay?"

"Sure, sure, Myron. I'll be there."

"Eleven sharp, okay?"

"Count on it, Myron. Bench. Big tree. Public Garden. Midnight."

"Jesus, Tom, stop rattling my cage. Eleven."

I hung up and would have laughed if there had been anybody to hear it. No way was I going to meet a guy in the middle of the Public Garden in the middle of the night. Particularly not a guy who had tried to kill me once already.

But then something else struck me. What kind of party would Cooper be setting up for me that the Hocker had to be there for, too? At the very least, it ought to be amusing to hear what the two of them had to say to each other while they were waiting for me. Shit, now I was curious.

But I couldn't scratch my itch till after dark, so I had all

186

day to play with Morty Limbach's software. I was in that honeymoon phase with my Macintosh, where you're still trying out new positions. It had been tough not to buy all the swell new programs in the catalogs and the computer magazines, the programs that will shave seconds every month off the minutes you spend balancing your check-book. Or they will once you've put in a couple of days figuring out the program and punching your lifetime financial history into the computer. And now, thanks to Morty, I could waste all this time for free.

Among his toys, Limbach had programs to organize your slides, do your taxes, score your music, correct your gram-mar, publish your own newsletter, write your own will, and, sure enough, balance your own checkbook.

I started out by installing a little program that would avoid screen burnout by switching over to shifting patterns while the computer was on but unused. I could even fill my screen with little dancing swastikas, if I ever managed to figure out the manual. Cooper was the one who made me think of it. For the moment, though, I went to work installing all kinds of new typographic fonts that would allow me to self-publish, if I should ever happen to self-write. And so it went till suppertime, when I heated up some lamb stew in the microwave and washed it down with India Pale Ale. After that I went back to playing with my new computer toys, till it was time to go.

I walked to Harvard Square and headed underground. Taking the T seemed wiser than running the risk of being towed, ticketed, or stolen on the streets around the Com-mon. By the time I got off the Green Line at Boylston it was twenty till ten and had been fully dark for a long time. There were streetlights around the outside of the Garden and at intervals inside, but once you got out of their reach it was hard to make things out. Myron had made a good choice. No one in his right mind would be out here at this time of night.

I left the path well before getting to the bench he had specified, and circled over the lawn toward it. Whenever I reached a bush or tree I stopped to listen. The only sounds were the regular undercurrents of the city outside the park—horns, sirens, traffic. When I got near the bench I stopped and listened again. Once I was satisfied no one was around, I climbed onto the bench, and pulled myself up into the tree. Most of the leaves were gone, but these were city boys who wouldn't think to look up into a tree. Even if they did look, they wouldn't see anything against the dark sky. Or so I hoped. Up about ten feet I found a perch that seemed comfortable.

It wasn't. After a minute the branch started to dig into me, and I had to shift around. It took me a little while longer to figure out that the only way to handle it was to crouch monkey-style, holding on to an upper branch to keep my balance, but with my weight on my feet where it belonged. Probably that's why we have arches, to curve over boughs. I lit the tiny light on my throwaway Casio. Just past ten. About an hour to go.

I waited and waited and waited. Very hard to wait, crouching in a tree. Better than sitting in one, but not by much. I took to counting seconds, one one hundred, two one hundred. Every three minutes I raised myself from a crouch to a semicrouch, to ease the knee joints. Twice people came along the nearby path. Once it was a man with a huge plastic bag of empty cans slung over his shoulder. The other time it was four young music lovers with a boombox. It was playing one of Screw U-2's greatest hits, "Power Dick." Some of the lyrics were a little hard to make out, but I caught, "Couldn't wait no more, had to have a lick first time she see my power dick." Thank God for the First Amendment, or we'd still be stuck with Cole Porter.

I waited, and waited some more. I checked my watch. Almost half past ten, another half hour to go. And then I heard footsteps and voices approaching. As they got nearer, I could make out Myron's voice first, sounding urgent, and then Westfall's, talking less. They stopped in front of the bench, almost below me. At first I thought Westfall was carrying a handkerchief, but then I made it out to be a cast on the finger I had broken. By now my eyes were so used to the gloom that I could see reasonably well by the light of the street lamp down the path. But the tree trunk and a couple of branches kept me from getting a clear view of the two men.

"He'll be here any minute, Mr. Westfall," Cooper was saying. "I told him ten-thirty."

Interesting. Why would he want the Hocker to show up a half an hour before me? An answer occurred to me, but I dismissed it. Myron wouldn't have the balls, now that he was self-employed.

"Hey, what if Bethany did see the guy that robbed me?" Westfall asked. "That's what I keep telling you, Myron. What that amounts to, seeing the guy, is absolute fucking zip."

"He says he'll trade for the guy's plate number."

"Which he got because he was following me the same time this thief was following me, too? Even if that's true, Myron, think the thing through, for Christ's sake. We get a number from Bethany, and maybe it's the number of some guy he's got a hard-on for, or maybe he just made a number up so I'll show him the suicide note and he'll look good to his boss. But suppose it's actually the right number, the right guy? We still haven't got shit, Myron. You were a fucking cop in the service. Even a military court wouldn't convict without more evidence than that. Fact it's not evidence at all."

"Hey, Mr. W—"

"Don't call me Mr. W, for Christ's sake, I told you already. It just sounds stupid."

"I'm sorry, Mr. Westfall . . ."

"How come you don't call me Hocker? You done it on the tape."

"Look, I'm sorry . . ."

"Now you want me to hire you back with a pile of shit like you're talking about here, that it couldn't convict a fucking dogcatcher?"

"No, sir, I'm not talking conviction here. I'm talking taking care of him personally, this guy that robbed you."

"Oh, sure, great. Like you took care of Bethany personally, huh? That was a brilliant move, you go behind my back and try to snuff some harmless fuck like you're the fucking Providence mob, and the upshot is I got to pay off two niggers for letting a Communist kick the shit out of them."

"It was a mistake in judgment, I admit it. That's what I'm doing here, Mr. Westfall, trying to make up for my mistake in judgment. Bethany's end of this agreement is that he goes after this guy, this mugger, and takes care of him. He's not a Communist, Mr. Westfall, honest to Christ. He was CIA in Laos, he's a good American. He knows how to kill."

"I wonder if you got any idea, Myron, just how crazy you sound. Let me tell you straight, since it's obvious by now this dickhead Bethany isn't coming, that the only reason I'm here is to get something for nothing. I got to give that suicide note to them sooner or later, I only been holding on to the thing to jerk that cunt lawyer's chain. So if Bethany's really got information on who robbed me, I get it for nothing. If he's got no information, which is probably exactly what he's got, then we both get nothing and it's a wash. But either way, Myron, you get nothing. What do you think, I'm going to put some asshole back on my payroll that runs around behind my back calling me an asshole in front of a TV camera? Forget it, Myron. We done business for a long time but no more, so just forget it."

"I'm sorry you feel that way, Mr. W."

"What's the matter you call me that, asshole? Didn't I just fucking get through telling you—"

A movement through the branches, and a dull noise, not very loud. Then a louder noise, like a duffel bag hitting the floor. Then Myron grunting with effort and saying, *"Ass, hole, ass, hole, ass . . ."* and the dull noise along with each word, like beating time. Around the trunk I saw a couple of feet, jerking to the same beat. As soon as it registered on me what was going on, I jumped.

I landed on top of Cooper, knocking him flat. With somebody under me I reacted without thinking, in the way I had been trained most of my life to do. I immobilized him, not that there's much to immobilize after 180 pounds free-falls ten feet onto your back. I jacked his right foot up to his wide butt, put my weight on the trapped leg, and took a look to see what we had here.

Some sort of small club was lying beside Cooper. He had used it to beat in the top of Westfall's head, as nearly as I could tell in the shadows. I finally remembered that I had a tiny Mag-lite on my key chain, and I risked shining its beam around for a moment. The thing on the ground was a blackjack with a braided handle. Its butt was an SS death's head, the kind that the fancy Nazi daggers have. The top of Westfall's head had looked black in the dark, but in the flashlight beam it was red, with a little white showing where Myron had beaten through the bone to the brain. I twisted the light off, and ran my free hand all over Myron. Nothing but his handcuffs, which were on his belt again. I took them off his belt again—the same handcuffs I kept using on him. "Myron, you dumb fuck," I said softly as I worked. He mumbled something. Still dazed, but coming around. Before he could make a fuss about it, I hand-cuffed him to Westfall's wrist. I tossed the key a few yards away, invisible in the darkness. I did the same thing with the blackjack, careful not to smudge up Myron's prints. Next I made myself go through the dead man's pockets to see if he had brought along the famous suicide note. He hadn't. Then I wiped my prints off the cuffs with my hand-kerchief and sat down on the bench to wait for Myron to come around.

"Oh, Jesus," he said when he did. He had just tried to move, and discovered that he was chained to Westfall.

"You dumb fuck," I said, again.

I don't think he realized I was there till I spoke, because he started, and turned to look at where I was sitting in the darkness.

"Oh, Jesus," he said. He was repeating himself, too. "I told you eleven."

"That's it, Myron? You kill somebody and that's what you got to say? Well, shit, I came early to get a good seat."

"Let me loose, Bethany," he said. "I can take a second mortgage on the house, honest to Christ. I got plenty equity in it."

Cooper's thoughts were moving in funny ways, but I tried to catch up to them. I said, "You got to be shitting me, Myron. I let you go, and you go straight to First Boston tomorrow, get a big pile of money for me? I guess I got a problem seeing how that would work out in real life."

I got up to go.

"Where are you going?" Myron said, sounding close to breakdown. "You can't just leave me here."

Actually that was exactly what I had in mind, having figured out by now what the purpose of this whole weird scene was.

"Why not?" I said. "You think for some peculiar reason the cops might happen to come by just about the time you told me to show up? And then it wouldn't be me they'd catch with the body, it would be you? Too bad, Myron, but basically so what? I don't give a shit if your Nazi ass gets reamed at Walpole for thirty straight years."

I turned and started walking again. I thought he might start crying or pleading, but there was a little more to him than I thought. I heard a dragging, hitching sound which had to be the live bastard dragging the dead one toward some leafless shrubbery ten or fifteen yards away. It wouldn't work, at least not for very long, but what else could he try?

I walked over to Charles Street where it cuts between the Public Garden and Boston Common and stood there to wait. Myron might have been the one waiting there, if only things had worked out better for him. I figured he would have arranged for the cops to come five minutes or so after I was due. Sure enough, the sirens sounded just after eleven. I headed across the Common toward the Park Street station.

It wasn't the nearest station, but it was where the Red and Green lines crossed. It was busy even at this hour, and consequently anonymous. The entrance to the tunnel that leads to the Red Line outbound is faced with dark red tiles, so it's like going down into a blood vessel. I sat on a bench to wait for the next train to Harvard Square. In the light I noticed a piece of whitish stuff stuck to the front of my black windbreaker, up near the shoulder. It was a piece of Westfall's brain, had to be. I knew how it got there, too, from hearing Gladys Williams talk about crime scenes. It isn't the impact of the hacking and battering that splatters stuff all around. It's the back cast, so to speak, of the weapon. Things fly off it. That's what the crime scene technicians call them, flyers.

It was a jacket I liked, but I took it off anyway. I drifted over to a trash can and dropped it in when nobody seemed to be paying attention. Let some other guy walk around with Warren Westfall on him.

Back home I thought about what Cooper was probably telling the cops just about now, and it came to me that I could use a friend with high credibility. And so I called Felicia Lamport, a poet who was married to a retired Episcopal bishop. She herself had never retired; being a poet is apparently a lifetime sentence. Years ago, Felicia had spotted me crashing the course on Gerard Manley Hopkins that she still taught at the Harvard extension school. She thought that sneaking in showed good spirit on my part, so she let me stay as long as I didn't tell any of her paying customers I was getting a round on the house. We have been friends ever since. A friend is somebody who throws on some clothes and comes over without being asked, when you call her in the middle of the night with a certain tone in your voice.

"I got myself mixed up with something earlier tonight, and it worked out different than I thought it would," I told Felicia when I had got her comfortably settled down with a hot chocolate. "It worked out pretty bad."

"Tell me about it," Felicia said. And so I got myself a beer and did. She was one of the half-dozen or so people I would tell the truth to, about something like this. Gladys and Hope were on the short list, too. In fact the whole list was women; I don't have much in the way of male friends.

"I saw plenty of people dead before," I said when I was done. "But this is the first time I ever saw anybody actually being killed."

Felicia leaned forward and patted my hand. It startled me a little. In all the years we've been friends, it was the first time I remembered her touching me. I managed a smile, she took back her hand after the pat was finished, and that was that.

"My mother used to raise rabbits in a shed out back," I said. "When she figured I was old enough to take my turn, eight or nine I guess, she sent me out to kill one for supper. Big Flemish doe about the size of a cocker spaniel, looked like to me. The way you did, you'd grab them by the small of the back, hold them up head down, then club them at the base of the skull. I knew all about that, saw my older brothers do it a hundred times. So I hoisted that doe up and gave her my best shot with the sawed-off hoe handle we used to use. She just hung there kind of dazed, but still moving. So I clubbed her two or three times more and she still wouldn't die. This was the rabbit from hell. Naturally my brothers are laughing like crazy all this time. I had to lay her out on the frozen ground so I'd have something to hit against and I kept whacking away till she finally died, and they kept laughing. Each time I'd whack, the rabbit's hind legs would quiver just like Westfall's."

"What a horrible story," Felicia said. "Now your story about tonight, I don't regard that as nearly so horrible."

"You don't?"

"Of course not. But then I've met Mr. Westfall. He was a very rude man."

I looked at her in surprise, and then had to laugh. "Felicia," I said, "you're too much."

"Why? He *was* rude."

"Yeah, but that doesn't carry the death penalty."

"It should. In fact, that should be the only permissible grounds for capital punishment. I must write Jesse Helms about that."

"Yeah, straighten him out."

"Seriously, Tom, you didn't kill the revolting Mr. Westfall and you tried to stop him being killed once you saw what was going on."

"I can't say I minded much, though."

"I can't say I'd mind much if one of Jesse Helms's friends

from the Klan killed *him*. Now, that doesn't make me a murderer, and you're not one, either, but that may not be what the police think. Consequently, if asked I shall tell them I spent a quiet evening with you, during which you tried in vain to sell me on the virtues of word processing."

"You don't have to do this, Felicia."

"I'm perfectly well aware of that."

"What will the bishop think?" The bishop was really an ex-bishop, or bishop emeritus, or whatever they call them in the Episcopal Church. As a kind soul and a believer in the perfectibility of man, he had a less realistic view of the world than his wife did. For instance, he had been glad to see the King James version of the Bible go out of use, because he figured his people would have an easier time understanding the new translation. Felicia hated the new version. Her view was that religion was poetry, not prose. Only a few people were able to understand it anyway, and the rest were better off mystified. Let them listen to the music of the language and do as their betters told them. The bishop would just listen to his wife's foolishness, and smile fondly, and go on believing what he had always believed.

"What will the bishop think?" Felicia repeated. "I shouldn't worry about it if I were you. The bishop has been defending himself very well for seventy-two years now. That's the way the French describe the ability to communicate in human speech, did you know that? True. Ask a Frenchman if he speaks some language or other, and he replies that he is able to defend himself in it. Don't you find that to be an interesting view of the function of speech?"

"Well, yes . . ."

"If someone should ask me if I spoke English, it would never occur to me to reply that I defend myself in it. I'd say that I delight myself in it."

* * *

The TV news readers were all over the story next morning, flies settling on Westfall's carcass. All three stations had pretty much the same story, as usual, and pretty much the same pictures, as usual. The pictures could have come from the stock footage of any TV station in the country: blue lights blinking, emergency technicians hustling a sheet-covered stretcher out of a wooded area at night. The cameras had got there too late to film Myron while he was still cuffed to his victim. Too bad. Great visuals. But all they got was the standard shot of a frightened piece of shit being shoved headfirst into a police car.

The story was a good one, not so standard. Rough-and-tumble corporate raider. (Rough-and-tumble *is the way they say* bully *on television.*) Worth listed by *Forbes* at $250 million. *(Sure. I knew a man who made the* Forbes *list at $125 million; he died the next year, leaving $8 million.)* Supporter of Reagan's Contras and other conservative charities. Brutally bludgeoned to death by a Nazi blackjack, being held as evidence. Assailant had evidently dragged his handcuffed victim to secluded spot not far from victim's luxurious Beacon Hill town house. (Shot of luxurious Beacon Hill town house. Shot of secluded spot.) Disgruntled former employee, Vietnam vet, charged with the murder. *(Fifty years from now, let some old fart in a nursing home beat another one to death with his crutch and TV will call him a Vietnam vet.)* Police alerted by anonymous caller to 911. (Tape played, with a transcript of the words moving right along underneath. Words used as visuals.) Police asking the caller to identify herself, to aid in prosecution. *(The voice sounded like Myron's wife's, assuming his wife was the woman who had picked up when I called his house. Myron evidently didn't know that all 911 calls were recorded, which everybody else in Boston has known since the Stuart murder case. Myron was even dumber than I thought.)* Suspect claims murder committed by man who jumped out of a tree and then handcuffed him to the victim. *(Lots of luck, Myron, with that ludicrous story.)* Handcuff key found nearby, where the accused murderer apparently lost it in the darkness. (Shot of the key in question.)

I showered and headed down to the Tasty, figuring I'd better be on hand for the calls as they came in. The first one was from the man who was technically my boss, Jerome Rosson. He was at home but just about to jump on the T. He'd stop off on his way to law school to meet me on the Holyoke Center terrace. I had time to finish my breakfast. I was eating oatmeal, which I ordered because they were breaking in a new cook and it's hard to screw up oatmeal. No matter what you do with the stuff, it still comes out wholesome and tasteless. The Mondale of cereals.

I had just picked out a place on the terrace when Rosson came up, hustling along with his hand already out to shake mine when he was still two or three paces away. Always a day late and a dollar down. I took his hand when it eventually got within reach. He shook it in a flash and then lit on the edge of the chair, as if he were going to take wing again in a second.

"While I was watching the news I got a call from the Boston homicide bureau asking me to get in touch with you immediately," he said. "Evidently this fellow Cooper told them I knew how to reach you. What the hell is going on?"

"You think I should talk without my lawyer present?"

"Huh? Oh, I see what you mean. Fine, I'll represent you. Now you're my client as well as my employee. Whatever you say is fully privileged under the client-attorney et cetera. So say."

"Cooper wanted to kill the Hocker for firing him, and he wanted to blame it on me. His idea was to leave the body there and have the cops catch me right near . . ."

When I had finished, Rosson stopped fidgeting for a minute while he processed the information. Then he leaned forward and started drumming on the cast-iron table with his fingers. "Okay, okay, okay," he said. "Why did Cooper go to all this trouble to nail you?"

"Because I was the one who got him fired."

"How and why?"

"As my employer, you might not want to know."

"Your employer just took a walk. This is your attorney speaking."

I told him how I had humiliated Cooper twice, getting him fired the second time.

"No real problem," Rosson said at the end. "If Cooper has any brains at all, he'll see that telling the cops what you did to him would just dig him in deeper. Give him a motive to frame you. But he doesn't seem to have any brains at all, does he? So he probably *has* told them. He will have said you got him in trouble twice, and last night you were doing it again. You killed his former boss and tried to pin it on him. Why did this guy always want to get you in trouble? the cops will ask. Good question. What's the answer?"

Well, because of what he said about Hope, for one thing. So I told him about that.

"Okay, fine," Rosson said. "But you didn't have to carpet-bomb the son of a bitch, did you?"

Rosson didn't have the whole picture, of course. He didn't know that Hope and I were lovers, and I wasn't going to tell him. Still he was right that I had overreacted. And I had thought about why, but I couldn't come up with the answer. I supposed the only answer was I did it because of who I am. And, like everybody else, I can't really figure out why I am who I am. Anyway, I gave him what was probably a piece of the answer. It went back to the time little street kids had picked my pocket in Saigon.

"I grabbed one of them," I said. "He was tiny, no bigger than an American first-grader. I could feel the bones in his arm, like chicken bones. He was scared to death, the little kid. What was I supposed to do with him? I held on to him a few minutes, feeling worse about myself all the time, then I let him go."

"Sure," Rosson said. "What else could you do?"

"Other things were possible. For instance, when I was bouncing Cooper around I asked him did he ever make people cry when he was an air policeman in Vietnam. He said sometimes kids. When they would steal from the PX."

"Long time ago," Rosson said. "Little late in the day for such a disproportionate reaction, isn't it?"

"Yes."

"Why did you do it, then?"

"Probably the same reason a dog licks his balls."

"Why's that?"

"Because he can."

Rosson chewed that over a moment, and smiled. "Well, maybe your reasons were good enough, whatever they were," he said. "Certainly it couldn't have happened to two nicer guys."

The professor and I were a little bit alike, as far as I could see. Maybe he couldn't wrestle fat bullies to the floor, but he made a career of stomping them to death in court.

"Right now, though, it doesn't matter why you did it," Rosson said. "Doesn't even matter *whether* you did it. Police aren't likely to care very much one way or another. But you better be ready to explain why you didn't call them after you overpowered the murderer."

"I wasn't around for the murder, actually," I said. "I showed up late for my appointment and left when I saw police all over the place."

"Well, it could work. Although it doesn't explain how Cooper got handcuffed to his victim."

"Hard to say. My guess is that Westfall got suspicious, and Cooper had to use the cuffs to drag him into the park. Beat him to death, and then couldn't find the key to the handcuffs. Result of which he got caught in the trap he meant to set for me."

We went over to one of the line of pay phones in Harvard Square, not old-fashioned booths but modern things with no roof to keep the rain off and no shelf to put your spare change on. Evidently the phone company isn't making as much money as it wants to from pay phones. So the company is making them as inconvenient and overpriced as possible, the same strategy the railroads used so successfully to kill off passenger service. Rosson arranged for the homicide detectives to meet us at two, in the reading room of the Harvard faculty club. "I don't think I've set foot in the club in over a year," he said after he hung up. "But all those old portraits on the wall ought to keep the cops polite."

Something did. The two detectives wrote down everything I said just as if it were true, and only seemed really interested when I gave them Felicia's name. "Lamport?" one of them asked. "Haven't I heard that name somewhere before?"

Probably he had, since the bishop was always getting hauled away limp from pro-choice demonstrations. But these guys didn't strike me as big libbers, so I thought I'd emphasize another one of his interests.

"Her husband is Bishop Lamport," I said. "The one who set up the big homeless shelter in East Cambridge."

"Oh, yeah," the detective said.

"You spent the night in your apartment with the wife of a bishop?" asked his partner, who seemed to be the smarter one.

"She's got probably thirty years on me," I said. "We're just friends."

201

How I could tell the detectives were satisfied with my story was that after a while they drew us into their circle, all pals, by telling us what they had on Cooper. "We're talking serious nut case here," the smarter one said. "The fucker—pardon my French, counsellor—anyway, this nutso had a Hitler room in his basement. His wife was scared to death of him. Know what he done right after they got married? Made her change her name legally to Eva. You imagine that shit?"

Then he got worried that we might not understand. "You get it, don't you?" he said. "Eva?"

"Hitler's girlfriend, right?" I asked. "Eva Braun?"

"Right. So Eva says—Eva Cooper I mean—she says her husband has money in his will for that Nazi guy that's a senator in Louisiana, what's his name?"

"David Duke," Rosson said. "I don't think he's a Nazi, though. I think he's a Republican."

"Whatever."

"But there might be some Nazi element in this killing," the professor went on, laying down smoke. "Westfall was supposed to be involved with a lot of far right-wing stuff himself. Could be worth a look."

"Ahh, we got all we need. You got a fired employee cuffs himself to his boss, then drags the son of a bitch into the park in the middle of the night and beats him to death with a Nazi blackjack and fingerprints all over it, well, you don't have to look much further."

After the detectives left, we set out across the Yard. Rosson was going to the law school and I had been headed for the stacks at Widener Library to educate myself about primogeniture. Passing all your money down to the first-born son was such an obviously stupid idea that I couldn't see why we ever gave it up. I was building up a file on primogeniture and inheritance in general for a possible chapter in the possible book I may possibly someday write. Possibly the title will be *What Makes Us So Dumb*.

But the business about David Duke and the will had just made me think of something else. "We were talking about Morty's will earlier," I said to Rosson. "Did he write it himself?"

"No, I wrote it."

"Were there any earlier wills that he might have written himself?"

"No, and that was strange, actually. A man with an estate that size, you'd expect him to have a will. But he said he had never had one before. Why do you ask?"

"Because I just woke up and smelled the coffee. I was going through some of his software yesterday, and there was a will-making program in it. Why would he buy a program when he already had a will?"

"And a lawyer, if he wanted a new one drawn up," Rosson said. "I don't know the answer."

— 12 —

INSTEAD OF HEADING FOR THE LIBRARY STACKS, I TURNED around and walked back to my apartment. I made myself a pot of tea and set to work looking for a will among Morty's computer files. Nothing listed on the directories of his data disks had a file name that suggested a will. I was just about resigned to calling up each file on the new disks for individual inspection, when it occurred to me that I might get a clue if I looked at the will-making program itself and found out how it worked. There was a tutorial that walked you through the process, and once I called it up I had my answer. To write his will, Morty hadn't bothered to go any further than the tutorial on the program disk. He had just filled in the blanks for names and numbers. The date at the top was a week before his death.

This time he had still left a million dollars to his old college and a quarter of a million to his prep school. But he had eliminated the bequests to his mother and the Poor Attitudes Theater Foundation. Half of the rest went to Nora Dawson ''in the hope that she will use some of it to continue support of the Poor Attitudes." The other half went to Leo Grasso, Jr. Nora I could understand, but Leo Grasso, Jr.? In Little Leo's eighteen months of life he must have earned more money than any baby in history. If Limbach wanted to leave his fortune to the two great loves of his life, why not split it between Nora and Kathy? And where was the actual will, anyway? What good was an unsigned and unwitnessed will, sitting in a computer? And if the will existed on paper, who were the witnesses?

Nobody at the Poor Attitudes had mentioned a will, but then I had never asked. I headed over to the mansion, figuring it would be the logical place for him to go for signatures. The troupe was rehearsing again, and I sat down prepared to wait awhile. But they were just about done, as it turned out. Ned Levine came over when they broke up.

"Doing any good?" he asked.

"I don't know," I said. "Maybe."

"Maybe us, too. We sounded okay today. Jesus, I hope things work at the gala."

"Ned, help me with something. Do you know anything about Morty's will?"

"Not really. I just witnessed it."

Simple as that.

"Anybody else know what was in it?" I asked.

"I don't know myself. He just showed me where to witness his signature on the last page, and I signed. I didn't read it."

"Who was the other signer?"

"Nora."

I went over to her and asked if we could talk someplace else. She took me to the backyard, where we crunched through unraked leaves to a couple of beaten-up old Adirondack chairs. We brushed the leaves off them and sat down.

"Did you read the will?" I asked.

205

"No. He just folded it up to the back page. There were only a few lines of legal garbage on the page I saw, and then the spaces for the signatures."

"You say 'it.' Was there just the one copy?"

"That's all I signed was one."

"Did he tell you about what was in it?"

"No."

"Did you ask?"

"Of course not. That was exactly the kind of thing I'd never ask him about, who his money was going to. Jesus!"

"Practically half of it was going to you."

"You're shitting me," she said. If she wasn't taken completely by surprise, she was a hell of an actress. Of course she probably was a hell of an actress.

"Must be millions," she said absently, thinking it through. "That doesn't leave me looking so good, does it?"

"Why not?"

"I'm the one who's sleeping with him. He dies during some kind of weird sex play. I inherit a fortune. What would anybody think? Shit, I'd think it myself if I didn't know different."

I didn't answer, and she thought some more. "What if I gave the money back?" she said at last. "Then nobody would think I did it, would they?"

"I doubt if you could give it back. You'd have to ask a lawyer. I guess you could give it away, though. Once you got it. But where's the will?"

"You don't have it? How could you know what's in it, then?"

"At the moment it's nothing but a bunch of magnetized oxide molecules on one of Morty's computer disks. Do you have any idea what he did with the hard copy?"

"Hard copy?"

"The actual pieces of paper. The document you witnessed."

"No. I never asked him about it again and he never mentioned it."

I called Professor Rosson from the Poor Attitudes House and told him about the missing will. "Sounds legal enough," he said. "There's a slight potential problem in that one of the witnesses was a beneficiary."

"She didn't read it, though. She and the other witness signed it one right after another, and all they saw was the back page."

"Well, that might help. In any case, the question probably wouldn't even arise unless the will were contested. The more serious problem is that, legally speaking, the new will doesn't really exist unless we can find it." He paused to think things through. "Even so," he said, "it certainly changes the way things look, doesn't it?"

It certainly did. For the first time, we had possible motives for murder. Nora and Kathy would get control of large fortunes from Morty's death, or at least might think they would. Teddy Elliman would be a major loser under the new will—or a major winner if it disappeared. The same was true of Sally Limbach.

"I guess you'd better come over to the office," Rosson said. "We need to talk about this."

When I got there he had just finished talking to Mrs. Limbach on the phone. "She didn't have much to say," he said, "but the way she said it was very interesting indeed."

"How do you mean?"

"Listen for yourself. I tape all my calls in case there's something I need to refresh myself on later. This one was definitely a keeper."

I heard my own voice, since my call had evidently been the one immediately preceding. Then the click as I hung up, and then whoever answered the phone at the Limbach house. Rosson talked his way past the woman, and then Mrs. Limbach came on the line.

"I'm afraid you'll have to call my attorneys, Mr. Rosson," she said. "Mr. Atwell or Mr. Parker, the elder Mr. Parker, at Longstreet Foxcroft Firth and Parker."

"It isn't really a legal point I'm calling about, Mrs. Limbach. Point of information, really. A family thing I thought you might be able to help on."

"I'm sure Mr. Parker—"

"I'm calling about your son's new will."

"Where did you . . ." It was a long pause. "You'll need to talk to Mr. Parker," Mrs. Limbach said at last. Click.

"Hardly legal proof, of course," Rosson said to me.

"She knows it exists, though," I said.

"Yes, and I wonder how? I didn't even know, and I was Morty's lawyer."

"Yeah, and what's that all about? Why didn't he have you draw up the damned thing? Was he afraid you might have disapproved of leaving the money to Nora and Little Leo?"

"I doubt it. He knew I thought Teddy Elliman was a pompous hustler, but that didn't stop him having me draw up the original will with Teddy in it. Morty listened to my reservations, but he went ahead anyway."

"This time he didn't want you to know, though. Why else would he have gone out and bought a kit and made himself a secret will?"

"Not so secret. Seems his mother knew about it."

"He didn't like her much," I said, thinking about the mommydeer of the Downdump files. "Could he have told her about the new will to hurt her?"

"Doesn't sound like Morty."

"After Morty's body was found," I said, "we know that his mother sent the Hocker over to his condo. To clean things up, I imagine. Considering how he died, no telling what might be lying around the house."

"Could be," Rosson said. "That's the way her dull and proper mind would work, all right."

"Well, we pretty much know the Hocker walked off with the so-called suicide note. So he probably walked off with the new will, too."

"And gave it to her?"

"Let's think about it. Did she know she was in the old will?"

"Morty told all the beneficiaries, yes."

"So she would have thought she'd get two million bucks when Morty died. I wonder if the Hocker knew that?"

"Too late to ask him."

"Suppose he did, though. What would he do? He has a piece of paper that could cost an old lover two million dollars. Sentiment probably wouldn't enter into it. He'd be figuring how he could get the most advantage out of the situation. What would that be?"

"Impossible to say," the professor said. "Too many unknowns in the equation."

"It's worth poking into, anyway," I said. Rosson didn't ask me what kind of poking I had in mind, and so I didn't tell him. For all I knew, he might have an ethics problem.

I was grubbing through the weeds down the side of an embankment a few blocks from the town house of the late Warren W. Westfall. So far my big find had been the body of a long-dead dog. A road kill I figured, until I saw that somebody had tied the dog's feet together with wire. The poor animal had fallen into the hands of a subcanine species.

."What you looking for, mister?" a kid asked from the top of the embankment.

"A remote," I said. "You know, one of those things you switch channels with."

"A clicker," the kid's buddy said. "Man lose his clicker."

"Help me look, I'll give you five bucks if you find it."

"Each?"

"Ten bucks to the kid that finds it. Five for the other."

It took twenty minutes, but finally they came up with it. "Which one found it?" I said.

"We both did," said the kid who had it in his hand. He was standing out of my reach.

"You kids should be in cancer insurance," I said.

"Huh?"

I gave them a twenty-dollar bill and they gave me the Hocker's garage opener. Next I went to a hardware store, bought the tools I needed, and loaded them into the trunk of the Datsun. Then I went to a parking garage on the corner of Ellery Street, drove up a couple of ramps, and parked next to a Sentra that looked about right. It had a couple of weeks' buildup of dust on the windshield, undisturbed. No one was in sight. I unscrewed the plates, tossed them into my trunk with the other stuff, and moved my Datsun down a level. Then I walked to a Greek restaurant a few blocks away.

The food was lousy, as I should have known before I went in. The only thing Greeks cook that's worth eating is pizza, which is Italian. But the meal took up enough time so the garage attendant wouldn't wonder why I had paid a couple of bucks for driving in and driving right back out again. When I did drive out, the new plates were on my Datsun. I headed toward Beacon Hill. My idea was to drive right into the garage of Westfall's town house, as if I owned the place. Once before I had broken into a house. That time was at night, and I was scared people would see me breaking in, and I was scared they would see any lights I put on. This time I figured the brazen approach might be less scary, but I was wrong. I was still scared.

It was dusk when I drove past the entrance to the alleyway the first time, scouting. No lights were on in Westfall's house, naturally, but rear windows in most of the other houses were lit. Around the block again, working up nerve. The second time I made myself turn the Datsun into the alley, and then I nosed the car in toward the garage. Not hard so far. I could still back out. I pressed the button on the remote and the garage door rose. Still not hard. The hard part was letting out the clutch and driving inside.

It was like my first solo flight. The part that takes nerve isn't landing; once you're up in the air, you've got to land. The tough part is on the runway beforehand, forcing yourself to push the throttle to the firewall and then holding it there till it's too late to abort your takeoff. That moment came now, when the garage door slid down behind me. The fear didn't go away; safe landings are a lot harder than safe takeoffs. But the choice to put myself in danger had already been made. I switched on the garage lights and took the tools out of the trunk.

People fixate on doors. Bars. Locks stacked one on top of another. Rings full of keys. Alarm wires. Barlocks. Next people think about windows. Windows have catches and latches, bars, shutters, wiring running around the edges. Westfall's house had those wires, along with decals to tell you the wires were there. But people don't think much about what's in between the doors and windows, which is walls. Anyone who's ever worked construction knows that you can walk through most walls in seconds using nothing more than a hammer and a pry bar. Really solid construction might hold you up for a few minutes. The walls between garages and houses are seldom really solid construction. As it turned out, I didn't even need to use the power tools I had bought.

I poked a hole in the half-inch wallboard with my crowbar, then used the bent end to enlarge it. Then I poked a hole through the wallboard nailed to the other side of the studs. The beam from my little Mag-lite showed a pile of dinner plates, so I had found my way into a closet or cupboard. I moved over six feet and did the same thing again. This time the flashlight beam showed open space behind the interior wall. I yanked off slabs of wallboard until I had made my own doorway. The studs were set on sixteen-inch centers, leaving me plenty of room to step through sideways. Finding my way with my little pocket flash, I turned on the lights beside the real door to the kitchen. There was some kind of a device beside the switch that probably deactivated the alarm. I didn't touch it, since I had carried out an end run around the system.

The house had three floors. I climbed to the top and started down, looking in each door. Guest bedrooms and bathrooms I didn't worry about for the moment, and left dark. I left lights on in the master bedroom on the second floor, and in a sort of library-study on the ground floor, off the dining room. These seemed to be the most likely rooms for papers to wind up in, unless for some reason you wanted to hide them in an unlikely place. But I couldn't see why Westfall would have felt any great need to hide the will and the suicide note. So I moved quickly through the master bedroom, looking only in the places that a man would be likely to put papers away. Nothing in any of the drawers, or on top of the bureau, or on the bedside tables. I headed downstairs.

The ground-floor study was lined with books that had been bought by the yard, unless the Hocker had developed into a big Trollope fan on his way up life's ladder. The sets of nineteenth-century authors looked odd on the book-shelves, which looked like shelves in an auto parts store-room, pierced steel bolted together in tiers. Apart from the books in their leather bindings, everything in the room and in the house itself was desperately modern. I found the will the first place I looked, in the top middle drawer of the large, white desk. The steel drawer ran out smoothly on steel runners, very industrial-tech or whatever the look is called. At a fast glance the will seemed to be the same as the one in Morty's computer, only signed and witnessed. I put it in the inside pocket of my jacket and gave the rest of the room a fast scan. No suicide note that I could find. It was time to get out while my luck still held.

I went back upstairs to turn out the lights, looking as I went to see if there was anything I wanted to steal. Since I had already done the crime, I might as well profit by it. But there was nothing in the whole house I wanted badly enough to pick up and take. Not one thing. Left to himself, the Hocker probably would have bought one or two things by accident that weren't totally repulsive. He must have had outside help, from a really top-flight decorator, to assemble a houseful of objects without ever once crossing over the line into good taste. His lovely home was as repellent as Bette Midler's in *Ruthless People*. To go even a step further, it was ugly enough to be featured in the Design section of the Sunday *New York Times Magazine*. I knew it because right there on the wall of the Hocker's dining room was a framed page from that very section, showing the Hocker's dining room.

And so I left the exquisitely appointed town house of the late insurance mogul, carrying with me nothing but huge inheritances for an eighteen-month-old baby and a former 7-Eleven clerk from Dorchester. It was a good feeling.

After getting back home from my burglary I felt silly with relief, but I also felt as tired as I used to feel after a major tournament. Both put the same steady strain on the nerves, as the organism kept itself constantly ready for fight or, in the case of burglary, flight. Like pain, it was tiring. Just as if I had been hurt, I wanted sleep. The only thing I had on for Friday was to drop by the parking garage and return the plates, if the Sentra turned out to be still there. It wasn't exactly an appointment, and so I didn't set the alarm when I went to bed, or I didn't think I did. I was surprised when it went off at quarter till ten the next morning, until I figured out that the telephone was what was ringing. I did the best job I could of saying hello.

"You sound as if you're half asleep," Hope said.

"Could be," I said. "A few seconds ago I was all asleep."

"I'm sorry."

"No, you're not. You're glad. You've already rowed four miles on the Potomac, got the kids off to school, and put in a couple hours at the office. You hate me. What's up?"

"Big developments. Developments, anyway. I just got off the phone with Herb Clymer, he's the house counsel for Pilgrim Mutual? I was bugging him about the alleged suicide note and he said we can have the damned thing. He's messengering it over to the Tasty, care of you. Your secret is safe with me."

"What secret?"

"Your address. That you don't really live in an all-night lunch counter."

"Oh, that secret. Look, how come they changed their mind and sent it to you?"

"Basically because Westfall died. I knew Clymer slightly when I was an intern years ago. Not too bad a guy, but not very assertive. He was scared of the old management back then, and I bet he was a lot more scared when the Hocker took over. All Westfall told his legal department was that he had a suicide note, and evidently Clymer didn't insist on seeing it. The first time he came across it was yesterday, when he was going through the boss's files. Tom, we won't have any trouble with that note. It's the same one you saw in the computer, the one that quotes the Cummings poem. I asked him about a signature, and all it's got is the initials, M. L., on a computer printout. Even Westfall couldn't have taken that note very seriously. He must have just wanted us to work for our money."

"Wanted *you* to work for it, you mean."

"Well, maybe. Although it's hard to believe after all these years."

"Believe it. Did Clymer say anything about Morty's will?"

"I was getting to that. Jerry Rosson mentioned a new will yesterday, so I asked. Clymer hadn't heard anything about it."

"I've got it right here, signed and witnessed."

"You do! Where'd you get it? Wait a minute. Do I want to know?"

"I don't know. Do you?"

"Probably not, right?"

"Good choice."

"But I do want to know who benefits from the thing."

So I told her, and she said, "That could be important to us, you know."

"To us?"

"To the ACLU, that us. I've been looking up cases, and there's a chance we could lose a lot of money even if it isn't suicide."

"How's that?"

"Without getting into the boring details between an accidental means and an accidental results policy, it's at least possible that the company could argue successfully that the insured voluntarily placed himself in a situation carrying a high risk of death."

"Actually this guy Unger, the shrink, he said autoerotic asphyxia probably isn't particularly risky. It's just that the only cases anyone ever hears about are the occasional ones that turn out fatal."

"That's one argument, all right," Hope said. "But I keep

215

coming across an odd undercurrent in practically all the decisions. The unspoken feeling you get from the judge is that this form of behavior is so disgusting that the victim deserved to die. Nor should he be allowed to profit from it.''

"Is that the kind of clear thinking you learn in law school?''

"No, but it's the kind of clear thinking you come across after you get out into the real world.''

"Assume you do get a judge like that, then. How does it cost the ACLU money?''

"Because of the double indemnity clause. If death followed as an expectable result from the behavior, we get a quarter million. If death occurred accidentally, we get a half million.''

"Is murder accidental?''

"From Morty's point of view, sure. The insurance company wouldn't even bother to argue otherwise.''

"You said the will could be important, though. What's the will got to do with accidental death?''

"For the first time, it gives us people who would gain from Morty's death. At least now there's a reasonable possibility of murder.''

"Well, it is murder. I've thought so ever since I talked about the death scene with Gladys and Nora.''

"But then it was a hard sell,'' Hope said. "Who would have murdered him? Everybody loved Morty.''

"Who would have murdered him now, either? Nora? Baby Leo? His mother?''

"All right, all right. But who knows? At least they'll profit from his death.''

"So will you. But I've got a real problem with all four of you as suspects. Where did you folks get the semen?''

"Maybe one of us had an accomplice.''

"We're getting a little far-fetched here."

"Well, I'm just basically flailing around."

"So am I," I said. "Time to try something else. I think I'll get Rosson to make a few calls for me, introduce me to the people at the 'Little Leo Show.' I might as well try New York. I've run out of people to talk to here."

— 13 —

LTV PRODUCTIONS WAS IN A FEATURELESS, ANONYMOUS block on West Twenty-sixth Street. The small and bare lobby was deserted except for a receptionist wearing a black leather jacket. She was blowing a bubble of gum. As I walked in, she managed to collapse it and get the gum back in her mouth instead of all over her face, which was better than I usually did in my own Fleers days. She had never heard of me, but she called upstairs and it turned out somebody had.

"My name is Iris," said the young woman in a sweatshirt and blue jeans who came down for me. "I will be your information person and your food person for today. Want some food? Come on, I want some food."

Iris took me up two flights of uncarpeted concrete steps with gray-painted steel treads and down a hallway to a table littered with boxes and bags of food. "Danish?" she said. "Bagel and cream cheese? Cranberry muffin? Chocolate chip cookie? Brownie?"

"I don't know," I said. "Got any carrot sticks?"

"This is a joke, right? I didn't even hear you say that. Next thing you'll want decaf."

"I always figured decaf defeated the whole point of coffee."

"That's what I like to hear. Black, huh?"

"Cream and lots of sugar."

While she got my coffee I loaded a paper plate with lipids and empty calories. "Way to go," Iris said. "Keep those arteries clogged."

"Why worry?" I said. "All my old man ever ate was Pop Tarts, and he lived well into his forties."

"There you go. Probably you've got many months of life to look forward to." Iris took a break from talking while she put away the last of a slab of coffee cake covered with frosting and almond slivers. She washed it down with Coke, and said, "But enough of this chitchat, Tom. May I call you Tom? Thank you. Okay, let's go for the VIP tour. As your information person, I will show you around and answer any questions you may have to the best of my ability. Which, if I may say so, is considerable. What I don't know about this show you could fit in a gnat's ass. Come on."

She took me down the hall from the food table and through a small door with a Do Not Enter sign on it. Behind it was a darkened room full of people looking at a wall of TV screens. "Teddy," she said, "this is Kathy's best friend in the whole wide world, Tom Bethany."

A balding man in his thirties looked up at me. "Teddy Elliman," he said. "Glad to have you." He smiled and turned back to the dozens of small TV screens that filled one wall of the room. The room was like a tiny theater, with long tables in four tiers rising up from the wall where the monitors were. Elliman, wearing a microphone, sat at the front table. Each place at the tables had its own small reading light on a flexible tube. The eight or ten people in the room were all busy, making notations on scripts, talking into the intercom, scanning the bank of monitors.

"All right, everybody," Elliman said into the mike around his neck, "scene one, page one."

"What does that mean?" somebody said.

"Means we're in the lock, briefly in the lock. Okay, positions, please . . . Bring 'em in on medium, yes, Donald, thank you . . . Three is going to two, three is on two . . ."

"Who's on first?" the man next to Elliman said.

The director smiled, but his concentration didn't break. "That cappuccino machine doesn't read in the close-up," he said. "Can't see the steam. Maybe a black one would read better."

"I can use the white one," said Iris, next to me.

"Take it home with you, dear," Elliman said. "Just make sure I've got a black one tomorrow . . . Charles, Charles, you're looking too far upstage for him to get eyes and he can't get in any farther . . ."

I sat and listened quietly, whispering a question now and then to Iris. The chaos started to come into focus. Elliman was juggling back and forth between cameras to get the most effective angles on each bit of each scene, and to give the illusion of action even when no one on stage was moving much. His assistants were taking note of whatever had to be done to incorporate the changes into the final product.

After ten minutes or so, Elliman halted operations while he conferred with his assistants over some problem he had discovered in the script. The images on the screens became undirected and random. A camera might be fixed on a corner of the set, the only movement coming when a stagehand or actor happened to cross its field of vision. A cameraman might focus idly on an actor's necktie or shoe, then lose interest and let the lens swing up to the ceiling.

"Want to go out on the set?" Iris asked. "I'll tell the

assistant stage manager who you are and then split, okay? Got a few things to do, but I'll be back."

The studio she took me to was a huge no-frills room with cinderblock walls and cement floors painted gray. Half the room was for the audience that would watch the final performance. Rows of metal folding chairs stood in the bleachers, which rose up from ground level. Two big TV monitors hung from the ceiling, so the live audience would be able to see what the camera was seeing. Big blue and white signs reading APPLAUSE hung down from the roof on each side of the bleachers, ready to light up whenever the director wanted to goose the audience. At least it was one step up from canned laughter.

The other half of the room, on the other side of the diagonal made by the front of the bleachers, held three brightly lit stages back against the far walls. One was a kitchen, one was a living room, and one was Little Leo's bedroom. Kathy Poindexter and a couple of other members of the cast were loafing around the living room set, waiting for things to get going again.

The sets themselves were relatively uncluttered, but everything in front of them and above them and on all sides of them seemed to be in total confusion. Lights hung down from the ceilings on steel stalks, wires and pipes ran all over the walls, thick cables snaked back and forth all over the floor.

"Okay, everybody, here we go again," said Elliman's voice over the sound system. "Positions, please."

The cameramen locked in on their targets. Assistants positioned huge mobile turrets on wheels. Sound men sat on top of the turrets, manipulating long booms that bent like fishing rods under the load of mikes the size of sash weights. The rods telescoped in and out to follow the movement on stage, so that the sound men seemed to be fishermen playing the actors as they tried to escape.

They did each scene over and over again, each time being called up short from the control room as Elliman spotted changes he wanted to make. Then they would start again, working in the changes, until he hollered, "Hold it a moment, folks," and changed some other line or movement or bit of business. Then they'd take it again from the top, each time getting a little further before the voice called them up short. It was like picking out a tune on the piano keys till you made a mistake and then starting over, each time getting a little further into the piece.

"Impressive," I whispered to Iris during one of her brief stops. She was all over the place, doing God knows what, but every now and then she'd check in to see if I was all right.

"What's impressive?" she asked.

"How complicated it is. Like playing a bunch of different chess games at the same time."

"I knew a guy in college who could do that," Iris said. "Except for that, though, he was an idiot."

"These guys don't sound like idiots."

"Teddy? No, he's no idiot. He's smart. A lot of the people in TV are smart, actually. It's amazing how they can turn out such crap."

"Is this crap, here?"

"If it is, it's pretty high grade. Maybe it's even art, who knows?"

"What makes the difference, then?"

"Kathy, basically. She's got, you should excuse me, the vision thing."

"Okay, people," Teddy Elliman's voice was saying from the control booth, "may I take this opportunity to thank you from the bottom of my heart. That's it till two o'clock. Have a good lunch."

"Hey, Kathy!" Iris shouted out. "He's over here."

Apparently Kathy Poindexter didn't have a Big Star

problem, because she looked up at her bright little gofer, smiled, and headed our way. But she was a Big Star, and you could see it even when she was out of the lights. She still looked like an image that came to life, probably because the image had imprinted itself on me before I ever met the person.

"Hi," the person said. "I won't shake, okay? My palms are all sweaty and disgusting. Kind of like armpits without hair."

That was a conversation stopper, as she noticed. "Don't mind me," she said. "Takes me a little while to get offstage. You're the estate lawyer, huh? You look more like a bodyguard."

"I used to be a bodyguard, actually. Part that and part pilot."

"Oh, yeah? For who?"

"Teddy Kennedy, back in '80. They hired me because I didn't look like a bodyguard. Maybe I grew into it."

"Whatever happened, you sure don't look like a lawyer."

"Rosson's the lawyer. I'm just doing research for him."

"What's to research? Poor Morty's dead."

"A lot of things are coming up. You have a minute to talk?"

"Hey, I'm the six hundred–pound gorilla. I have all the minutes I want. Let's go to my dressing room."

Her dressing room wasn't very elaborate—just a small room furnished with a leather couch and three leather sling chairs. Doors were open into a bathroom with a shower, and a large walk-in closet. A lighted makeup mirror was on one wall, with a dressing table in front of it. Nothing was on the table, and the bulbs were gone from three of the sockets around the mirror.

"It's nonfunctional," Kathy said, when I flicked the switch beside the mirror and nothing happened. "Actually all the makeup is done down the hall in the makeup room.''

On the floor beside the dressing table was a vase made out of purple plastic. It held a huge floral arrangement, waist high. The flowers were plastic, too—the kind of thick-petaled artificial flowers that had tiny ridges on the edges of the leaves, left by the molds back in Taiwan that made them. The colors looked just a little wrong to be any kind of flowers I knew. A handwritten card was attached to one of the leaves by a paper clip. "To the sweetest, prettiest little gal in the whole wide world,'' it read. It was signed "Leo.'' On the old "Leo Grasso Show,'' whenever Kathy would show mild resentment over his latest insult or mistreatment, Leo would slip into a total-phony mode and say, "Now, don't you be like that, honey. Why, you're the sweetest, prettiest little gal in the whole wide world.''

I thought the paper clip was a nice touch, but I didn't say so. Instead I dropped a rock on Kathy Poindexter's foot, to see what she would say:

"Morty left your son half his money.''

What she said was, "What!'' And then, after a pause, "Oh, shit. Is there any way to keep it out of the papers?''

"I think once a will is probated, it's a public document. Why would it matter if it was in the papers, though?''

"You mean because they're both dead?''

I nodded, like an unprepared student who's just been fed the answer by his teacher but doesn't understand it. Both Limbach and Westfall dead? Huh? If I kept my mouth shut, maybe she'd feed me the explanation, too.

"No, not because they're both dead,'' Kathy said. "Because it ruins the show's whole goddamn MacGuffin.''

"MacGuffin?''

"Premise, gimmick. It's the 'Little Leo Show.' Once people know he isn't Little Leo, there goes the show.''

I nodded again, just as if this made sense. As in fact it

was beginning to. She hadn't been talking about Limbach and Westfall being dead. She meant that Limbach and Leo Grasso were dead. "Maybe you'd better tell me about it from the start," I said. Maybe she saw me as representing Morty, which in a sense I did, and maybe that made me seem to be a logical person to confide in. In any event, she did tell me from the start.

Her father had taught Latin at Milton Academy and died of a brain tumor when she was eleven. That was the end of the fancy house on campus and the prospect of a fancy education as a faculty kid. Her mother had wound up in a clerical job at Harvard, with two daughters and very little money. Kathy wound up at Cambridge's giant high school, Cambridge Rindge and Latin, which is right down the street from Harvard geographically, but a long way away in practically every other sense. She did drugs and hung out at Harvard Square. I had probably seen her there dozens of times during those years, just another faceless girl in uniform. Pink hair moussed into spikes, black clothes, costume jewelry turning her thin wrists and neck green.

Most of the freaks were no more than pathetic, harmless dropouts with nothing more in their future than bills, dead-end jobs, and dropout kids of their own. But there was talent on the Square, too, here and there and now and then. The singer Tracy Chapman, for one, had come off those streets.

"The first job I ever had, you know what it was?" Kathy said. "You ever see the guy that used to get out of chains in that little plaza there, in front of the bookstore? The escape artist guy? I was the one that wrapped him up in the chains. Hey, don't laugh. I was in show biz." After dropping out of high school for good and leaving home, she took a more or less regular job at the comedy club on JFK Street, Catch a Rising Star. It wasn't even waiting tables, since she was too young to serve drinks. She only washed dishes and cleaned up, but at least it gave her an excuse to hang out and make a pest of herself. And listen.

Days, she'd sneak into drama lectures or workshops until she got caught. Or she'd do guerrilla theater with friends, making up characters and situations on the T, or on the sidewalk. Robberies, lovers' quarrels, skits about reunion or parting, whatever came to mind.

Kathy drifted into the Poor Attitudes before Morty showed up on the scene. Back then the company was a shifting collection of dropouts and misfits who sneaked into unused MIT classrooms at night for rehearsals. "When Morty showed up he kind of gave things a center," she said. "There was a place to live if you needed one. We had an actual phone number, you imagine? Once our picture was even in the *Globe*. We were big time. We got forty bucks a week walking-around money. In theory it was each person's split from what we made in our appearances, but actually we practically never brought in that much. Morty made up the difference.

"We were working like hell, taking iron tablets to keep our energy up, running around performing for anybody who'd watch us, making a little name for ourselves, getting word of mouth. At last it felt like I was getting somewhere. Pretty good, huh? Well, I fell all apart. Completely. Go figure. Sell on the good news, huh? Now I've got a broker, that's the advice he gave me once. I knew exactly what he meant. All my life I been selling on the good news."

Mark Unger had already become Morty's psychiatrist. Morty called him to get Kathy out of her room. She hadn't left it for three days, even to go to the toilet. She went in a plastic diet soda bottle with the neck cut off, and emptied it out the window. Unger talked her out of her room and into analysis. A few months later he moved his offices to where they were now and eventually began seeing other members of the company as well. With Morty quietly picking up the tab, as I already knew.

Next came an affair with Morty.

"At first mostly I felt sorry for him," Kathy said. "He had all of us but at the same time really he didn't have anybody, you see what I mean? We got to where we'd hang around together, keep each other company, and one thing led to another. I could tell he really wanted to, but he didn't dare ask. Well, maybe he wasn't such a big turn-on, but I said shit, why not? This is a nice guy, he's done a lot for me, for all of us. Even the shrink thought it was a good idea."

"You asked Unger?"

"Not like I was asking permission, no. But I mentioned Morty seemed to like me, and he told me it might be a good thing for both of us. Romantic, huh?"

And so they became lovers. Once or twice a week he'd visit her in her downstairs bedroom, or she'd spend the night in his place in Boston. "Very low key," she said, "but kind of sweet, in a way. So brilliant me, naturally I went and pissed in the punch bowl."

Leo Grasso had come roaring into town from six years of working construction in New York while he failed over and over again to get into show business. "Tell me it isn't luck," Kathy said. "Not one of the dumb sons of bitches in this town saw what Leo had until he went off to Boston and got lucky. Before that the best he ever got was a few gigs in comedy clubs, fifty bucks a night, and that was it for six years. Still, he would have stuck it out in New York forever, or at least till he died in the gutter. Only reason he came to Boston was because he got fired from his construction job for doing drugs and his sister in Belmont said he could stay with her and her husband for a while. Which her husband thought was a really swell idea, on account of Leo of course was the original house guest from hell.

The brother-in-law kicked him out after two weeks. Somewhere Leo heard about Poor Attitudes House and like they say, the rest is show biz history. Eighteen months later he's back in New York and every slimy bastard in the industry is kissing his ass. Mine too, as far as that goes."

From the start Kathy and Leo went together like ketchup and fries. "When we were working it was like we were inside each other's heads," she said. "I'd throw some totally outrageous line at him and before he opened his mouth I knew what he'd say, and he knew what I'd say back to him after that. People talk about on the same wave length, but it's more than that. I don't know what it is, how you can be totally inside two heads at once, both of you. But I can tell you one thing, it only works onstage. Don't ever think you can bottle that shit and take it home with you."

Nevertheless they got married at Cambridge City Hall. Her wedding ring was one of the little steel gaskets that go on the base of a spark plug. Kathy thought it was cute at the time. "Actually I shouldn't bitch," she said. "Maybe Leo never did buy me a real ring, but there was nothing cheap about him once he hit it big. As quick as you handed money to him, he'd get rid of it. Like it was red hot. One afternoon I saw him drop twenty-one thousand bucks. A couple of sandwiches and a half-dozen beers for the two of us, and the rest on gifts for everybody he could think of."

But he was erratic and violent, too. He wanted total submission, obedience, and adoration from everyone around him. When he didn't get it, he bullied until he did. "There was a lot of that in him at the best of times," Kathy said. "But it was worse when he was into the booze and the pills. The first time he slapped me around was three days after we were married. He had put away pretty near a case of beer and he asked me to go out after some more. I told him fuck you, and he came out swinging. Fortunately after a couple of good ones he missed and fell down. Soon as he hit the floor he went to sleep."

"What did you do?"

"All he was wearing was skivvies, so I opened the windows and locked him in. We were living in one of those upstairs bedrooms in the Poor Attitudes House and it was January. I went back down to my old bedroom on the ground floor, so pissed off I didn't care if he froze. Naturally he didn't. Leo's a horse. Was a horse."

That set the pattern. Leo would belt her around, verbally or physically, until she left him for her hidey-hole downstairs. A day or two later he'd talk her back upstairs again, with charm, humor, tears, apologies, anything that worked. Then whatever had brought them together in the first place would keep them together for a few more weeks, and whatever drove them apart would drive them apart again. But they were always together onstage, the sum greater than its parts.

"The more hostility there was between us offstage," Kathy said, "the better the act seemed to work." And the better it worked, the better the rest of the Poor Attitudes company became. There were more gigs, bigger crowds, more money, more newspaper stories and magazine profiles, more young talent lining up to join the troupe. Morty got to thinking the time had come for a resident director, and at Yale Drama School he found Teddy Elliman.

Meanwhile Kathy was going like a yo-yo between the second floor and the ground floor of the Poor Attitudes House, depending on whether she loved Leo that week or hated him. And Morty, still carrying the torch, heard her crying through the door one night downstairs, after Leo had slapped her around again. He knocked to see if there was anything he could do. There was. "Morty wasn't real exciting, but he was real sweet," Kathy said. "Sweet was what you wanted, after a little bit of Leo, off flying on one thing or another. It was a crazy time.''

"I can imagine.''

"Oh, yeah? Well, imagine this, for crazy. Imagine I miss my period and the timing was that it had to have been Morty, all right? Do I go down and get scraped out like a normal person, which would have been my fourth abortion? No, not this kid. This kid figures she'll carry Morty's baby to term, it's just what Leo needs to turn him into Mr. Nice Guy. You believe anybody could believe shit that dumb? Well, I did. And the funny thing is, it sort of worked. Leo figured now I was pregnant I might break, so he stopped beating up on me. He was actually *excited* about having a kid. It was amazing.''

"Let me make sure I got this right. Leo figured it was his kid?''

"Yeah, thank God. Leo could be scary enough, just being normal Leo. I think he actually might have gone nuts if he learned his wife was having somebody else's kid.''

"Nuts how?''

"Shit, I don't know. Killed somebody, even.''

"Killed who?''

"Me? Morty? Himself? Who knows? You got to remember, when Leo was normal, what was normal for him, he was what anybody else would consider over the edge already.''

"How about Morty? Did he know it was his baby?''

"Not then.''

"When?''

"I didn't mean for him ever to know. I figured things were complicated enough already, okay? I hadn't even told Leo I was pregnant by the time we got our big break and came here to New York. I was only three months gone, and it didn't really show so you'd notice. Not that Leo would notice a little thing like that anyway, as long as he had a few lines and a couple of six-packs on ice. I didn't tell him until pretty near the end of the fourth month, and by then the show was in its sixth week and already you could tell we were all going to have more money than the fucking pope. That's what Leo always said, more money than the fucking pope. Is the pope really rich?''

"I don't know. I'm not Catholic."

"Me neither. But Leo was, so maybe he knew. Anyway, Leo is all excited and even turned into a more or less good guy, like I said. But Morty still doesn't even know I'm knocked up. He only learns when everybody in the world does, when we finally write the pregnancy into the story line of the show."

"You never told him he was the father?"

"The fact is, I felt like such a complete shit when we took off for New York and left Morty behind that I was too ashamed even to say good-bye. Let alone tell him I was carrying his baby."

"He must have guessed, to judge by the will."

"He found out when he came to New York for Leo's funeral."

"What did he say when you told him?"

"I wouldn't have ever told him. He figured it out for himself as soon as he saw Little Leo in the flesh instead of on the tube. I mean, that kid doesn't hardly have any of *my* genes, let alone Leo's."

"Leo never saw the resemblance to Morty, though?"

"No, and I used to wonder why. What I figured, it must have been because he watched the baby grow up from day one, when they all took like Winston Churchill. So he got used to the idea that this is what a kid of Leo Grasso's looks like. But when Morty first saw Little Leo in living color, the kid was starting to look like a human being, you know? So he spotted the resemblance right away. In fact, the day before Morty died he showed me a snapshot of

231

himself at the same age. The two of them could have been twins."

"What was his reaction to finding out he had a son?"

"Pride. He couldn't get over it, you know? What, me, little Morty? A father? No big deal, I tell him. Anybody can be a father. Shit, even Danny Quayle's a father. And I'll tell you something else, Morty, check *this* out. Danny Quayle's *father* was a father.

"Morty goes yeah, poor Danny Quayle's father, huh? But *my* kid, what a kid! A star and he's not even two yet. A male Tracy Ullman. A white Eddie Murphy. Michael Jackson without the surgery. Hey, you suppose the kid can sing, Kath? How about dance? I'll pay for the lessons. Here old mom is, trying to calm this looneytoon down, but forget it. Morty's the first guy ever had a kid, and he's on a roll. I never saw him that excited before. Shit, he wanted to *adopt* the kid. You believe it?"

"What did you say to him?"

"I said, Morty, this kid doesn't need adopting. He's got this like *mother*, see? And this mother, she's off of food stamps now. She's got her own place, and in fact the kid has got his own room and his own British nanny and a chauffeur and a big fucking Reaganmobile stretch job a block and a half long with mirror windows and its own phone. So actually, Morty, this kid is scraping by okay without a daddy. But you can be his Uncle Morty and come around at Thanksgiving."

"You didn't really say that, did you?" I asked.

"Well, I didn't say it as smart-ass as that, naturally. The truth is, I was kind of touched."

"Did he offer to marry you?"

"He said he would if I wanted to, but he was in love with somebody else."

"Nora."

"You know about them, huh? Anyway, that was part of

his adoption idea. He would marry her and they would adopt Little Leo."

"Jesus."

"I know. Man comes up to you and says, uh, Look, Mom, why don't I just take that poor little fellow off your hands and give him a good home for a change? Little offended, maybe? But from Morty it didn't bother me. I knew where he was coming from, that he was just too excited to think things out. When I walked him through it, though, he realized why we had to keep quiet about it."

"Why?"

"For the show! We've got a contract with the audience, is the way Teddy Elliman puts it, and he's right. The audience doesn't even know there *is* a fucking contract, but break it and they'll know it fast enough. A really big part of our particular contract, maybe the whole goddamn thing even, is that this is a real baby born to these real parents, and now it's really without a father. You ever read about a show back in the fifties called 'The $64,000 Question'?"

"A little, yeah."

"Well, their contract with the audience was that the contestants were regular people just like you and me, answering real questions. You remember what happened?"

"It came out they were coached, and the show folded."

"You got it. They broke their contract, and the show folded. You have any idea what we're talking about here, if the 'Little Leo Show' folds?"

"Not really."

"Let me tell you, then. There's twenty-two shows a season, which means good jobs for all these people you see here. Particularly me. I'm taking seventy-five thousand dollars a show out for myself. Don't bother to do the arithmetic. That's one-point-six-five million."

"Holy shit."

233

"Not yet. Holy shit comes later, when I sell it into syndication. Cosby got five hundred million bucks."

"That's a lot of money to take chances with, all right," I said.

"I hope Teddy's wrong, but on this one I don't think he is. When it comes out about Little Leo's real father, the show is fucked."

"Why should it come out?"

"You said wills are public."

"Only if somebody is interested enough to go look at them. Rich people die every day, but how many stories do you see about their wills?"

"You're saying it could just sit there in the files?"

"Could. Even if it came out, leaving dough to a kid doesn't necessarily make you his father."

"Oh, yeah? Think you could sell that argument on the checkout line down at the A&P? Inquiring minds want to know."

"First they have to know where to inquire. But I guess you're right. If the *Enquirer* ever learns about the will, they might make a mention of it all right."

" 'Little Leo Secret Son of Pervert Pop,' " Kathy said. "Jesus, that's all we need."

" 'Pervert Pop' is good, yeah. Or maybe 'Murdered Millionaire.' "

"You think Morty was murdered?"

"I'm pretty sure, actually."

I told her what I thought but couldn't prove.

"Who had any reason to kill Morty, though?" she asked.

"Could it be somebody who wanted to protect the show, maybe? Who else besides you knew that Morty was Little Leo's real father?"

"Nobody but Teddy Elliman. Unless he told somebody else, and I doubt if he did. He was scared shitless as it was."

234

"Of what?"

"That it would get out. Because of all that stuff I told you, about the contract with the audience."

"How did he know himself who the baby's father was?"

"He figured it out and then came to me with it."

"How did he figure it out?"

"It was when we were on location that time in Boston, the week Morty died. Morty got to playing with the baby on the set, and I could see the moment it hit Teddy. He looked at the baby and Morty together, and then he looked over at me. He didn't say anything till later, but that was when he knew."

"What did he say later?"

"Just for God's sake to be sure Morty didn't tell anybody. He had a shit fit when I told him about the adoption scheme, but he calmed down when I told him I had cooled Morty off about it."

"Teddy would lose millions if the show went down the tubes, right?"

"He'd lose his job, that's all."

"I thought director-producers, et cetera, I thought those were the guys that got rich."

"Those are just titles. Words, just like all that shit you read about how the 'Little Leo Show' was Teddy's personal brainstorm."

"It wasn't?"

"It was my idea."

"Why let him take the credit?"

"I don't give a flying fuck who gets the credit, as long as I get the cash. Listen, you know how I held on to my first real job, cleaning up at the comedy club? Every night after closing I had to blow the assistant manager. I was sweet sixteen. Point I'm making is that I've had to take a really lot of shit along the way. And along the way has been most of my life, even after we moved here to New

York and started to make money. Talk about eating shit, try being married to Leo.

"Anyway, Teddy didn't come up the way I did. He went to Yale, he never learned that money talks, bullshit walks. Teddy is willing to settle for bullshit, fine. Go for it, Teddy."

"So you're the real owner of the show?"

"I'm it. Sounds awful to say it, but when Leo died it gave me the chance to get just amazingly rich."

"What does him dying have to do with it?"

"Well, when we came to New York the network held all the cards and we had none, right? So naturally they fucked us. Eventually we could have blackjacked a lot more dough out of them than the original contract was for, but the show was still theirs. We had points, but they fuck you on the points. Only the producers make the real money."

"Who were the producers?"

"The network."

"Did you buy them out?"

"Much better than that. They bought me out. When Leo died they paid me off for the old show and I was free. So I turned right around and sold them the 'Little Leo Show,' produced by LLTV. 'LL' is Little Leo. Which is me. Everybody here works for me, including Teddy."

"He doesn't have points?"

"If he did, I'd fuck him out of the money for them. That's what we do, us producers. But he doesn't."

"So he's just on salary?"

"Basically, yeah. A hell of a big salary, forgive me, Leo."

"What does that mean?"

"Leo couldn't stand Teddy, all right? That's why he left him back in Cambridge. I couldn't stand him much better, tell you the truth, but after Leo died I figured I could use him. I'll tell you something, Bethany. Producing, directing, all that shit sounds glamorous. But what it is, ninety percent of it, it's dealing with unions, hiring and firing, worrying about lighting, equipment maintenance, depreciation, payroll deductions. Going to meetings with network scum, putting together budgets, kissing ass at City Hall for licenses and permits. Let Teddy do it. Maybe Teddy *is* an asshole, but he's a smart asshole and he works like a bastard. So let him tell *People* magazine he's a genius if that's what turns him on. It doesn't come out of my pocket."

"Does he like you, too?"

"I imagine he hates me. Teddy's one of those guys that thinks he's the only smart person in the world and the rest of us are just cattle. But here's this dumb cow, me, that's his boss and won't even give him a piece of the show he thinks he invented."

"Does he really think that?"

"Oh, sure. Guys like him make up their own worlds. Nasty little freak."

"Freak?"

"Sure. That's another reason he probably hates me. One time back in Cambridge Leo was working on a character he used to do, an American Nazi. So we go to this leather bar in Allston for ideas, and shit, there's Teddy, this genius from Yale. He's sitting at a table in a leather bar with some big, hairy Harley-Davidson fuck. Teddy had this collar on, like a dog collar, and the guy with the beard was holding the chain. Teddy made us promise never to tell anybody else about it, but Leo naturally never let him forget it. Sometimes he'd just come out with a little bark, arf, and nobody but Teddy would know what he meant. Or he'd snap his fingers and then say, 'No, Teddy, not you.' "

"How did Elliman come to be in New York the day Leo died?" I asked.

"He was looking for a job with us."

"Get one?"

"Shit no. Leo couldn't stand him."

"Which Elliman must have known. Why bother to ask the guy for a job, then?"

"You never know till you ask, do you? I couldn't stand Teddy, either, but I hired him."

"Was Leo autopsied?"

"Autopsied? Oh, I see where you're going. Leo tells Teddy fuck you, you can't have a job, and practically immediately winds up dead. Tell you the truth, it never crossed my mind Teddy could have done it. For one thing, Leo was a horse, like I told you. He was twice as strong as most guys, maybe five times as strong as Teddy. And he used it. He was a fighter. No, put it out of your mind. What's he going to do, hold Leo down while he chokes him with a chunk of roast beef?"

"That's what it was? The papers just said a sandwich."

"Roast beef sandwich with roasted Italian peppers and fried onions. Watching Leo eat one of those beauties, it was enough to turn you vegetarian. He had them cut the meat about an inch thick, at a deli around the corner. And he *was* autopsied, yes, to answer your question, and a chunk of that meat was what killed him."

"Is it okay if I talk to Elliman?"

"Sure."

She went to the door, opened it, and hollered for Elliman in a voice they could have heard outside on the street. He came to the dressing room door a minute or so later, looking unhurried. But he came.

"Did I hear my name, very faintly?" he asked.

"This is Tom Bethany," she said. "He represents Morty's estate. Needs to talk to you, okay?"

"We should be getting going after lunch on the diaper service scene."

"If we have to, we'll get started on it without you. Tom here, give him whatever he needs, will you? I got to go get Little Leo away from his fucking nanny anyway, before she gets him talking like William F. Buckley."

When Kathy Poindexter had disappeared, I motioned Elliman to a chair just like it was my office. And I closed the door to the hall. Maybe it would make him think of visits to the principal's office or something.

Elliman was a young man of medium height, balding, and with a bad color. He had the kind of snapping-turtle nose that Dick Tracy had. The skin was drawn tight over his features, making you conscious of the skull beneath. He had small bones, with a little too much flesh on him, so that his polo shirt pooched out over the waistband of his chino pants. The whole impression wasn't of sickness, but of unhealthiness. The sort of man you'd expect to be in and out of hospitals and finally to die of something or other in his forties or fifties.

"Brilliant talent," he said, gesturing at the door Kathy Poindexter had just gone out of. "Well, tell me what I can do for you, although I can't imagine what it could be. I don't know thing one about Morty's death."

"Not much mystery about his death," I said. "He died of autoerotic asphyxia, according to the police and the medical examiner. But the insurance company is trying to get off the hook by claiming he killed himself, so we're looking into Morty himself. Did he strike you as suicidal?"

"Not even remotely. As a matter of fact, he seemed unusually animated in the days before his death. I suppose you know we were up in Boston for a shoot that week, and saw a good deal of the Poor Attitudes people?"

"What was he animated about?"

"I couldn't say."

"About learning that he was Little Leo's father?"

"Kathy told you that? Well, then, I guess I *can* say. Certainly. That was what he was animated about."

"Kathy says you were kind of animated about it, too."

"Well, of course I was. If a thing like that got out, it could destroy the show. Absolutely destroy it."

Elliman paused for a moment. "I believe I begin to see what this is all about," he said. "In that case, then let me tell you something Kathy may not have told you. Apart from my paycheck, which I could equal or surpass almost anywhere in this business, I have absolutely no financial interest in the survival of the 'Little Leo Show.' A paternal interest, yes. Little Leo himself may be Morty's baby, but the show is mine."

"That's a pretty strong interest."

"I suppose you're suggesting that people have killed to protect their offspring. Well, mine didn't need protection. Once Morty was over the first flush of his enthusiasm for his bizarre adoption scheme, he understood perfectly well that it was in nobody's interest to advertise his proud parenthood."

"Do you have any children yourself?"

"No. Do you?"

"I've got a daughter, but I haven't seen her for a long time. She's in Alaska."

"How sad for you."

"Don't be scared of me, Teddy."

"Thank you very much, but I'm not in the least scared of you."

"Sure you are. You'd be crazy not to be. You know I represent the estate. That means I know that Morty's will gives you control of a big pile of money. And I'm asking questions about the guy's death. So you're scared of me, and that's why you're telling me to go fuck myself."

"Can you really do that? I'd be fascinated to see it."

I smiled, sunny as the Ronzo himself. "There you go again," I said. "Hey, calm down. Really. I don't think you killed him. I don't think anybody killed him. Look, I've talked to three people who were on the scene, and I've

240

seen the police photos and I've read the lab reports. The guy came all over himself before he died. What could it be but autoerotic asphyxia?"

"Hanged men have been known to ejaculate."

"Just a little seepage into the urethra, but not a real ejaculation," I said, expanding a little on what Gladys had told me. "Probably caused by the muscles relaxing, same reason the bowels let loose."

"Really?" said Elliman. "What a revolting comparison."

"Anyway, what I'm saying here is that nobody killed anybody and let's be friends. Okay?"

He looked at me, watchful but at least not making smart-ass remarks. I tried to calm him down a little more, and then sent him off to have his lunch. By then Kathy Poindexter had came back with her famous baby. "Where's the nanny?" I asked.

"I told her to bug off so I could have some quality time with the kid," she said, setting the baby down on the floor. "There you go, Leo. See what you can find down there in the real world." The baby went toddling off happily, looking for stuff to taste.

"I think I can see why your husband and Teddy never got to be beer-drinking buddies," I said. "I don't think I really brought out the best in him either, tell you the truth."

"Yeah, I doubt it, too. Teddy may like to play-act in leather bars, but real rough trade scares him shitless."

"You mean me or your husband?"

"Both of you."

"Well, you're the expert."

"On Leo, maybe. Not on you."

"You're the expert on rough, though. Anybody who could fuck a network."

She grinned like a little kid. Almost like a little kid. "Hey," she said, "networks need fucking."

Suddenly she jumped up from the couch she had been sitting on, horror all over her face.

"Take that thing out of your mouth!" she shouted.

But it didn't sound like a six hundred–pound gorilla to Little Leo. It sounded like it was only his mom, so he kept right on chewing the bristles of what he had discovered in the bathroom.

"Now you put that down this instant," she said, advancing on the baby with her hand held out. "Give the toilet brush to Mommy."

"A few years ago she was a street kid and now she's screwing a TV network out of hundreds of millions of dollars," I said. "Aren't you impressed?"

I had phoned Hope at her Washington office to tell her what I had learned on my trip to New York about leather bars and bastard sons and contracts with the audience.

"I'll tell you what impresses me even more," Hope said. "Kathy was shrewd enough to see right away that Leo Grasso was worth more money to her than Morty Limbach could ever be."

"That's pretty harsh."

"What did you think it was? Love?"

"Actually I did."

"You liked her, huh?"

"Yeah, I did."

"Well, you could be right. You've met her and I haven't."

"You will. Or I hope you can come up, anyway. She's sending you an invitation to be her guest at this Poor Attitudes gala week after next."

"What is this gala thing, anyway?"

"Supposed to be a boost that the 'Little Leo' people are giving their old alma mater. But Elliman said it was more than that. Evidently LLTV has plans to produce other shows. What Kathy's got in mind is to build the Poor Attitudes into kind of a farm club for her TV production company."

"You're going to be there, of course."

"Of course. I'm an integral part of the whole thing."

"Then I'll try to be there. Wait a minute, though, Bethany. What do you mean you're an integral part? Are you going to do a little dance or something?"

"Better than that. I got to thinking and it suddenly hit me. Hey, kids, we've got a barn and some old clothes in the attic! Why don't we put on our *own* show!"

"I think I like the little dance better. What do you mean, 'your own show'?"

"Well, just a skit, really. I've been talking about it with the guy who's sort of the honcho for the Poor Attitudes. Ned Levine."

"What kind of a skit?"

"What's all this suspicion, Hope? It's only a harmless little skit."

"Tell me about it."

"Well . . ."

"Go ahead. Spoil the surprise."

And so I told her what I had in mind. I had even written down a page or two of dialogue during the train ride back from New York. Fortunately Ned was around, to change the stuff into workable form.

"That's a really twisted idea," Hope said when I was done.

"I know. I'm kind of proud of it myself."

— 14 —

HOPE HAD BEEN ABLE TO COME UP WITH SOME BUSINESS IN Boston that brought her up the day before the gala. Friday night, then, we were at the Border Café in Cambridge, waiting for Gladys and Nora. The two of them had been getting pretty tight over the past few weeks. When Gladys had handed off one of her former boyfriends to Nora, it had been a big success. Nora and the guy had been double-dating with Gladys and one of her present boyfriends. Anyone else might have found the situation a little awkward, but not Gladys.

"Things like that, you've got to just charge right in and not give a shit," she had explained to me once. "Pretty soon nobody else does, either." That was probably good advice, like Larry Bird telling you just aim for the basket. But it wasn't useful advice, since most of us aren't Larry Bird or Gladys.

Here she came toward us with Nora, not leading Nora but Nora not leading either. Neither woman gave the matter a thought, I don't imagine, but they crossed the dining room on separate but equal courses so that they arrived at our table at the same time.

I introduced everybody and then the discussion turned to me. This is what generally happens when my platonic women friends meet my nonplatonic one. There's no sexual tension, and so everybody can get down to business. Which is to discuss me as if I weren't exactly present, the way you might discuss the dog, or a child playing by himself off in the corner.

"You're lucky to have him," Gladys said to Hope. "He's not so bad."

"No, he's not," Hope said. "As men go, he's a pretty good one."

"I almost made a run at him myself, but fortunately we both had better sense."

"He told me."

"Oh, yeah? He talks to you about stuff like that? Most of 'em don't."

"Hi," I said. "It's me."

"Shut up," said Gladys. "We're talking."

So I shut up, until the waitress came around. Then they let me give the order, although they wouldn't let me pay.

"This is on me," Nora said. "I'm practicing up on how to be rich."

"You may not be rich for a year or more," Hope said. "We lawyers sit on your money for at least that long."

"I'm rich already. Professor Rosson told the bank about the will and they loaned me ten thousand bucks against it. The main thing, though, is that they gave me a credit card, too."

Nora pulled out a cheap nylon wallet with a Velcro flap and showed us a Visa card. "I never had one of these suckers before," she said. "Well, that's not completely true. This guy I was going with, he stole a woman's purse once and had me charge some stuff on her cards. Actually that was more fun than having your own, but this is pretty good, too."

Then the excitement went out of her, and she said, "Jesus, the poor guy's only dead what, a month or so? And here I am laughing it up. Buying for the crowd with his money."

"Hey, we talked about this," Gladys said. "He didn't leave you the money so you'd sit around and feel guilty all day. Why should you feel guilty? You didn't kill him."

"I guess not."

"No guess about it. We talked about that, too."

"About what?" I asked.

"Oh, shit," Gladys said, "Nora had some crazy idea she was the one who made him kill himself."

"He didn't kill himself," I said.

"What I told her. Honey, ask Tom yourself. No matter how upset the poor guy was, he couldn't possibly have killed himself over it. On account he didn't kill himself."

"Wait a minute, here," I said. "What was he upset about?"

"Because I was stupid enough to tell him about Asshole and me," Nora said. Asshole was what she called Dr. Unger.

"You told me you didn't tell him," I said.

"She was scared people would blame her," Gladys said.

"What's everybody going to think?" Nora said. "The poor guy feels like shit already because I won't marry him, so what do I go and do, brilliant me? I tell him things are even worse than he thinks. Your pal the shrink used to screw me, so why not jump off a bridge or something, baby? I'll take care of all that nasty money for you."

"You didn't even know you were in the will," Gladys said.

"Who's going to believe that, with my signature on the goddamned thing?"

246

"Well, I believe it," I said, and I ninety-five percent did. "Tell me exactly what you told Morty."

While we were waiting for our food, she told us. The day before Morty Limbach died, he and Nora had been hanging around the 'Little Leo' company, in town for the shooting of the Boston episode. They were both half-drunk, and Morty was after her again about getting married.

"Did he mention anything at all about Little Leo?" I asked.

"Little Leo? No, he was talking about getting married."

"Little Leo didn't come up in any connection?"

"No, but Unger did. Morty told me that he discussed marriage with Asshole, and he thought it would be a good thing for the both of us. Hey, I'm sorry, but when I heard that, I went totally ballistic, all right? I'm hollering at Morty, 'He's supposed to be a marriage counsellor now, that asshole? You know that goddamn couch you lie on, Morty? You know what else he uses it for?' Anyway, that kind of thing. Jesus, I even gave him a blow-by-blow on how Unger conned me into doing it."

"How?" Hope said. "I mean, if you don't mind saying. I have a professional interest in sexual abuse of patients by physicians."

"Okay, have you ever been in analysis?" Nora asked.

Hope shook her head.

"Well, it's a weird kind of a head trip. You want this guy to like you, the way you wanted your teacher to, or your dad. Only it's hard to figure out whether the guy does or not. He's hiding there behind you and whatever you throw at him doesn't bounce back. Hey, daddy, I wet my pants again. Nothing. Father, I committed bad actions. No, not with myself. With the whole goddamned football team. Nothing. Hey, I did it with a couple of German shepherds, too, all right? Still nothing. You see what I mean?"

"I think so," Hope said.

"You're getting more and more desperate to get some sort of a reaction out of this guy. If you can't get his attention by telling him how bad you are, what can you do? He'd have to pay attention if you put out for him, right? Give him your warm little bod for a present, and then maybe he'd like you. This is a regular stage in analysis, not that I knew it at the time. The shrinks call it transference.

"So anyway," Nora went on, "I'd be lying there on that couch like a little kid three times a week, trying to figure out what daddy wanted me to say. He seemed to want me to say whatever I really felt, and what I was really getting to feel was I wanted to play house with him. So at last I said it. 'Well, okay,' he says. 'But we got to go at this carefully. You understand I'm really not your daddy, don't you? You understand this is therapy. We're just working this thing through, getting it out of your system. Long as you bear that in mind, I guess you can touch it if you want to.' Jesus, was I dumb."

"Not dumb," Gladys said. "Just fucked up."

"Same thing."

"No, it's not."

"I think maybe it is," Nora said. "I been thinking about that. This kid used to live down the street from us, looked dorky just like Woody Allen? I knew him all through school. He worked hard, still all he got was B's. So he's pretty dumb, right? Maybe not at Harvard, I wouldn't know. But in the Dorchester schools, that's dumb. You show up most days, you turn in most of the work, you get A's. Anyway, the guy marries in the faith, a little Jewish girl named Sylvia that's just as nerdy-looking as he is. Only they think each other is just perfect. Now the guy works behind the counter in his uncle's jewelry store and she does the books. Guy's as happy as a pig in shit."

"What's your point here?" Gladys asked.

"My point is he doesn't go around making jokes about what a nerd he is and making movies where he bangs tall Gentiles. He doesn't think he's a nerd and he's happy banging a short Jew. Who's dumb? Him or Woody Allen?"

"I don't know, now that I think of it," Gladys said. Neither did I.

After dinner, Hope and I walked down Brattle Street toward the Charles Hotel. It had been your standard non-summer day for the Boston area—dark gray skies, gusts of wind driving occasional cold rain, temperatures in the high thirties and low forties. A climate hostile to all forms of warm-blooded life. Few people had the poor sense to be out on the streets, and we were glad to reach the warmth of the lobby.

First thing on reaching her room, Hope called home. I offered to leave, but she gestured me to stay put. For twenty minutes she went over her children's day with them, and then talked briefly with her husband.

"He said it's good for me to get up here once in a while," she said after hanging up. "Said he knows how much I enjoy Boston. I wonder if he knows."

"He could. But knowing and having your face rubbed into it are two different things."

"I wish you two could be friends, you know it? Doesn't that sound funny?"

"No. I wish it, too."

"What your friend Gladys says about barging right ahead as if you didn't give a shit, she could be right."

"She is right, for her. Neither of us is her, though."

"I liked her a lot. I liked Nora, too. Poor thing, criminally abused."

"What's the crime? Isn't she a consenting adult?"

"Consent isn't always a usable defense. For instance a child isn't considered capable of giving her informed consent, under the laws of most states. She can say yes, but the man is still guilty of statutory rape."

"Going to a shrink doesn't turn you into a child, does it?"

"A good question. Actually, it's one of the questions that I kind of assembled into a package to justify this so-called business trip. The Massachusetts legislature is considering a bill to criminalize sexual contacts between psychotherapists and patients. Our people up here oppose it on exactly your point. That consulting a mental health professional doesn't make you a child, incapable of informed consent."

"What do you think?"

"I don't know. That's why I've been talking to Toby Ingersoll and his people in the Boston office. Their argument is that it isn't worth making a felony out of it, when it's already professional suicide."

"Word gets around, huh?"

"Worse than that. In the last couple of years, five Massachusetts psychiatrists have lost their licenses after patients brought sexual abuse suits against them."

"Then maybe Toby's right. If it ain't broke, don't fix it."

"Maybe he is. On the other hand, how do you think Nora would vote on the question?"

The Prince Restaurant is on old Route 1 in Saugus, maybe twenty minutes out from Cambridge. That stretch is a sort of time capsule from the late thirties and early forties, when Route 1 was the main artery between Maine and Florida. More than a thousand miles of schlock, Felicia Lamport once told me, practically solid with souvenir shops in log cabins or plaster wigwams, roadside reptile farms, and lunch counters shaped like giant hot dogs. In this great tradition, the Prince Restaurant was topped by a leaning tower. The neon sign on it said Tower of Pizza.

"It's more attractive than my wildest dreams," Hope said

when she saw the sign. "I understood you to say it only had a leaning tower of Pisa on top."

On the south side of the building was an entrance marked Comedy Club, which was where Ned Levine and three other actors from the Poor Attitudes had been holding our secret afternoon rehearsals for the past week. The concept, as we say in show biz, was mine. But the execution, which is the part that counts, was Ned's.

Hope and I pulled up for my show business debut in my crummy old Datsun, which was maintained a lot better than it looked. Underneath the rusted, dusty hood everything looked and acted brand-new, thanks to the attentions of Bob MacKinnon and his crew at MacKinnon Motors. I learned during my poor days that it was cheaper by many orders of magnitude to keep an old car in perfect shape than to buy a new one.

For contrast I parked next to a silver-colored stretch limo that had cost some bloodsucker two years' wages for an honest man. The thing was about double the length of my car, an artifact from the days when it was morning in America for a certain few people. As Walter Mondale said to deaf ears during the '84 campaign, a rising tide lifts all yachts.

"Opening night," I said. "I'm kind of excited."

"You really think anything's going to come of this bizarro scheme of yours, Bethany?"

"I don't know, but it can't do any harm. If Morty died accidentally, then the skit will be meaningless to everybody. If he was murdered, then the murderer will have to figure I know exactly how he did it. And if I tell the police how, they won't have any trouble proving who."

"You think he'll rush up to the stage and confess on the spot?"

"I just figured I'd fart in church, see how the different people react."

251

There was a small pileup of people at the door of the club because Kathy Poindexter herself was at the entrance, greeting everyone personally. "Terrific, great . . . Of course I do . . . Glad you could come . . . Glad to meet you . . . So glad . . . Appreciate your support," and so on.

The Comedy Club was a long room, with the stage half-way down one side. This meant you couldn't play to the whole crowd at once, Ned had explained to me. You were always leaving out half of the audience. To get around this, he had arranged for movable partitions to divide the room in two. The half where you entered was set up with service bars and sideboards for the food. Kathy had ordered up the kind of affair where a chef was carving from a steam-boat round of beef and the jumbo shrimp made a pink mountain in a cut-glass bowl the size of a wash basin. Beyond the partition were tables and chairs where the guests could keep on drinking later, as they watched the show. The arrangement of the partition put the stage in one corner of a newly created square room, like home plate in a baseball diamond. That way the actors could play to the entire crowd at once.

Cutting the size of the room down with partitions was also a way to give the appearance of a full house, as I knew from my old days on the road with political candidates. And the audience for the gala wasn't large. The idea hadn't been to get the most, but the best. In this case, that meant local entertainment critics and their bosses from the various papers, magazines, and television stations, television producers and newscasters, booking agents, columnists, publicists, and editors. These were the important people as far as the Poor Attitudes were concerned. To make them feel that they really were important, celebrities were included, too—a couple of dozen of Boston's political, business, and society royalty. College presidents, mayors, congressmen, the lieutenant governor, the attorney general, multimillionaire high-tech entrepreneurs, that kind of thing.

All of them were there, of course, to see Kathy Poindexter and Little Leo. Of the two, Leo was the bigger draw. The baby was smooshing around a plate of hors d'œuvres while his nanny kept swabbing him down with a napkin to keep him as nondisgusting as possible. The guests kept crowding around him. The kid had star presence, no doubt of that, but then most babies do. Probably it's in our genes to pay attention to babies, or else they would have been left behind every time we broke camp to wander off after a new supply of roots and grubs.

"I hate this bullshit," said a low voice behind me. Kathy's. "The only way I can do it is to play a part. A ditz part."

"You're doing good. You'd make a hell of a cruise director."

"I know I'm doing good. I knew I was really into the role when I was nice to Morty's father without puking."

"Which one is he?" I asked.

She pointed out a man with a face weathered ruddy by the sun or by alcohol. Most likely both. "Putting in a cameo appearance between regattas," she said. Limbach, like me and perhaps a quarter of the other men present, wore a tuxedo. The rest wore dark suits.

"The Limbachs both love me now," Kathy said. "That's what's so unbelievably cool about being a big star. Some of the world's biggest shits suddenly just love you."

"How about introducing me to Limbach, then?" I said. The elder Limbach did seem to love her. Once he had done that for a moment, Kathy said, "I'd like you to meet a friend of mine, Tom Bethany."

"Wonderful gal," Limbach said as she moved off to bubble at somebody else. "Just wonderful. Tom what was it?"

"Bethany," I said, and this time it registered.

253

"The detective person?" Limbach said.

"No, I'm not the detective person. I'm just doing some research for Professor Rosson."

"Unusual research, I'd say."

"How is it unusual?"

"I'd be interested to learn how you came up with this so-called will of my son's."

"Me? I came up with it?"

"Come on, fella."

"No, no, you come on. Why do you think somebody had to—" I paused and leaned on the words—"come up with it?"

"What's that supposed to mean?"

"What it means is why wouldn't Professor Rosson be the one to *come up with it?* He was Morty's lawyer, wasn't he? Wouldn't he have the will in his files? Well, wouldn't he, Limbach? Why would you think the will was somewhere else? Huh? Where did you think it was?"

"Now listen here—"

"What made you think it was in that other place, Limbach? Somebody tell you? Who? Why?"

"I don't like your tone one bit, young man."

"You started it with tones. 'Detective person.' Give me a break."

"I think you'd better leave now."

"Why should I leave? I'm invited. You don't like it, leave yourself."

He turned to do just that, and I said to his back, "I'm sorry about your son." That turned him around again.

"I doubt that very much," he said.

"Well, don't. You had a son to be proud of."

"Thank you for your opinion."

"No problem. Here's another opinion. You shouldn't be ashamed of how he lived or how he died. He should have been ashamed of you."

This time I was the one who turned and walked away, not quite sure what that had been all about. It was more than Limbach being snotty. It wasn't just ice cream cones thrown down on sidewalks, nice guys finishing last, lonely kids collecting snakes. It was all the slights and snubs and injustices that make the enlisted men and the officers of the civilian world fear one another on sight. I want to say hate, but fear is more honest. On both sides.

"What's wrong?" Hope said when she saw my face.

"Nothing. I lost it with that asshole Limbach, that's all."

"Over what?"

"I don't know. Yes, I do, too. It just came to me. I lost it because of Marian Peterkin's mother. I was a sophomore in high school and Marian Peterkin showed up in our class after Christmas because she was kicked out of some fancy boarding school and she couldn't get into another one till next fall. Her parents were New York City people and they just parked her up in their summer place. Mostly the housekeeper was the only person with her. We went out maybe four or five times and I think I only met the mother twice. The last time I was going to go out with Marian, the housekeeper answered and she hollered upstairs, 'It's Tom Bethany.' Then it was like a relay, with the mother passing on the message. Only she changed it a little. She said, 'It's that Tom Bethany person, dear.' "

"Loud enough for you to hear, obviously."

"Yeah, obviously."

"What did you do?"

"I closed the door and walked away, and I was too ashamed ever to ask her out again."

"And that's why you lost it with Limbach just now?"

"He asked me if I was the detective person."

Hope put her hand on my arm. "Sorry you lost it?" she said.

"No."

"Good," she said. "The hell with them. Pilgrim's lawyer, the guy I used to know? He told me the only emotion the Limbachs showed over Morty's death was because they thought the sex angle reflected on the family. When West-fall suggested it might be suicide, they jumped at the idea and did everything they could to help him."

"Like letting him into Morty's apartment so he could grab the will."

"Right."

"Let's think about it. Morty dies, and Morty's mother immediately figures she just came into two million bucks. Westfall finds the will, and presumably tells her that she gets nothing. Westfall makes the will disappear. Now Morty's death is worth two million bucks to her all over again."

"You don't really think she killed her own son?"

"I don't know what to think. But what she knew, Hocker Westfall knew. And I've still got it in my mind that the guys that tried to kill me came from Westfall. Maybe he was afraid I'd find another copy of the will. Which in fact I did, once I looked inside Morty's computer."

"Sounds pretty thin to me."

"Well, so does every other theory I've got. Still, maybe somebody should keep an eye on the Limbachs, too, during my little skit. Would you mind doing that?"

"What should I look for?"

"I don't know. I'm just doing what we producers do, looking for audience reaction."

"Am I really going to hate your show, Bethany?"

"You might. It's got some dirty words in it."

"Shit, I knew I was going to hate it."

Kathy and the other members of the two troupes were urging people through the entrance in the partition to the half of the room where the entertainment would be. People could carry their plates in, which a lot of them did. There were place cards, and most of the guests milled around

256

finding their assigned tables. We didn't have to look, since I had assigned my own place as well as a few of the others. Dr. Mark Unger was at a table slightly in front of me and a little off to one side so that I could see him almost in profile. I had set Gladys Williams up with a good view of Teddy Elliman. And Rosson was at the same table as Kathy Poindexter, which he was pleased about. I hadn't included the Limbachs in my seating arrangement, but they were near enough to us so that Hope would be able to keep an eye on them.

When the waitresses had had time to fill everyone's drink orders, Kathy Poindexter left her table and went up to the small stage. Once everybody was quiet, she raised her microphone.

"Morty Limbach is dead," she said, and stopped. It got their attention.

"He was a gentle, decent guy, which is something you don't see that much of in this business. It made him happy, really happy, to see somebody else get ahead. You don't see much of that in this business, either. Maybe in any business.

"I was one of the people he helped to get ahead. So was Leo Grasso. So was Baby Leo, even if he's too little to know it. The rest of us, though, we're big enough to know it. The people who came with us from the Poor Attitudes to the 'Leo Grasso Show.' The other performers that Morty encouraged and supported over the years. The Poor Attitudes performers who are going to entertain you tonight. We all know it.

"I've been very lucky. A few years ago I was hanging around Harvard Square, sometimes panhandling, sometimes even sleeping in the street. I don't panhandle anymore. I don't have to sleep in the street. Being rich, being famous, being a star, it all came from Morty Limbach. His decency. His generosity.

"Maybe you think it didn't all come from that. Maybe you think my talent and my ability had something to do with it. Well, thank you if you think that. But there are dozens and dozens of young people just in the Boston area alone with just as much talent and ability. You'll see some of them here tonight. The main difference between them and me isn't talent. It's luck.

"Morty Limbach was my luck. I want him to keep on being other people's luck, too. So I signed the papers just this morning that set up the Morty Limbach Foundation for Creative Theater. It starts out with two million dollars in funding, which is really only a small part of the luck Morty gave me. And I'll add a dollar for every dollar that any one of you contributes. The foundation's official mission, as far as the IRS is concerned, will be to keep Poor Attitudes House alive as a place where the talented young performers in the Boston area can have the same chance Leo and I had. Its real mission, as far as *I'm* concerned, will be to keep Morty Limbach alive."

She bowed her head for just an instant, too brief to be prayer but giving the hint of it, and stepped down from the low stage. She hurried back to her table with her shoulders a little hunched, as if she were flinching from the applause that came as soon as the audience woke up to the fact that she was through. By seeming to run from applause she had doubled it.

"See what she did?" I asked Hope. "She's starting to give Morty back the money he left the baby."

"I didn't think of that. Of course that's exactly what she's doing."

Ned Levine had come onstage during the applause. He wore the same Rorschach T-shirt I had first seen him in, unless he had a collection of them. When the noise finally died away, he smiled at the crowd and said, "Well, this evening's performance peaked kind of early." Then he introduced the first piece. I had seen it in rehearsal, the skit about the couple on a date who got lawyers in to draw up a presex contract. So I had heard all the jokes, but everyone else was in the mood to enjoy the skit, and did.

Ned got back out onstage, then, and talked about the troupe, and about the nature of improvisational comedy. Which he explained wasn't what this last skit had been, but which was what we'd be seeing from now on. First would come the charades routine, charades being the form of improv that people were the most familiar with. For that reason, perhaps, the charade also went over well with the audience. And then Ned came out again to introduce our own special little number, his and mine, which he said would be true improvisational theater. Which was a lie.

"Okay," Ned said, "what we're going to stage here is a holdup. And what you folks are going to do is tell us what to hold up. What about it? Who's been stuck up?"

"America," someone called out.

"America?"

"Yes, the S & L bailout." Presumably an academic wit had just been heard from.

"Okay, America," Ned said unenthusiastically. "What else?"

"Filene's basement."

"Okay, good. Filene's basement."

"A pizza parlor."

"A topless bar . . ."

"A laundromat . . ."

"A sperm bank," someone shouted. Me.

"A sperm bank! Who said that?" Ned pointed me out, making sure everyone would know where the idea had come from. "Let me just say, sir, that you have a genuinely sick mind."

Three or four other suggestions came from the audience, and then the players huddled off to one side, as if they were discussing which one to build on. Then a frizzy-haired blonde left the huddle with a chair in hand and sat down facing us. From rehearsals, I knew her name was Audrey Herman. Audrey made as if she were working at an imaginary desk while the actor named Harvey came through an imaginary door and stood in front of her. It was all going according to the script:

DONOR: This the First National Sperm Bank?

NURSE: You the ten o'clock? *(Looking down at schedule)* The Donald? *(Donor nods. Nurse drains the last of an imaginary coffee cup and hands it to him.)*

NURSE: Fill 'er up.

DONOR: Right here?

NURSE: Go ahead and whip it out. I'm a nurse. *(Donor starts to do so, when Robber bursts in and grabs him around the neck while threatening the Nurse with an imaginary gun.)*

ROBBER: Stick 'em up! *(Nurse and Donor obey, although the Donor is in obvious distress from the strangle hold the Robber has on him. As the other two speak, he fights silently for breath and his hands lower slowly to his sides.)*

NURSE: Are you crazy? This is the First National *sperm bank!*

ROBBER: I don't give a rat's ass what you call it, sister. Hand the dough over in unmarked tens and twenties or this guy gets it. *(Holds gun to Donor's head.)*

NURSE: You can't kill that man!

ROBBER: Why not?

NURSE: He's already dead. *(Robber notices this is so and lets Donor fall to the floor.)*

ROBBER: Shit, what am I supposed to do for a hostage?

NURSE: You idiot! You've killed the most brilliant business-man in America. His sperm was worth a fortune.

ROBBER: Huh? Who is he?

NURSE: Donald Trump. He used to get two million bucks a wad.

STRANGLE HOLD

ROBBER: Jeez, what kind of broad would pay that kind of money for somebody else's sperm?

NURSE: Women married to rich morons. Oh, shit, here comes Mrs. Quayle now.

MARILYN: I've come to pick up my order of Trump sperm. Wait a minute. Isn't that The Donald on the floor?

ROBBER: He's just resting. *(Aside to Nurse)* Keep your mouth shut, sister, and I'll split with you fifty-fifty. *(Back to Marilyn)* If you could just step into the other room with my nurse for a minute, give Mr. Trump a little privacy . . .

MARILYN: Of course. *(They turn their backs while the Robber retrieves the fallen coffee cup from the floor, turns away from the audience, and goes to work.)*

ROBBER: Okay, ladies. All set. *(They turn around again.)*

MARILYN: Sorry to interrupt your nap, Mr. Trump. Mr. Trump?

ROBBER: He went right back to sleep, I'm afraid. It took a lot out of him.

MARILYN: *(Looking into the cup the Robber has handed her)* Doesn't look like much to me.

NURSE: Hey, you know what they say about The Donald, don't you?

MARILYN: No, what?

NURSE: *(Breaking into the old Brylcreem song)* Trumpcreem, a little dab'll do ya. Trumpcreem, a little dab'll do . . .

ROBBER: Yeah, I know it don't look like much, but there's millions of them little suckers in there. So if you'll just hand over the dough . . .

MARILYN: Not so fast. I've got to check it first.

ROBBER: *(Looking into the cup)* Looks okay to me.

MARILYN: *(Shoving an imaginary purse protectively under her arm)* Yeah, well, you're not getting my wad till I'm sure this is The Donald's wad. I'm taking it to the Cambridge police for a DNA test.

ROBBER: Okay, lady, have it your own way. *(He shoots Marilyn dead and grabs her purse as she crumples, then shoots the Nurse dead, then shakes the purse upside down. Empty. He shoots himself dead.)*

261

And that was the end of our skit. All four players popped back up to their feet, bowed, and exited to applause that did my producer's heart good.

"My God, Bethany, have you no shame?" Hope said. "A little dab'll do ya?"

Probably this called for some sort of response, but I was suddenly in a hurry. Dr. Unger was on his way out the door.

— 15 —

THE BEST I HAD FIGURED ON WAS SOMEONE ACTING VISIBLY nervous or angry, and even that would have been a long shot. People don't register emotions as much in real life as they do onstage or in books. Most of us learn pretty early about poker faces. Unger had worn one, certainly, almost from the start of the skit. Of course, since the other people had been laughing, maybe his poker face itself amounted to a display of emotion. He smiled at the end, though, when he said something inaudible to his table mates and got to his feet.

And now he was out the door. I gave it a moment or two, so he wouldn't spot me behind him.

If I had thought someone would actually leave because of my little skit, I would have parked near the exit, facing out. As it was, I was just getting my car out from behind the stretch limo as his red Mercedes 350 SL turned right on Route 1 toward Boston. He was almost out of sight when I got on the highway and floored it. The old Datsun failed to respond with a surge of power, but eventually I got it up to seventy and began to gain on the red sports car in the distance.

On the way over the Tobin Bridge Unger and I were in the left lane, with me hanging back a good ways until I woke up to the fact that he wasn't in the left lane anymore. He had drifted over into the right, without bothering to signal and was in the process of drifting farther to the right, off onto the Storrow Drive exit ramp. I couldn't drift anywhere myself, since a fast-moving carload of kids had come up on my right. By the time I could switch lanes, Unger was gone and I was headed for Cape Cod. There was only one thing left to do, so I did it.

I shouted, "Aw, shit!" out into the night.

The next exit took me into the maze of poorly lit streets and baffling signs around the Callahan Tunnel entrance. By the time I got out of all that, Unger could have been well on his way to pretty much anywhere. But it figured that he was on his way to his office, since Storrow Drive was the logical way to the Poor Attitudes House. When I finally found my own way to the mansion, I could see the Mercedes parked out behind, where the driveway ran around to the rear. The car was empty, and the lights were on in Unger's top-floor office. I parked in front of a hydrant and walked up the drive. As I stood outside for a moment, wondering what to do, I heard his steps on the stair. Since there was no other place to get out of sight, I stepped to one side of the door so that it would hide me when it opened. In a minute Unger came out and started toward the car, carrying what looked like a carton full of files.

I went through the open door fast, and on up the stairs. I was in his office when I heard him coming back up. This time I hid in the bathroom, which was down a short hall from his office. I listened to him rummaging around for a while. "That cocksucker," he said at one point, as he slammed things back and forth. Probably he meant me.

After a while I figured I'd better find out what was going on, so I left the bathroom and moved quietly down the hall. Unger's back was to me. He was slipping something into the inside breast pocket of his dinner jacket, something he had just taken out of a drawer.

"Hi," I said.

He jerked as if I had touched him. When he turned and saw who I was, he started to bring himself a little bit more under control. "Where did you come from?" he said.

"The bathroom."

"But . . . I mean . . . how . . ."

Fair enough, since the last time he saw me I had been sitting in a comedy club in Saugus.

"Doesn't matter much," I said. "I got here, Mark, and now here I am." I figured it was all right to call him Mark; doctors like to call everybody else by their first names, and fair is fair.

"Just what the hell are you trying to pull, Bethany?" he said.

"Mr. Bethany."

"What?"

"Call me Mr. Bethany."

"The fuck I will."

"Oh, pretty soon you will. What were you putting in your pocket, Mark?"

"None of your goddamned business."

"Come on, give it to me." We would have looked out of place in a schoolyard, two grown men in tuxedos. But we wouldn't have sounded out of place. I held out my hand and moved a half-step toward him. Unger took his best black-belt stance.

"Give me a break, will you?" I said. "What are you, the Karate Kid?"

The best way to deal with a club or a chain or just about any kind of a blow is to get inside it, where the other guy can't get a good shot at you. If I could get my hands on Unger, none of his kicks and blows could work, and all of my tricks would. So I shot fast for his right leg and he had to grab onto me for balance.

I had him on the floor in a second, and in a cradle in another second. The cradle is a hold I used a lot in high school. I was meaner then, for one thing, and I didn't know too many other holds yet, for another. It's almost impossible to force a man's shoulders to the floor with a cradle, but it's easy to grind your skull into his temple until he lowers his shoulders to the mat just to stop the pain. I didn't care about pinning Unger, but I wanted him to know I could maim or kill him, and to think I might. I leaned into his temple pretty hard and said, "I told you, call me mister."

He groaned but said nothing, so I made him groan some more. He was a lot tougher than most people, certainly than Cooper. But finally he said "mister."

"Mister Bethany," I said, keeping up the pressure.

"Mister Bethany," he gritted out.

I turned him fast, jacked his right foot up to his buttocks and kept it there with the weight of my body. I forced his left arm up between his shoulder blades and held it there first with one hand and then the other while I searched him. Inside his jacket I found a little dark blue book that I didn't recognize till I turned it over and saw the gold lettering on the front cover. The last time I got a passport was so long ago that they were still green and a good deal larger than this one. I tossed it up on Unger's desk and went through the rest of his pockets. Apart from his wallet and regular pocket junk, all I found was four audiotapes. I threw the cassettes on his desk, too. I left the rest of the stuff on the floor for him to pick up. It would do him good to have to bend over and pick things up.

I let go of Unger's arm and leg but stayed on top of him.

As soon as he realized he could move without pain, he twisted violently to escape. I shifted my weight a little so that he couldn't get out from under. He tried again, and again, and again. "You beginning to understand, shithead?" I said.

"Understand what?"

"That there's not a goddamned thing you can do?"

He tried again, and I moved slightly to keep him helpless.

"I don't even need my hands, Unger. You notice that?"

And I didn't. Once a good wrestler gets on top of a nonwrestler, all he needs to stay there is the weight of his body, shifting a little each time the other man begins an escape movement. To anybody watching, it looks as if the man on top isn't doing much but lying there. To the man on the bottom it's a mystery that makes him mad at first, and then frustrated, and finally fearful. He's up against a force he can't understand and can't fight. There's a total helplessness and loss of control, as if he were zipped up in a sleeping bag with people sitting on him. When I figured he had received the message in his bones as well as his brain, I got up and sat in the armchair at the head of his couch, the one he would sit in during sessions while the patient lay down. Unger got to his feet, and headed toward the chair behind his desk.

"Not there," I said. "On the couch."

"What is this, anyway?"

"On the couch, goddamn it!"

I started to get up, and he sat on the edge of the couch.

"Lie down."

"Listen . . ."

I grabbed a fistful of his hair and pulled him down. As soon as I let go, he twisted his head to look at me, opening his mouth to speak. I was out of my chair before he could do it, and had him by both ears. I put my face right up to his, way within his space.

"Listen, you prick," I said, spitting the last word out, spraying him a little. "You lie there and shut the fuck up till I tell you different. So far you're not hurt, but jerk me around and you will be. You know I can do it, don't you?"

Unger nodded.

"You believe I will?"

He nodded again. "And I will, too," I said. "It'll be a present to Morty. The more I learn about Morty, the more I like him. The more I learn about you, the more I think you're nothing but a piece of slick shit. Let's see what you got on those tapes."

I went over to the desk for them, and then sat back down in the armchair that Unger used when he played wise healer. It looked as if he might have preserved some of his best roles on tape, too, judging by the way he had his armchair set up. It would have given him easy access to the controls of the tape deck during sessions. I leaned over to open the cassette compartment and felt something dig into my thigh. It turned out to be the hospital call button that Unger used to buzz the downstairs door when patients rang. I shoved it down between the cushions, out of the way—and then I fished it out again. I looked at where the cord came out of the chair, and where it lay in loose loops beside the chair, and where it was attached to a jack in the baseboard. And I knew exactly how Morty had died.

I put the cassette into the machine and pressed down Play. The tape was marked N. D., and it was Nora Dawson's voice that came out, sure enough. Hers and her doctor's.

"I want to, sure," she said. "But it feels funny, you know?"

"Because I'm your doctor?"

"I guess. But it's more than that, too."

"You mean I'm more than your doctor? Someone else, maybe?"

"I don't know. Do you think my feelings for you are mixed up with . . ."

"What do *you* think, Nora?"

"Well, maybe. Could be. You don't look like him."

"I'm not him, am I?"

"No."

"Of course not. But you think the feelings you've developed toward me might somehow resemble the feelings you had toward him as a little girl?"

"What do you think?"

"We're concerned here with *your* feelings, Nora."

"Well, maybe they do. Resemble them."

"Maybe. But I'm not him. No maybe about that, is there?"

"No, you're not him."

"If you had those same feelings toward me, they wouldn't be improper in any way, would they?"

"No."

"So it isn't the feelings themselves that disturb you?"

"No."

"It's the focus of those feelings?"

"Yes. I mean, your own . . ."

"Your own what?"

"Well, father. You're not supposed to . . ."

"Then it's the focus that you feel is inappropriate?"

"Well, isn't it?"

"If the focus is your father, yes."

"Well, isn't it?"

"You'll have to make up your own mind. Is it?"

"I just don't know."

"Is your father alive?"

"You know he's not."

"So he can't be sitting here, can he?"

"If he is, he's got a pretty good shot at 'Geraldo Rivera.' "

"We've talked about the use of humor as a defense, haven't we?"

"I'm sorry."

"So if he isn't sitting here and someone touched you, it couldn't be him, could it?"

"Of course not. Obviously."

"Close your eyes."

"Why?"

"I want to try something that might help. I want to help you to identify the nature of the experience of touching with the evidence of your senses, not with your Oedipal feelings toward your father. No, hold still. Now. That touch would have been inappropriate coming from your father, clearly. But not from a lover, would it?"

"No, not from a lover."

"This doesn't mean that I am your lover, Nora. I'm merely attempting to help you distinguish between the feeling of love and the focus of that love. To experience the feeling as an abstract, unrelated to an inappropriate object. There. No, keep your eyes closed. Let the feeling dominate. Cut it loose from any object. Let the feeling float free. Let it be a corrective emotional experience. That's it, darling . . ."

At the beginning of the tape, Unger had tried once to rouse himself from the couch, to explain. I grabbed another fistful of hair, though, and wrenched him back down in position. I held him there while the tape rolled, so he would remember not to interrupt. There were jumps in the tape. Apparently he had spliced together the good parts from many sessions. It went on and on. I kept my grip tight enough on his hair to be painful, only partly because I was disgusted by him. More than that I was disgusted at myself, because I found myself being aroused by the pictures the voices made.

"Do I have to?"

"We've already discussed this, Nora. Before you can be entirely free in your sexuality, we need to work through the complete range of sexual experience."

"It'll hurt, I know it will."

"Darling, logic tells you an object this size won't hurt if you relax your muscles. I'm thoroughly lubricated—"

That was it for me. I clicked the switch and the voices stopped. I let go of Dr. Unger's hair. By now you could hardly tell it had ever been blow-dried.

"Can I sit up?" he said.

"No."

"Can I say something."

"No. Shut up." I watched the tape, which was still rolling. I had hit the Stop button in the same motion as the Play and Record buttons, hoping it would sound to the psychiatrist like a single noise. But the machine was still recording over whatever was left on the tape. It didn't matter. What I had already heard was enough.

"You're something, you know it, Unger?" I said. "Some poor little bird with a broken wing comes up here for you to fix it. So you butt-fuck her."

"It wasn't like that," he said before he could think. And then he stopped, remembering he was dealing with a crazy man who didn't want him to talk.

"Go ahead. How was it?"

"There are circumstances, certain patients, not many but some, where a sexual relationship between doctor and patient can have definite therapeutic benefits."

"Oh, yeah? How far would you let one of your patients get with a bullshit rationalization like that?"

"Look, sometimes it can be difficult for the nonprofessional to follow—"

"Sometimes it's hard for the professional, too, huh?

271

From what I understand, the Massachusetts Psychological Association wants to make shit like this a felony."

"In certain circumstances that's true."

"In exactly the circumstances on those tapes. Four tapes, different initials. I guess you've got four different patients on them. Any one of those tapes, they'd lift your fucking license before they even got through listening to them."

"Those tapes are protected by law under the doctor-patient relationship."

"Get real, Unger. You think I give a fuck about the doctor-patient relationship?"

"Look, we can settle this easily enough. I'm pretty sure I have a thousand dollars, right here in the office."

"I've got tapes that can ruin you and you're offering me a thousand dollars? Get real, I told you."

"Two thousand, then."

"It isn't just I can ruin you, Unger. I can put you in Walpole for killing Morty, and you goddamned well know it. You wouldn't be running if you didn't figure out my little skit."

"There's nothing you can prove."

"Come on. I just go to the police and I say, Hey, listen, officer, you want to be Sherlock Holmes? Just check the come on Morty's shorts and see if it really came from him, okay?"

Of course nobody kept semen samples, but Mark Unger wouldn't know that. He did know a little bit about logic, though.

"That wouldn't prove anything," he said.

"Prove somebody else was there."

"Yes, but who?"

"I don't know," I said. "Let's see."

I had my equipment out already, having given a little thought to this improvisational skit, too. I snatched his arm without warning and used it to twist him over onto his belly. "Ouch," he said when I pricked his thumb with my penknife. "What are you doing?"

"Lab sample for the cops to match." I blotted up the bright drop of blood with my handkerchief and put it on the desk. Once I was back in my armchair, he turned over and raised himself up on one elbow so he could look at me. Testing the limits like a kid with his old man, to see how much I'd let him get away with. He licked a little blood from his thumb and pressed his forefinger on the tiny puncture to stop the bleeding. He looked at the handkerchief, with its big scarlet spot.

"DNA," I said. "Probably you don't remember too much from medical school, but I bet you know about DNA testing."

"Anybody could have put my semen there."

"Oh, yeah? What do you do? Pass it out at parties?"

"None of this proves murder. It just doesn't."

"Well, maybe you're okay, then. Maybe you can convince the shit out of a jury, what do you think? Tell them you walked in there and found the guy strangled so you figured what the hell, he's dead, he won't mind if I give him a little squirt or two of Dr. Unger's White Root. Yeah, it could work. I'd buy it."

"The burden of proof is on the prosecution."

"Oh, I bet the proof would be there once somebody told the cops where to look. What I'd tell them, I'd say this is how it happened. Saturday night or Sunday morning Morty calls up all pissed off because his shrink mind-fucked his girl into going to bed with him. Let's talk it over at the office, you say. So Morty storms on over, hollering about how he's going to do this, going to do that. Kick you out of your office, lift your license, sue the shit out of you. This is a guy that's got the money to follow through on it, too. So you loop the cord from this call button around his neck and kill him. Then you drag him downstairs while everybody else is sleeping it off as usual. Lock him inside Kathy's old room with his own key. Go buy an extension cord the same diameter as the one you killed him with, so it'll match the marks on his neck. Where do you go for an extension cord on Sunday? Probably one of the twenty-four-hour places, right? Li'l Peach or Store 24. Easy enough to check. Find the clerk who worked that shift. Get him in to pick you out of a lineup. Match the fingerprints on the cord with yours . . ."

"They wouldn't find any fingerprints."

"You wiped them off?"

"I'm not an idiot, after all."

"Sure you are. What's it going to tell the cops, that there's no prints on the cord? You think Morty would have wiped the fucking cord himself?"

Unger didn't say anything. Probably he didn't have anything to say. Probably he felt stupid.

"Actually you did a half-assed job all around, Mark. You didn't rig things right for autoerotic asphyxia. You should have got out some of Kathy's old panties and left them around. You should have picked up a copy of *Hustler* at the Li'l Peach, left it beside him. Or at least a mirror. The half-assed job you did was good enough for the cops and the medical examiner, but it wasn't good enough for the insurance company. They figured things didn't really compute, not for autoerotic asphyxia, and they might be able to save a buck by claiming it was suicide. Which is what brought me in, and now you've got to start coming to grips with things, Mark."

"Listen, let's think this through," Dr. Unger said. He was sitting up on the couch now, facing me, on the same level. I let it go, to show that now we were equals, bargaining together. No more dominance games.

"We should be able to work our way through this and into a stable, enduring relationship," he went on. "You're an intelligent man, Tom. Turning those tapes over to the ethics board isn't productive behavior from your point of view. Neither is sending me to prison."

"What is productive? From my point of view, naturally."

"Well, in prison I'm worth exactly nothing from your point of view. Out of prison, on the other hand, I have a flourishing practice that produces close to two hundred thousand dollars a year." This had to be way high, but I let it go.

"How much of that would I have a stable relationship with?"

"Ten percent. Plus the two thousand we already agreed on, for the tapes."

"Fifteen percent."

"Twelve and a half."

"Actually, let's forget about the stable relationship, Mark. I don't want to marry you, and worry all the time about waking up with an extension cord around my neck. I just want to fuck you once, and move on. Where's your two thousand?"

"In my safe over there. That thing is a safe."

"Go open it."

He got up and went to a two-drawer oak filing cabinet with a lamp on it, over by the wall. The bottom drawer turned out to be a dummy, which hid the front of a safe. I got a glimpse of the dial before he squatted down and began working the combination. After a minute I heard the handle clank. An instant later I saw something blue-black in his hand as he rose and whirled. Run from a knife but charge a gun was Jimmy Hoffa's advice, and I took it. I was hardly up out of my chair, though, when the gun jerked in Unger's hand as he yanked at the trigger. But there was no explosion. I kept going. Unger was grabbing at the revolver with his other hand. I went for it, too.

He got the safety off before I grabbed his wrist, but the

gun was pointing at the floor when he finally got it to fire. With my hands on him I could feel the recoil myself as I took his arm down and him with it, rolling him forward and smacking his back hard into the floor. It shook him into harmlessness, and the gun was out of reach back where we had started tussling, but I was still powered on adrenaline. I got a hammerlock on Unger and dragged him to his feet. I kept him locked in it, hard, while I let my system slow down. When the danger that I would kill him was over, I let him go and went to pick up the gun.

"My neck," he said, sounding frightened. "You broke it."

"No, if I broke it, I think you'd be paralyzed. Actually, I don't know, though. Maybe I did break it. But probably I just fucked it up. Dislocated, maybe. What do you think? You're the doctor."

He didn't answer, maybe because he was afraid to. I sounded crazy even to myself, babbling away, coming down off my homicidal high. The psychiatrist kept on standing there, his black bow tie still miraculously tied while I sat down in his armchair and started to fiddle with the baby-shit brown call button that Unger had swiped as an intern. Finally it gave me an idea. I pulled the slack out of the cord, and then ripped it loose from the junction box.

"What are you doing?" Unger asked.

"Shut the fuck up," I said, and he did.

I tossed the long cord onto the armchair and went to see what Unger had left behind in the safe when he took out the gun. There were various business and legal documents, which I didn't bother with. And there was an envelope that had that unmistakable size and feel of cash.

"Take it," Unger said.

I opened the flap and counted the neat sheafs of new hundred-dollar bills. "There's twenty thousand in here," I said.

"That's all right. Take it all."

"Yeah, I will."

"Fine. Listen, just leave the tapes with me and we're even, okay?" I had three of the cassettes in my pockets. The fourth was still in the tape deck, still rolling.

"No, I'm going to put the tapes in the trash."

"Well, okay. I guess that's okay."

"Also I am going to hang you from that light fixture in the ceiling."

"Tom, let's talk this thing through. We're not in any hurry here. We can take our time deciding what's best for everybody."

"What's best is I hang you from that light fixture."

"Why, Tom?"

"Well, Mark, you tried to shoot me. So I'm going to hang you from that light fixture." I went over to the door and locked it, taking the key. I didn't want him running away before I could hang him. Then I picked up the gun and the bloodstained handkerchief and put them in my pockets, too.

"Killing me isn't going to solve your problems, Tom."

"No, I guess not."

"What are your problems, Tom? I might be able to help you work them through." But it didn't come out the soothing way he meant. It came out tight and scared. And my new therapist was holding his neck a little funny. Maybe I *had* dislocated his neck some. I certainly hoped so.

"Well, Mark," I said, "my basic problem is finding something to tie your hands with. If the guy's hands aren't tied behind him he gets to clawing at the rope, and shit like that. That's why you always see the hands tied in the movies."

"There's probably something downstairs you could use to tie me with, if that's really what you want," Unger said in the phony-reasonable tone you use to a drunk or a child. Or a madman. "Why don't you go down and look?"

"No, this ought to do," I said. I had found some package tape in the desk. "Nobody could break this stuff. Come on over here. Well, shit, all right, don't."

I went to him and brought him back to the desk with a come-along hold. He screamed when I bent him over the desk with his hands behind him, although I hadn't done it hard enough to hurt him. Maybe he *was* having a problem with his neck, sure enough. When I had his hands taped together behind him, I let him straighten up. Once he saw I wasn't going to stop him, he got as far away from me as he could get and stood with his back against the wall. He watched in silence as I climbed up on a chair and tied the end of the extension cord to the heavy old fixture that was anchored solidly into the ceiling. Then I got the white pages and the yellow pages out of his desk and piled them on the floor just under the dangling cord.

He gave psychobabble a final try when I dragged him over to the little platform I had made. "It doesn't make sense to put yourself in the same fix I'm in, Tom," he said. "Killing doesn't solve anything."

"You wish you hadn't killed Morty Limbach?"

"That's exactly what I'm telling you, Tom. I let myself be dominated by the same unproductive emotion you're feeling now, Tom. Anger. I let anger take over, and I regret that now."

"Right. Get up on those phone books."

"Tom, think about this."

"Otherwise I'll break both of your fucking eardrums. I used to watch the Meo do that to NVA prisoners in Laos. You just clap on both ears at the same time, real hard. The way they screamed, it must hurt like a son of a bitch."

I had only heard of that but never seen it, and it was probably bullshit like so much else we heard over there.

Like the restaurants where rich Chinese ate the brains out of live monkeys with special spoons. Still, the eardrum story was a good one, and it got him up on the phone books. I put the loop over his head and tightened the knot under his left ear, just where Morty's knot had been. The bell was dangling down on Unger's chest, the same way the socket had dangled on Morty's.

"Please," he said. "For God's sakes, Tom . . . Mr. Bethany?"

I kicked the phone books out from under him.

— 16 —

O_{H,"} said Unger, in a little, surprised voice.

At first I thought he was surprised over finding himself still alive, just standing on his toes after his short drop off the phone books, but then I smelled it.

"Jesus, Unger," I said, "you filled your pants, didn't you? That's really disgusting. My God, you must be practically forty years old."

He was too scared to say anything, which probably meant that I had managed to apply Nixon's madman theory effectively. The notion Nixon had was that you could scare the other guy into backing down if you could convince him you were deranged. It helped, of course, if you were.

Maybe I was, too, I thought as I sat in Unger's chair while he stood on tiptoes to keep from strangling. He was right when he said that I felt anger, but I didn't so much feel it just because he had killed Morty Limbach or even because he had tried to kill me. What I felt about those things was an almost artificial anger, something I felt because I knew it was how you were supposed to feel. But that wasn't what made me angry enough so that I had been able to convince a psychiatrist that I was insane. It was what Unger had done to troubled women who came to him for help, and my anger about that was all the stronger because it wasn't pure. It was mixed with lust and envy. There's a mind-fucker in all of us when it comes to women. Maybe in them when it comes to us, too, but that doesn't let us off the hook. Just means there's two hooks.

Meanwhile, there had to be a limit to how long Unger could stay up on tiptoes, after taking his three-inch plunge off the phone books. Probably I should get somebody over here to turn him loose. I called Lieutenant Billy Curtin at his unlisted home number, which he would no doubt be irritated to know I had, since I wouldn't give him mine. I had got the number from Gladys.

As the phone rang, I wondered how a man like the lieutenant would answer. Military/bureaucratic?—"Curtin here"? CIA/paranoid?—"Five-seven-three-three-six-nine-four"? Beacon Hill?—"Curtin residence"?

"Hello," Curtin said.

So I said hello, too, and then said who I was and what I had been up to lately. He listened quietly, just asking me to stop now and then while he made a note of something. When I was getting ready to tell him about my home taping, a thought struck me.

"Hold on a second," I said. I looked at the machine and the reels were still turning slowly. One of those 120-minute cassettes. I clicked it off and smiled up at Unger. He didn't smile back, but then he was strung up on tiptoes with his shorts full of shit. I hoped I had managed to do lasting damage to his view of himself. Two could play at mind-fucking.

"I'm back," I said to Billy Curtin. And then I told him about the tapes.

"I don't know that much about the rules of evidence," I said at the end, "but you could use something you picked out of the trash, couldn't you?"

"Whose trash? Where?"

"Well, say it was down at the end of the block where they're doing some construction work and they've got a dumpster out on the public sidewalk. What if you looked in that dumpster and found a murder confession on tape? You could use that, couldn't you?"

"Oh, yeah. Provided there wasn't any evidence on the tape that any coercion had been used."

"On that, you might want to listen to them, you know. Might be a section toward the end that you wouldn't have any real need for."

"You didn't hurt the fucker, did you?"

"I think he sprained his neck a little, attempting suicide."

"You better explain that, Bethany."

"Well, when you get here you'll probably find him with a rope around his neck. An electric cord, actually. Tied to a light fixture in the ceiling. Wouldn't that give you probable cause?"

"Probable cause for what?"

"To arrest the son of a bitch. Looks to me like he was trying to hang himself. Isn't attempted suicide a crime?"

"I don't give a shit about that, but I do give a shit about murder. He better be alive when I get there, Bethany. Not like last time."

"Oh, he will be," I said, hanging up.

The first time I ever had dealings with Billy Curtin, he had gone along with covering up a murder. Expecting him to do the same thing again would be too much. If Unger strangled accidentally after I left, or even if he actually did commit suicide, Curtin would be after me for it. Too bad. Here I had gone and set everything up just the way Unger had for Morty. Now I'd have to spoil it.

Unger seemed to be trying to say something.

"What the fuck do *you* want?" I asked, looking over at him. Right away I saw what he wanted. His calf muscles had given out, and he wanted to breathe. I pushed the phone books toward him. When the pile touched him he felt feebly for its top with one patent leather shoe, and then climbed aboard to safety.

"Had enough?" I said, just as if I cared whether he strangled. But I climbed back up onto the chair anyway and undid the noose from his neck. Then I retied the cord, to the hands I had taped together behind him. I made it so that his arms were pulled up high, bowing him forward. His position wouldn't be comfortable, but I knew he'd try very hard to hold it till Curtin got there. The alternative was dislocated shoulders. Then I got down off the chair and went around the room picking up this and that. The tapes, a large manila envelope to put them in, the smaller envelope with twenty thousand dollars in it. I left behind the fired gun carrying Unger's prints and the handkerchief with his blood on it.

"Hey, Mark," I said when I was done. He raised his head a little, obediently, and waited. I was going to ask him if he thought anybody would care when he went up for murder, except to be glad. But the hell with it. When he saw that I wasn't going to say anything after all, he let his head sag back down.

Hope wasn't back from the gala yet when I got to the Charles. I let myself into her room and stretched out on the bed in my clothes, feeling sort of sour and heavy about things. She came in a quarter of an hour later while I was still lying there in the dark. As soon as she switched the lights on and saw me on the bed, she picked up on my mood. She cut the lights and came over to the bed. "What happened, Tom?" she asked.

Telling her made me feel a little better. On the basis of just the facts, leaving out the atmospherics, the evening had been a success after all. "I think you're okay from the legal point of view," she said when I was done. "For the moment, the Poor Attitudes House belongs to the estate, and you're an employee of the estate. You found a door standing open, and you called the police. They don't need a search warrant under those circumstances. Of course I don't know how Lieutenant Curtin decided to handle it."

"I can guess," I said. "If he takes the hint I give him, he'll put it in his report that he found a guy who tried to commit suicide with a gun. Only the guy's hand was so shaky he missed. Then he rigged a noose to hang himself, but the lieutenant fortunately got there in time to save him."

"Well, if he's as smart as you say he is, he'll be able to keep his story straight. That's something I've always really hated about the law."

"What?"

"The way it makes liars out of policemen. In a sense, lawyers like me force them to lie. We do it because we think we have to do it to keep the system from slipping entirely out of balance in favor of the state. And so policemen think they have to lie to keep it from dipping too far in the direction of the defendant. If God were running the show, a good cop like Curtin could hand Unger directly over to the warden and justice would be served."

"How about guys like Westfall, who don't actually break any laws?"

"To God, Westfall would have been a career criminal and spent his life in jail."

"Speaking here as God, you think he deserved the death penalty?"

"Maybe he deserved it, but I don't think anybody should get the death penalty."

"That's what he got, though, and it seems to me I gave it to him. Standing in for God."

"Come on, Bethany. How do you figure that?"

"Look, I was pissed at Westfall for what he said about you. But instead of taking it out on him, I went downstairs and pushed his pet Nazi around. Then I set it up so Cooper's own staff would come in and find him humiliated. I did everything I could to hurt him and destroy his authority."

"And he tried to kill you for it, didn't he?"

"Yes, he did. Cooper tried. Not Westfall. So I humiliated the son of a bitch all over again, this time with his boss. And got him fired."

"So next he tried to kill his boss, instead of you. And he succeeded."

"Right. And none of it would have happened if I hadn't acted like some macho teenage asshole in a goddamned street gang."

"So now you feel as if you were the one who killed Westfall?"

"Sure. In a sense."

"Pardon me, Bethany, but that's bullshit of purest ray serene. People get pushed around every day without trying to kill somebody over it. People get fired every day without beating their boss to death. If you respond to life's little problems by killing people, then you're a murderer. But you didn't kill anybody, Bethany. Cooper did. So he's the murderer."

"I created the situation that set him off, though."

"So what? Both the law and common sense recognize predisposition as a defense against charges of entrapment, which is exactly the charge you're bringing against yourself. And he plainly had a predisposition to murder."

"Who can say?"

"I can. I defended lots of guys like Myron Cooper when I was a public defender. Ask your friend Curtin about them. It's never the first time they did whatever they did. It's just the first time they got caught."

"Maybe."

"No 'maybe' about it. How did Cooper just happen to know those two guys that tried to kill you? What had he used them for before?"

"Maybe you're right. Maybe he's Jack the Ripper. But Westfall was the one who wound up dead, not Cooper. Did Westfall deserve to get killed?"

"Why not? Come on, Bethany. Why do you think he hired a Nazi bully like Cooper in the first place? Guys like Cooper and Westfall can spot each other all the way across the crowded room. Westfall was a criminal himself and he hired Cooper to do crimes for him. Then Westfall wound up being killed by his own bomb, like one of those terrorists. That's all there is to it."

"Yeah, you're right. You're right about all of it. I agree with you."

"You do? Then what's been going on here? Why have you been bleeding all over yourself?"

"The truth? I was afraid."

"Of what?"

"That you'd agree with what I was saying."

"I'd agree that you killed Westfall by brutalizing Cooper?"

"Well, yeah. Like that."

"You brutalized him, all right."

"No question of that."

"And if he had brought assault charges the way he should have, you might be serving thirty days right now. I wouldn't be happy about it, but I wouldn't figure it was a big failure of the criminal justice system, either."

"Me neither. It's the risk I took."

"But Cooper didn't bring charges, and lacking a witness

to the alleged assault, the law is helpless. Which I'm glad about. In fact, I'm glad about the whole incident."

"You're glad I—"

"Yes, I am. I'm glad you committed a crime against the peace and dignity of the Commonwealth of Massachusetts by feloniously assaulting the person of the said Myron Cooper."

"Why?"

"Because you did it for me."

"That seems a little short on logic, counsellor."

"It is. Come over here."

It was football weather still, with the leaves crackling under your feet on the sidewalk. In fact, Harvard was about to play Holy Cross that very day, as I remembered when the noise of the Harvard band came through the open windows of Hope's hotel room at an absurdly early hour Saturday morning. Except for the time they got up, the Harvard band was my idea of the perfect band. They met behind the Freshman Union before dawn on game days and then walked around the streets for an hour or so beating on things and blowing into other things. From the sounds, you had to figure they never rehearsed. On-the-job training seemed to be all they had. After wandering around the streets making noise for an hour or so, they went away somewhere till they reappeared at Soldiers Field for the game. At halftime they put on disorganized and obscene marching routines, or at least they used to be obscene until the administration cracked down a few years ago. Somebody should have fired the administration on the spot and turned the university over to the band. The bandsmen had a much better approach to being stewards of a great tradition.

Hope's flight back to Washington wasn't till late in the morning, and so we could have slept in. But there we were awake, thanks to the band. After a certain time had passed, Hope said something.

"Did I hear you right?" I asked. "Did you just say, 'mmmmm'?"

"Yes, I did. I said, 'mmmmm,' all right."

Suddenly she was up and sitting on the edge of the bed, perfectly naked. Naked and perfect.

"Come back here," I said, but I knew I was beaten. When Hope makes up her mind to charge forward into the day, that's it for torpor. Torpor is a dead duck.

"Come on," she said, stripping the covers off me. "Let's go out for breakfast."

"Can't. No place open."

"The Tasty's always open."

"Yeah, but they don't squeeze the orange juice fresh."

"Up!"

"Jesus. Can we at least take a shower?"

"All right, but no funny stuff, Bethany."

A couple of cab drivers were in the Tasty when we got there, and Joey Neary was behind the counter. It was quarter to seven. Joey saw me come in but ignored me completely. He gave all his attention to Hope, who deserved it. She wore a loose rust-colored sweater and a Shetland wool skirt and she looked terrific. I still had on my tuxedo, with the collar open and the tie hanging loose. "This guy actually knows you?" Joey said to her, and she nodded. "Amazing," he said, shaking his head.

He checked the eggs popping in grease on the grill to see if they were inedible yet. They weren't, so he turned back to us. "What'll it be, miss?" he said. "Bethany here always gets the quiche."

Before she could answer, the pay phone rang and he beat me to it. "Yeah?" he said. "Yeah, he's here. Minute." I took the phone from him.

"Whattaya, live in that fucking place?" a voice said. Billy Curtin's voice.

"Good morning, Lieutenant."

"It is, actually. Holy Cross is going to kick the shit out of Harvard in a few hours, and your buddy signed a statement."

"He did?" I couldn't imagine he had been that dumb.

"Yeah, he couldn't wait. What the hell did you do to him?"

"Just mind games. What did you do to him?"

"Mind games, too. I had him sit on newspapers so he wouldn't get shit on my car seat. Then we had a lot of trouble getting things organized back at headquarters, couldn't seem to get hold of clean clothes or a place for him to change in. Tell you the truth, though, by that time he had already practically given up. Keeping the load in his diapers just hurried things along a little, but basically right from the time I walked in he wanted to get it over with. Apparently he believed your DNA bullshit. Plus on the way in I picked up the tape you made. Plus he had to figure we'd find the guy that sold him the cord. Turned out he did get it at the Li'l Peach. Anyway, he just wanted to change his pants and tell his problems to somebody."

"Still, you'd think he'd have the sense to shut up till his lawyer got there. Doesn't he watch TV?"

"A lot of guys get tired carrying it all around. Once you grab 'em they just want to unload it, get it all over with. And you know another thing that helped a lot? He didn't want all his shrink pals to find out he was fucking the merchandise. Any chance of keeping the tapes out of it? he kept asking. Sure, I said. You got my word on it. Sign right here and there won't even be a trial."

"Any chance of keeping *me* out of it, Lieutenant?"

"Why not? One hand washes the other. Supposing I do keep you out of it, though, what have you got for me?"

289

Oh, shit, I thought. I knew what was coming, of course. I had just thought Curtin was different.

"What would you be interested in?"

"I'm interested in something Unger claimed he had in the safe."

Now it was in the inside pocket of my dinner jacket. "In the safe, huh?" I said, stalling, not wanting to hear what I was about to hear.

"I told him I figured it was horseshit, you want to know the truth," Curtin went on. "I told him he'd never prove anything was missing from his safe, and it was my personal belief that there wasn't a goddamned penny in there. But I'm still interested."

"How interested?"

"About fifty percent interested."

"Yeah, well, okay. That sounds good." Shit, shit, shit. Ten thousand dollars was reasonable under the circumstances. But still . . . say it ain't so, Joe.

"I think it's generous," Lieutenant Curtin said. "On my part, that is."

"Sure. How do you want to do this?"

"A check is fine."

"A *check?* You're shitting me, of course."

"Here's who to make it out to. You got something to write on?"

I fumbled out the envelope of cash and signaled Joey for a pencil to write on it with. "Go ahead," I said, and started copying down the instructions. "How do you spell *crones?*" I said, and he told me. When he was done I had down: Crohn's and Colitis Foundation of America, 444 Park Avenue South, NYC, 10016.

"You thought this was going to be something else, huh?" Curtin said when I got through reading the address back to him. "Well, why not? What do you really know about me? Jackshit, am I right? Which is just what I really know about you. So you better send me their receipt here at headquarters. Not a copy, the original."

"This thing is a disease, right? Something you have?"

"My niece Bridget. Eleven years old. Four operations. Break your goddamn heart. Well, fuck it. Why talk about it?"

So he hung up.

Coffee was in front of us and Joey was overcooking a new batch of eggs when I sat back down at the counter.

"You looked like it was bad news for a minute there," Hope said, "but I guess it worked out, huh?"